GREEK
SHADOWS

BLUE FEATHER BOOKS, LTD.

To the Amazon Spirit that dwells inside each of us.

ALSO WRITTEN BY K.C. WEST & VICTORIA WELSH AND
AVAILABLE FROM BLUE FEATHER BOOKS:

❖ SUPERSTITION SHADOWS

❖ CELTIC SHADOWS

COMING SOON:

❖ CANYON SHADOWS

www.bluefeatherbooks.com

GREEK SHADOWS

A BLUE FEATHER BOOK

BY
K.C. WEST AND VICTORIA WELSH

GREEK SHADOWS

Copyright © 2008 by K.C. West and Victoria Welsh

Cover design by Ann Phillips
Cover photograph by Andi Marquette

A Blue Feather Book
Published by Blue Feather Books, Ltd.

www.bluefeatherbooks.com

ISBN: 978-0-9794120-8-0

First edition: November, 2008

Printed in the United States of America and in the United Kingdom.

Acknowledgements

Greek Shadows is the third book of our series, but Kim and PJ are still running around loose inside our brains. Luckily, we have several people to help us corral and curtail their antics before too much mayhem occurs.

Our thanks to our publishers at Blue Feather Books (Emily and Caitlin) and our editor (Jane Vollbrecht). You found the glitches and made sure they were fixed.

We send kudos and gratitude to Arly, Bill, Connie, Lisa, Mary, Mistra, and the others on the online forum. You read our books, wrote reviews, and offered expert advice when we needed it most.

Supplying us with daily love, patience, and support were Victoria's life partner and her Arizona neighbors and my family and Maryland faithful.

A big old western hug and a plate of red and green chilis to Andi Marquette, author of *Land of Entrapment*, for the use of the photo that became our gorgeous cover, thanks to the magic of the Blue Feather art department.

Finally, our deepest thanks and appreciation go out to you readers. Bless you all for taking these characters and their stories to your hearts. Keep telling us what works and what doesn't. We love hearing from you, and we hope you enjoy book three. It offers a fresh locale, some new and returning characters, one or two adventures, plenty of romance…and… Amazons galore.

Hugs as always,
KC (kcwest2004@hotmail.com)
Victoria (vctrwelsh@gmail.com)

Chapter 1

Kim and I peered through the tinted glass of the limo as it sped up to the parking access for Logan Airport's E Terminal.

"Oh, shit." I grasped her hand. "There's a bunch of reporters camped out waiting for us."

"How the hell did they find out about this trip?" Kim's brow furrowed. "Never mind, honey. When we get to the entrance, just put your head down and keep moving forward. Your father and I will protect you."

"I know, and I appreciate it. But this is where my controlled breathing for stress relief will be useful."

In the seat across from us, Dad shifted. He removed his cell phone from a leather holster on his belt and dialed airport security. After requesting a contingent of guards, he looked at me. "Mitch and I will handle the questions and run interference for both of you."

"Thanks." Even though his news was reassuring, I continued to focus on my breathing.

Kim still gripped my hand. "We'll get Pup, our luggage, and ourselves onto that plane as soon as possible."

The vehicle threaded expertly through narrow lanes of taxis and shuttle buses. Walter and Mitch had chauffeured our family for decades, and Mitch was a superb pilot. I had no doubt about their abilities. Unfortunately, I couldn't control my pounding heart or my sweaty palms. The thought of mingling with a crowd of curious and nosy reporters was enough to unsettle me.

I took another deep breath, grabbed the leash of our seventy-pound half wolf, half German Shepherd, reached for my daypack, and prepared to run the gauntlet.

As the limo screeched to a stop, Dad and Mitch clambered out to serve as human shields. The reporters swarmed around us, firing questions. Cameras whined and whirred like pesky blowflies, hovering just beyond our reach. My father countered each question with a loud, "No comment."

Kim was standing in front of me. She held one hand behind her back, palm towards me, and I gave it a quick squeeze. We had devised this way for her to connect with me in public if I should fear an anxiety attack threatening. Sometimes, if the concern level was low, I only tickled her palm, and sometimes, like today, I needed a more tenacious connection.

Several Airport Security personnel arrived, muscling their way into the crowd to escort us.

Pup tensed beside me. When I paused to stroke his head, I could feel as well as hear a menacing growl rumble through his body. He must have sensed that these pushy humans didn't have our best interests in mind. "Easy, fella," I told him, trying to reassure both of us.

Kim reached down and took another section of his leash. "Just keep moving forward. We're almost to the door."

A camera flashed to our right. "PJ, this way! Just one more."

"What happened in Wales?"

Stuff I'd rather forget about right now.

"Were you kidnapped?"

I closed my eyes, trying not to remember. Yes, damn it.

"Were you raped?"

I opened my eyes and focused on Kim's hand on the leash. That's none of your business.

"Are you pregnant?"

Jesus. Enough, already.

The absurd interrogation continued. Kim and I plowed our way through the crowd, managing to keep our silence.

At the terminal entrance, an overzealous member of the press stuck a microphone in Kim's face. "Dr. Blair, a question, please?"

She glared at him. "Get that thing away from me."

Don't make her any madder than she is already.

"But just—"

"I said get it out of my face. Now!"

Don't push her, asshole.

"Is it true you two are lovers?"

Sweet Jesus, now you've done it.

Kim dropped her carry-on and seized the lapels of his sports jacket. "Back off, damn it!"

A photographer captured the action, and Kim reached for the lens of his camera.

"Hey, watch it," he spluttered, dropping the camera into his bag. He snatched up a smaller one, probably thinking it would be harder for her to grab.

Dad stepped through the circle of reporters now blocking our path, retrieved Kim's carry-on, and addressed the mob. "Move along, people. We have no comment for you. My daughter and her colleague must board a plane."

Again the photographer raised his camera. Clearly, the guy had a death wish.

Kim shoved him and his equipment to the concrete.

"Shit! You broke my camera, bitch!"

Several other photographers had captured the action.

I pinched the bridge of my nose, feeling the beginning of a blinding headache.

Kim pulled me close and pushed us both through the terminal's electronic doors. "You come at us again, buddy," she called over her shoulder, "and I'll break your ugly face."

"Kim, please, let it go." I'm not sure she even heard me. We were in the terminal, though, and I hoped that distance would diffuse the situation. A few more seconds out there, and things could have turned really scary.

Another squadron of security people came to our rescue, flanking us as we regrouped inside. I had no time to look at all the ocean creatures embedded in the mosaic floor tiles. The jellyfish and the eel were favorites of mine, but the "Atlantic Journey" recently installed at Logan would have to take a back seat to our own journey across the Atlantic. We moved swiftly with the current of security personnel who guided us through customs and hurried us out to the Curtis Foundation's corporate jet.

Kim and I had just enough time to hug Dad and say our good-byes before racing up the portable stairway with Mitch to join his co-pilot, Richard Swanson, and Richard's wife, Stacie. Stacie and Richard had already loaded our archaeological tools—including a pair of brand new Marshalltown 4.5-inch pointing trowels and some high visibility measuring tape—and prepared the cabin for our unexpected trip. When Mitch joined them, they started the pre-flight check.

Kim and I settled Pup in his crate in a corner of Dad's onboard office. Once we were airborne, he would be allowed in with us in the main passenger lounge.

I sank into one of the spacious seats, dropping my jacket and the daypack holding my laptop onto the seat behind me. The main cabin could accommodate twelve passengers. Seats were arranged in three rows of two, on either side of a wide center aisle. I had selected a window seat in the middle of the right side, thinking that Kim, with her longer legs, might enjoy the extra room on the aisle.

She placed her computer case next to mine, slipped out of her jacket, and collapsed into the buttery-soft leather seat beside me. I heard her shoes hit the carpet with muted thuds. She slid her hand along my arm. "That was amusing."

"For you, maybe."

I could hear the whining pitch of the jet engines coming to life. It was a comforting sound after what we had just been through.

Stacie stepped into the cabin and stowed our gear in the overhead compartment. I don't know what she thought about our relationship, but she treated me as she always had, like a kid sister, and she showed Kim the utmost respect and consideration. We felt we could relax in her presence, which made for more comfortable flights, especially on long ones like this.

Stacie hovered over us, making sure our seatbelts were securely fastened. "Quite a commotion back there. There's never a dull moment with you two, eh?"

"You know us, Stacie. We try to keep things lively."

"A little too lively, if you ask me," Kim said, her eyes still darkened with the remnants of her anger.

I sighed. "It's getting worse, and it's been like that ever since we returned from Wales. I'm glad to be leaving the country for a while."

Kim intertwined her fingers with mine. "You and me both, kiddo."

Stacie moved toward the rear of the plane, and I heard her working in the compact galley.

"What about you, tiger?" I gave our joined hands a playful tug. "You were ready to pulverize that reporter."

"I was ready to kill him."

"That's what worries me, Kimmy. If you remember, it was just a few months ago when you beat your former lover into pulp."

"And, under the same circumstances, I'd do it again. She was hurting you. What was I supposed to do? Anyway, I'd rather not talk about her any more." I could still hear traces of anger in her voice, and the expression that flitted across her face was a mixture of fury and fear. "It's over now."

"Yes, it is. Over and, I hope, forgotten."

This reservoir of rage that Kim sometimes tapped into had me concerned. I longed to have her talk to me about it, but with Stacie moving up the aisle behind us, I let the issue drop.

"Is the cargo loaded?" I asked her.

"All set."

"And I trust you stocked up on cashews this time." Both Dad and I had a fondness for that particular snack, so it wasn't unusual to have a critical shortage.

"I think I saw some just now when I checked the food supply. Let me make sure." Stacie returned to the galley, and we could hear cupboards opening and closing. "I forgot that your father flew to San Francisco for a meeting last week." Another door slammed shut. "Ah, here we go." She was a bit breathless when she returned to our seats. "I'm afraid there are only two pounds left, PJ. That will have to hold you until we can ship some more over."

"Only two pounds?" Kim shook her head. "She'll have that polished off before we reach cruising altitude."

"Oh, hush." I tried to swat her, but she grabbed my wrist and held on.

"Take it easy, little one." Her voice dropped to a seductive whisper, and she pressed the back of my hand to her lips. "You know I'm only kidding."

It seemed to me that Stacie pretended not to notice Kim's action and my sharp intake of breath. "I'll let them know you're ready for takeoff." Seconds later, she returned, took her backward-facing seat, and fastened her seat belt, while I took a few more calming breaths.

Geez, Kimmy, what you do to me.

Should our desires get the best of us I knew the bed in the stateroom was available, although Kim and I had always been reluctant to use it. I don't think we could get beyond the fact that we'd be making love in my father's bed, even if we would be thirty thousand feet above the ground at the time.

The engines revved, we taxied, and took off. As soon as we reached cruising altitude, I pulled off my running shoes and took a blanket from the overhead rack, spreading it over us. Stacie released Pup, who promptly curled up on the floor between Kim and me.

We'd had time enough to gather our passports, clothes, and data we thought we would need for the trip, along with dosing Pup with a mild sedative and collecting his papers from the vet. Sandy Arnold, Kim's former student, and a member of our Superstition Mountain expedition, had e-mailed us with a proposal to make this flight in order to lend him support on his current project. The message gave us little warning, but his brief highlights of the undertaking intrigued us enough to accept his invitation and join him, or at least find out in person what was happening. He provided us with just enough information to pique our curiosity, and he knew just the right amount of bait to use. We had to scurry to prepare for the project with no idea how long we would be gone.

This would be a different experience for Kim. In Arizona, where we searched for evidence of a lost tribe of Amazon warriors, she was the project leader and Sandy worked for her. Now, we were going to join his project. This time around, we'd be working for him. I had no doubt that we could handle it, though. We respected Sandy and appreciated his expertise in ancient Greek Archaeology.

I raised the arm dividing our seats, slid into Kim's welcome embrace, and pulled the blanket up around us. With a contented sigh, I closed my eyes, feeling her gentle kiss on the top of my head and her fingers brushing through my hair.

"Get some rest," she said. "I have a feeling that once we arrive we'll be caught up in Sandy's dream."

"Mmm. You rest, too, love. You need to unwind." I listened for her even breathing and felt her heartbeat settle into a slow, steady tempo. At least one of us had drifted into a trouble-free rest. My sleep, these days was anything but restful.

* * *

My thoughts returned to the past couple of weeks. Kim and I had decided to visit Dad in Boston, then spend a few weekends with him in Newport, Rhode Island, where we swam in the pool, took long walks on the beach, and relaxed in the summer home that had been in the Curtis family since before I was born.

Our visit to Boston was more than a pleasure trip for me. My experiences in Wales, earlier in the summer, had left me with some recurring troubles. I was able to suppress it for a while, but then I started having nightmares and flashbacks about the kidnapping and the attack. I think it scared Kim to realize that I was so rattled. She and Dad insisted that I seek professional help.

My father had a therapist in mind. He'd met Dr. Susanna Armstrong several years ago at a charity function near her home in Lexington, Massachusetts, and I think they had bumped into each other on and off since then, because his e-mails would occasionally mention her.

At first, I resented the idea and his parental interference, but Kim urged me to try it for all our sakes. To my astonishment, I discovered that I liked Susanna, as she insisted I call her, and she helped me feel at ease right away. Her area of expertise was not anxiety and trauma, however, so she recommended another psychiatrist. Scott Fleming was personable, gentle, and had an office right in Boston, close to Back Bay.

I made great progress during my sessions with Dr. Fleming, but I kept up my association and friendship with Susanna, visiting her a few times a month to talk informally in her home office, just off the town center with its Minuteman Statue on Lexington Green. Thick damask drapes muted outdoor traffic sounds, while we sat sipping juice in matching leather recliners. The gentle ticking of the Seth Thomas clock on the mantle over the gas fireplace encouraged me to relax and unburden myself with Susanna.

Now, hundreds of miles away from that refuge, I drifted above a blanket of muslin-colored clouds, snuggled in Kim's loving embrace. I could easily remember Susanna, during an early visit, sitting across from me, her compassionate gray-green eyes holding my gaze, as she tapped her pen against her cheek, rimless glasses perched on the bridge of her thin, straight nose. She often wore pastel-colored silk blouses and dark slacks that showed off her slim figure. I wondered if Dad's interest in her had been merely professional.

"You were saying, about your nightmares?" Susanna had prompted me.

"They're usually one or the other, and sometimes they overlap."

"The man in the cottage in Wales who attacked you, and the unwelcome advances from Kim's former lover?"

I shuddered, remembering. "Yes. First that man and then Terry Simms. She and Kim were involved for several years until she left Kim for a younger woman."

Susanna made some notes on her pad. "Do you want to talk about any of the attacks? The one with the man, perhaps?"

I sipped some juice and took a steadying breath. "He made crude remarks and watched me. Even when I was blindfolded, I could sense him, undressing me with his eyes."

"I see."

"He'd put his hands on me—on my butt and my breasts— whenever he could." Tears formed at the corners of my eyes, and I paused to wipe them. "It's one thing for that to happen when you're free to walk away or avoid someone, but when you have no escape and your hands are tied, you feel pretty helpless."

"That's understandable. And you felt helpless?"

"Yes."

"Did you ever give up hope?"

"I got pretty desperate one night, after I heard them talking about killing me."

"And the one man said he would rape you first?"

"Yeah, in his own delightful way." My voice thickened. Susanna sat up quickly and handed me the box of tissues.

"How did you feel then?"

I blew my nose and considered the question. "Frightened, of course. But angry, too. Angry with myself. It was my fault I was in that position."

Susanna seemed surprised. "You think you deserved to be raped?"

"No, not that. It was my fault I got kidnapped. I didn't listen to Kim or our bodyguards. I went out on my own when I had been warned and knew better."

"How did that make you feel?"

"Guilty, I guess. I think I still do."

"And the attack from Terry. What were you feeling when that happened?"

"With Terry, I felt stupid."

"Oh?"

"I should have figured her out. She and Kim were…"

I paused to wipe my eyes. Frequent bouts of weepiness only added to my lack of confidence.

Susanna shifted in her chair. I noticed her forehead wrinkled in thought, probably trying to pull all the clues of my story together, much as I would assemble broken artifacts at a site lab and construct a plausible history for them. During the past weeks, we had talked about my first meeting with Kim in Arizona, our work at the Amazon burial site, and the realization that we had fallen in love with each other after starting as adversaries. I touched on my mother's sudden death in a plane crash, my estrangement from Dad, and our reconciliation after some wild and wooly years of rebellion. I knew there were lots of juicy issues for a therapist to consider, but my immediate concern was Wales, so I focused on that.

"For quite a while, Kim wouldn't let herself get interested in anyone, romantically. Then, as improbable as it seems, she fell for me. We managed to find the best in each other, and before we knew it, we'd broken down our barriers and fallen deeply in love."

"Tell me more about her." Susanna's words had been all the encouragement I needed.

"Kimberly Blair saved my life—literally and figuratively. I can't imagine living without her. She's the smartest, kindest, most loyal, and most beautiful human being on the planet. When we're together, the world is brighter and my life is complete and meaningful. She brings out the best in me, giving me direction and purpose. I love her with every fiber of my being."

"I believe you, PJ." Susanna remained silent for a moment and then asked, "What about Terry?"

"Terry tried to rekindle Kim's interest in her and failed. She attempted to break us up and came on to me, but I turned her down."

"In what way did she try to break up your relationship?"

"By using our insecurities against us."

She was quiet after that, so I figured I was supposed to continue. I twisted my tissue and forged ahead. "Kim is older than I am. It sometimes worries her that I might lose interest, or that she'll get sick and become a burden."

"Is her age a problem for you?"

"Hell, no! Not for me. I love her just as she is—gray hairs and all."

"Okay. What did Terry think she could use against you?"

I felt my neck and cheeks heat up. "I'm not as... um... experienced in the art of loving a woman."

"You feel inadequate?"

"I suppose."

"Terry told you that you were inexperienced?"

"She made me think Kim would prefer a more experienced lover, someone capable, like herself."

"Has Kim given you reason to think you aren't capable?"

"Oh, God, no... nothing like that. We never had any trouble until we found Terry's underwear in our dresser drawer, and we each thought the other had been unfaithful. That's when we had our first big fight and Kim left." I swallowed hard, remembering the pain.

"Anyway, when Terry came to the room later, I told her to leave, but she got aggressive with me in a sexual way. I tried to fight her—I really did." Tears blinded me, and my voice cracked, as it all came flooding back.

Susanna offered me the box of tissues again. "Do you blame yourself for her attack, PJ?"

I dabbed my eyes and shook my head, unable to speak.

"It's okay. Take it easy. You had two traumatic experiences close together. Each one in itself was enough to unbalance even the strongest of women. You're entitled to be upset."

*   *   *

Now, it was weeks later, and we were thirty thousand feet above the Atlantic Ocean. I sat up suddenly in my seat. I must have squeezed Kim's hand because her eyes flew open, and we shared a startled look.

"Oh, geez. I'm so sorry I woke you. I had a dream… it's just those awful memories." I patted her cheek, brushing my lips against hers. "Go on back to sleep, okay?"

Chapter 2

I had only been dozing off and on, but admitting sleeplessness to PJ wouldn't have helped. She would only worry about me, and she already had so much to resolve in her own life right now. I soothed her back to sleep with a few calming words. Then, remaining alert, I watched over her, marveling at the strange and wonderful way destiny had brought us—two such different human beings—together. We hadn't planned on falling in love; I never thought I could love anyone again. Yet, here we sat, her hand inside mine, our fingers intertwined, holding us together like the weave of fine cloth.

I shifted slightly and gazed through the window. Beneath the wings of the sleek, private jet, the Atlantic stretched from horizon to horizon; a restless, endless, empty sea. What would await us at the other end of that sea?

I had gone without sleep much of the time since we received Sandy's e-mail and follow-up call. Our time in Boston had been hectic enough without the thought of another assignment, but Sandy had persuaded us to drop everything and join him.

PJ's father, Frederick Lane Curtis, had agreed, saying, "You both need to be involved again in what you do best."

It had meant a hectic few days of preparation. And then, there was that ugly business at the airport with those damn reporters. I had been lost in thought and came to in a cold sweat when PJ squeezed my hand. In addition to my concern for her, I was having frequent nightmares—frightening replays of the night that Terry assaulted her. Visiting a shrink was not my idea of fun, but I had promised to meet with Dr. Armstrong, mostly to please PJ.

Dr. Armstrong was a pleasant, attractive woman who lulled me into a sense of ease as I relaxed in her office recliner. "Just tell me in your own words," she had said, "what bothers you most about the events in Wales, especially about what happened between you and Terry."

I wondered if Dr. Armstrong was using some form of hypnosis on me because words came pouring out, despite my determination to keep silent. It was no wonder that PJ held her in such high regard.

"My former lover was in excellent physical condition," I told her, "but I found the strength to pull her off PJ and literally throw her across the room."

She leaned forward, pad in hand, pen poised. "Have you ever lost control or harbored such anger before this?"

My shoulders shifted against the recliner, and I pondered her questions. "A few times. I can remember losing it when I was a teenager and some boys threw firecrackers at my dog."

"Okay." Dr. Armstrong made some notes. "Anything more recent?"

"I'm sure I've had arguments with colleagues over the years, but I don't remember doing anything physical. Oh, there was that incident with PJ's so-called fiancé, Stephen Cresswell."

"Yes, I'm aware of that episode. Apparently, all of the members of your crew felt some form of outrage over how he treated PJ." She leaned back in her chair and crossed her legs. "So, apart from those few instances, you've been able to keep your anger in check until now?"

I noticed that my palms were moist and that I now had a death-grip on the arms of the recliner. When did I get so tense? I took a deep breath and forced myself to relax. "Uh, yes. I've always thought that it took a lot to make me lose my composure. I pride myself on being self-controlled."

Dr. Armstrong tapped the pen against her chin. "But things changed that night?"

"Things definitely changed."

"Why is that, do you think?"

My hands flexed along the recliner's arms. I flashed back to our bedroom in Wales, PJ bleeding, but fighting Terry with her last ounce of strength. Sweat formed on my forehead and neck. The rage emerged in full force. "It was PJ," I blurted out. "The woman I love more than life itself was being attacked and in pain. It's like this fury possessed me." I swiped at my eyes. Much to my embarrassment, the sweat had changed to tears. "That night, I realized I had the ability to kill."

Dr. Armstrong quickly added more notes to her pad, pushing the box of tissues in my direction. "Do you think you could have killed Terry, if you hadn't been interrupted?"

"I really don't know." I dabbed at my eyes and blew my nose. "I do know that I wanted to tear her apart, to punish her." I took a ragged breath. "So yes, I guess I would have killed her if we'd been left alone."

"And how do you feel about that?"

"It frightens me. No matter what Terry did, I had no right to make myself her judge, jury, and executioner." I wadded the damp tissue into a ball. "But when I broke her nose, and her blood spattered over me, the desire to kill was so strong. I was like a shark attracted to blood in the water. I've read where some human behaviorists believe that we're all capable of murder."

"And now, recalling those emotions, how do you feel?"

"Like I said, it scares me, but perhaps what they say is true— that it's always there, lying dormant inside all of us. The urge to protect those closest to us is equally strong in human or beast. So are we so very different?"

Dr. Armstrong leaned back in her seat. "That's a very interesting question, Kim. There are many schools of thought on that subject. I tend to think that humans and animals have a lot of common traits, especially when love enters the picture and, as you say, the 'urge to protect what is near and dear' to us is threatened."

"Loving someone has caused me pain in the past. Then, when Terry left, let's just say I was reluctant to ever put myself in that position again."

"Understandable."

"But this new love… with PJ."

Dr. Armstrong waited and then gave me a little nudge. "Yes?"

I felt tears threaten again. "It's painful, too, for different reasons. I don't want anything to happen to her. I can't bear the thought of losing her, of losing what we have."

"Kim, I don't think I'd be betraying a confidence if I told you that she feels the same way about you. What you two have is a very special bond. It's precious, but it needs space to grow and strengthen."

"That's hard to do. Especially now, when she's so fragile."

"We're working on that. Give her time. She's more resilient than you think."

I sighed. "If you say so."

"Besides, she's worried about protecting you from yourself."

We stared at each other for several long seconds.

"I'm here because I love her, and I made a promise to her. I can handle it."

Dr. Armstrong glanced at the clock and stood up. "Our time's just about up, and I can tell that you're not eager to return."

I rose and shook her hand. "No offense, but you're right."

She held onto my hand an extra beat. "I feel I can help you, but the choice is yours. Know though, that should you ever feel your control slipping, I'll be here for you. I believe in the power of love, Kim."

* * *

The muffled roar of the jet's engines lulled me into a light sleep. I awoke quickly when PJ stirred and snuggled back against my shoulder. I pressed my lips to her forehead and whispered, "I would gladly kill, or be killed, to protect you."

My thoughts strayed to Terry, and again I felt the familiar burning anger inside me. I hoped she was out of our lives forever, because if I were to ever see her again, I don't know how I'd react or what I'd do. Blodwyn Jones, the young police sergeant who had been so helpful to us in Wales, had kept in touch. She wrote that Terry had skipped bail and, though missing, remained actively wanted by the Welsh authorities. My former lover was smart. She wouldn't likely risk coming anywhere near us in the future.

Without moving my upper body, I stretched my legs. It had been a wet summer and I was feeling it in my joints. "What about that?" I whispered, my lips brushing PJ's forehead. "You have an old woman on your hands. But, by the Gods, you know how to make me feel young and frisky."

"Mmm, I love having you on your hands," PJ said, opening her eyes.

We giggled over her risqué comment and might have done more, but Stacie came into the main cabin and asked if we would like some tea.

"Earl Grey," PJ said, without hesitation. "And some cashews." She straightened up and stretched. Her body was lithe, like a cat, and when she stretched that way it always sent my aging hormones racing.

"You okay?" I asked.

"Uh-huh. You?"

"Raring to go."

"You know, I was thinking about some of the things Susanna told me—about what happens to us in life. How everything is the starting point for further growth."

"I suspect she's right."

Stacie brought us a tray of tea, a plate of shortbread cookies, and the Curtis specialty, cashews. We enjoyed our snack with the bright sun shining into the interior of the cabin. The window broke the rays into hundreds of rainbow-colored lights.

"It'll be good seeing Sandy again," PJ said, using both hands to cradle her cup.

I remembered the young man who had befriended her and helped her through her first uneasy days in Arizona. "He really wanted you, you know, until we discovered each other."

PJ laughed. "Yeah, I guess he did. And for a while, I was tempted to get involved with him, but I came to my senses and set my sights on you instead."

I squeezed her thigh. "And, I'm glad you did."

She took a sip of tea. "Besides, I was way too old for him. I would have stunted his growth."

"Probably." I took a long swallow and bit into a cookie.

"Do you remember the look on Sandy's face when he walked in on us that day in camp? Your shoulder was bothering you, and I had you strip to the waist and lay face down on the cot so I could give you a massage." She nodded, smiling. "There I was, straddling your hips. I don't know what he thought was going on, but the look on his face was priceless."

"Yeah, I remember. I don't know which of us was more embarrassed, him or me."

"True."

"So," I said between bites of crumbling shortbread, "do I stunt your growth?"

PJ stared into my eyes, perhaps trying to determine if my question had been serious. "You know better than that," she said. "I need someone with experience and wisdom to keep me grounded."

With my mouth so full I couldn't respond, other than to plant a kiss on her lips, leaving a trail of crumbs, which I forced myself to clean up.

PJ put her cup down. "I love you, even if you do rein me in at times."

"I rein you in? That's a joke."

She gave my ribs a swift poke.

Stacie came to remove our tray, and PJ nestled against me, falling asleep almost at once. She was relaxed, despite having gone through so much. I wanted to believe that she was getting over this bad spell in her life. Everything that had happened to her was, in effect, due to her association with me, a fact that made me feel lousy. I gazed over the top of her head through the jet's small window.

Beneath us, the Atlantic moved unceasingly toward its destiny, mesmerizing me with its vastness.

Despite everything that happens to us, we are just microscopic bits of a huge global picture that includes that expansive ocean beneath us. Do we really know what the future has in store for us any more than we know all that lies beneath those endless waves?

Every day, oceanographers encounter new forms of life. It's hard to believe that ancient mariners once believed that sea monsters lurking beneath the surface could sink their frail vessels and send them to watery graves.

Could we say for sure though, that there were no hidden dangers, no slithery creatures waiting for just the right moment to surface and destroy?

My entire body tensed.

How could I be sure that some day the monster inside me wouldn't burst forth and destroy not only me, but those who were nearest and dearest to me?

Chapter 3

"We're here," I said softly, acknowledging Stacie's instruction to fasten our seatbelts in preparation for landing. Leaning across PJ, I looked through the window, anxious to catch an early glimpse of our destination. From this altitude, I viewed wooded mountains, olive groves, vineyards, and picturesque villages. The plane banked into its landing pattern. I awakened PJ with a light kiss, receiving an inviting moan as her lips responded to mine. "No dear, not now. We're getting ready to land."

PJ opened one eye. "Damn." Her lower lip jutted outward. "You were giving me ideas."

"Later, I promise."

Stacie took Pup to his flight cage and secured him for landing.

PJ sat up, peering through the window with eyes not quite focused. "Is that the Island of Lesbos?"

"Yes, but I believe that the correct pronunciation is Lesvos. It's the third largest of the Greek Isles."

"Then all those white buildings with colorful roofs—that must be Mytiline?"

"Must be." I watched her eyes take on a gleam.

"Lesvos, the birthplace of Sappho, the poet," she said, with a hushed reverence in her voice. Then, she turned to me and hunched her shoulders in girlish delight. "Isn't that exciting?"

"Yes it is." I paused, catching her enthusiasm, but feeling a little guilty.

Was this the right time to tell her? I wondered. I'd better do it and get it over with.

"PJ, I've been here before."

"Oh. I knew you'd been to Greece, but I didn't realize that you'd come here." She was apprehensive now, as if bracing for bad news.

"Yes. Terry and I sailed to several Greek islands on a holiday. I didn't enjoy the trip much. We were already coming apart, though I didn't realize it then."

PJ's eyes flashed. "That was all in the past. This is now." She touched my cheek. "It's exciting for me to be here with you, and I'm going to make sure you enjoy it this time."

"How could I not enjoy it with you beside me?"

I was relieved to discover her old enthusiasm was returning. Perhaps this was what we both needed—to get back to work and give our minds something to think about other than the events in Wales.

* * *

Sandy was waiting for us when we walked into the terminal. He had matured since we had last seen him. He had gained some weight, though most of it was muscle, and sported a blond mustache on his suntanned face. Dark glasses, now perched atop his head in a bed of wind-blown fair hair, had created white circles around his eyes.

He waved and waited for us to clear customs, then flashed that familiar grin when we joined him at the side door of the building. "Hey, Doc, PJ, it's great having you both here." We exchanged hearty hugs and kisses.

"Good to be here with you," PJ and I said at the same time. We looked at each other and laughed.

Sandy joined in. "Geez Louise, you two have been together so much that you're even talking in couple-speak."

"Yeah," PJ said, "and we're both beginning to look like Pup here."

"You look great, both of you. I mean all three of you." He bent to greet Pup and seemed delighted when Pup apparently remembered him. "How did you get him into the country so easily? I thought there'd be all sorts of quarantine to go through."

"It's convenient having one of the wealthiest men on the planet for a father," PJ said, "and one who has the ear of politicians worldwide."

"Must be. How is Frederick, anyway?"

"Couldn't be better. He and I are doing fine, too. We've mended a lot of fences and admitted that we were both to blame for all the lost years."

He gave her another hug. "That's great news. I'm happy for you, and for your dad."

"So what's the big news that you couldn't tell us about when you called?" I asked. "You know we really had to dash to get here on such short notice."

Sandy held up his hand. "I know, and I'm sorry for that, but I didn't want to blab everything on the phone. I was sure when you got here and saw what I'm dealing with, you'd forgive the inconvenience. It's right up your alley, Doc. This is Amazon country, you know."

"Amazons?" PJ's eyes widened. "Don't get her started on them again."

"Okay, maybe not Amazons." Sandy's eyes sparkled as he spoke.

I felt a close affinity for those warrior women, despite PJ's continued reluctance to accept my connection with them. My experiences in Arizona had revealed that my life-long search for the Lost Tribe was something I was compelled to undertake, as if it were preordained.

"It's nice of you to invite us to join you in your discovery, Sandy, but why, if it's that important, do you want to share it with us, or anyone else for that matter?"

He looked around, giving his mustache a few idle strokes. When he answered me his voice had dropped to a conspiratorial whisper. "Frankly, my motives are selfish. I need your expertise. It's way too big for me alone. I need your years of experience."

I wondered if PJ was falling for this flattery.

"Okay, stop buttering us up and tell us about it," she said.

"All in good time." He led us through the side door and out onto the tarmac. "First, let's get your personal baggage stowed in that chopper over there." He indicated the smaller of two blue and white helicopters standing nearby. "Your supplies and tools can go in the other one." The larger helicopter was clearly designed to carry freight. "Afterwards, we'll grab a cup of tea. Are you two still into Earl Grey?"

"It's still our beverage of choice," PJ said. "Let's do it before I wet my pants in anticipation, okay?"

"Got it," Sandy said. "I'll grab my briefcase and meet you at the refreshment stand." He nodded toward a small, white stucco building with a blue-tiled roof and several outdoor tables.

The heat of the sun was tempered a little by the Etesian wind blowing strong from the north. It seemed like a good idea to enjoy some refreshments before moving on to another location.

Sandy caught up with us just as we sat down at a small, round, wrought iron table with a glass top. "No, over there," he said, pointing to a larger table, one that was shielded by a blue and white patio umbrella. "I have some pictures to show you, and I need more space to spread them out. It'll be quieter over there, too."

We moved and requested some tea and baklava.

While waiting for our order, I noticed how well the blue panels of the umbrella and the roof tiles blended with the brilliant azure of the sky. As I studied my surroundings, PJ and Sandy chattered on about trivialities, gossiping like a couple of teenagers, making me aware of the difference in our ages. Such moments were fleeting, however. I had only to make eye contact with PJ to be rewarded with a loving smile and know that we shared a bond that transcended age.

When our refreshments arrived, Sandy played the role of the perfect host by pouring our tea.

PJ took a bite of the baklava. "Mmm, delicious," she said, smacking her lips over the honey-and-nut-filled pastry. She selected a large piece and forced it between my lips. "Try it, you'll love it."

When I had chewed enough to speak, I agreed with her. In fact, if Sandy hadn't been sitting across from us right now, I'd have licked the honey off her fingers. "Must be full of calories, though."

"Don't worry about calories. Sandy will soon have us working off all this decadence." PJ glanced at him. "You will, won't you?"

"Absolutely."

When we had consumed the last crumb and drained the final drop of tea, we pushed our plates and cups to one side to make room for Sandy's pictures.

PJ and I shared a look. "It's about time," she said. "I think I'm about to burst with curiosity, but it's no good rushing him."

"Yes, he always was methodical in his work, but at the same time he had a flair for the theatrical."

Sandy's lips twitched. "Okay, I hear you. It's time to let you in on my discovery. Before I say anything, I want you to look closely at these pictures and tell me what you think. Take time to study them before answering." Barely able to contain his excitement, he arranged the pictures on the table, carefully keeping them in order.

I raised an eyebrow. "These are aerial photos."

Sandy nodded. "Right you are. I knew there was something big here, but it took aerial shots to clue me into the probable location."

We studied the pictures for several minutes. Then we glanced at each other and back at Sandy.

"Whoa," PJ's eyes widened. "This is impressive. If it's what I think, it appears to be bigger than the one on Crete."

"Right again, and we're almost there." He sat back and fingered his mustache. "We'll be breaking through any day now, and that's why the rush to get you here."

PJ stared at him. "Who knows about it, besides the three of us?"

"Your dad."

"Frederick?" I asked.

PJ seemed as shocked as I was. "Why didn't he tell us, instead of allowing us to fly out here without a clue?"

"He wanted to surprise you," Sandy said. "And we did, didn't we?"

I exhaled. "Surprise us? I'll say you did."

"Who else, besides my dad?"

"Obviously my crew knows that we're onto something important."

"Wow." PJ and I looked at each other, still not absorbing all of the possibilities.

"Congratulations." I extended my hand to him. "If this turns out to be what you believe it is, it will assure you a place in history. You know that don't you?"

A flush colored his cheeks. "I haven't given much thought to what happens later."

"I would if I were you, because it will likely become your life's work." I looked again at the photographs. "Are you ready to devote that much time to this project?"

Sandy was silent as he seemed to contemplate the job that lay ahead of him. Then the excitement returned along with his customary modesty. "As long as I have you both to help and guide me, I'm ready."

"Have you considered the downside?" PJ asked. "What if your interpretations are wrong, and this proves to be nothing at all?"

"Being wrong isn't part of my plan."

"I had to ask," PJ said, getting up and going around the table. She kissed him on the cheek. "Congratulations, good buddy, I always knew you'd be famous someday."

"You've done an amazing amount of work in a short time," I said. "I'm proud of you."

*   *   *

Kim stood up. "If you two will excuse me, I'm going to let Pup get some exercise." She nodded toward a nearby park area, now practically deserted. "Do they allow dogs along there?"

"As far as I know, they do," Sandy said.

She touched my arm in passing. "Stay and have some more tea. I'm sure you two have lots to talk about, and I won't be gone long."

Her hand lingered on my shoulder. I gave it a kiss before she and Pup left on their walk.

"So, how have you been, really?" Sandy asked me, waiting until Kim was far enough away to be unable to hear him.

I had a hard time meeting his gaze. It reminded me of the first time I had met him at Sky Harbor Airport in Phoenix in the fall of 1999. I had toyed with the idea of seducing what I thought then was a shy, young man. What a mess I was in those days, determined to screw everyone in sight. Now, I was the bashful one. "I'm working things out, but it's been a rough few months."

His hand slipped across the table to take mine, comforting me with the warmth of his touch. He waited until I looked up and held his gaze. There was so much compassion in his expression that a lump formed in my throat, and I blinked back tears.

"I was really worried about you and Doc. That was an awful thing to happen to the two of you. Please know that I love you both. If there's anything I can do for you, anything you need, just tell me."

"Thank you." I put my free hand on top of his. "Your e-mail messages said as much, but please don't say any more, or I'll start blubbering. I seem to do way too much of that these days."

With a final squeeze, he released my hand. "I understand, and I'm sorry to bring back unpleasant memories." We both watched Kim and Pup in the distance—two legged and four legged stick figures exploring the far reaches of the park. It was several seconds before he spoke again. "How is Doc taking all this? She seems quieter, more intense, and a little distant."

I poked at a sticky drop of honey on the table, focusing all my attention on it. "It was hard on her. We're both going through therapy to come to terms with everything." I managed to look up at him. "Her issues are different. After she and the police rescued me and I was out of the hospital, she came close to killing Terry. I think she would have if Dad hadn't intervened. I know it scared her, but she won't talk to me about it." I took my napkin and rubbed the sticky spot. "We're not quite at the stage where we can discuss it comfortably."

The waiter brought a fresh pot of tea, so we busied ourselves with refills and more snacks. Before long, I heard Pup panting up the path behind me. I lowered my hand and he nudged it with his nose, gliding his tongue across my knuckles. "Hey, guy, where's my best girl, huh?" I scratched behind his ear. "Did you chase her away?"

"Almost," Kim said, breathlessly. "We must have checked out every bush, flower, and tree—some more than once." She poured water into a saucer and put it down beside Pup who lapped it up with gusto.

I stood and stretched. "Now it's my turn for exercise. You two stay here and catch up on old times. I have to find the loo."

"Loo?" Sandy looked puzzled.

"That's British for powder room," Kim said.

"Oh, right."

"When I finish that, I'll check on the cargo loading."

Sandy stood and protested that his crew would attend to that.

I pushed him back into his chair and kissed him on the cheek. "I need to say good bye to our air crew, too, so you guys stay put. I'll be back in a bit. And thanks, cowboy, for the tea and sympathy."

*　*　*

"What is it, Kim?" Sandy must have noticed my silent and bemused expression.

"I'm not sure what to make of that bushy fuzz growing under your nose."

His hand flew to his mustache with unconcealed pride. "You don't like it? I thought it made me look older, more distinguished."

"I guess," I said, not very convincingly.

"PJ said it tickled when I kissed her at the terminal."

"Yeah, I noticed you two locking lips. I wondered if I'd need a crowbar to pry you apart."

He looked at me. "You're kidding, right?"

"I am."

"Good. Then I can tell you that she's a mighty pretty lady, in case you haven't noticed." We both watched her walk into the terminal.

"Oh, I've noticed. Just don't forget she's my pretty lady."

He looked back at me, throwing his hands up in surrender. "I hear you, Doc. You don't have to worry. I loved her; still do, but the best man... er, person won."

I took a sip of tea and peered at him over the rim of my cup.

"You two look good together. I can tell how much you care for each other, and I wish you both a ton of happiness."

"Thank you."

We finished our refreshments, Sandy paid our bill, and we walked toward the helicopters. They stood in awkward silence, their rotor blades in a perpetual pout position. Most of the supplies were already loaded into the larger of the two. A helicopter on the ground is an ungainly thing, I thought, lacking the sleek appearance of a jet or the look of what it often is in flight—a life-saving craft racing toward an accident scene.

"I'm a bit worried, Doc."

I forgot about the pouting helicopters. "Oh?"

"PJ looks kind of tired... and way too serious."

"She hasn't been sleeping well. Neither of us has, but we're getting the help we need. We'll work it out. Just give us some time."

He kept his eyes on the door to the terminal.

"This will help, you know. Our being part of your project, getting back to work again."

"Good." He turned to me, putting his hand on my arm. "If there's anything I can do, anything at all..."

"You're a good friend. Don't think you're not appreciated."

"Then, I hope that when you guys know all the facts, you'll want to be part of the team."

"After you called, we talked of little else. We had to see for ourselves what had you so excited. We can't wait now, after viewing your pictures, to be fully briefed on the project."

For a moment, he looked like a little boy who had stashed a pet frog in his pocket.

"But there's more than that, isn't there? There's a gleam in those blue eyes." I watched a flush come to his cheeks. "Uh-huh. If I didn't know better, I'd say maybe you're in love. Again."

His head bobbed. "Um, there's this girl. Her name is Irini and she's Greek. You'll meet her soon enough."

"Congratulations."

"Not yet." His entire face reddened. "I've been thinking of popping the question, but I haven't gathered the courage."

"So it's serious."

"Yeah," Sandy said, pulling on his mustache, "I guess so."

PJ returned, and any further discussion on the subject was curtailed as we boarded the helicopter for the ride to the west side of the island. Once underway, I could see the landscape changing. The vineyards and olive groves disappeared, and we found ourselves flying over an arid landscape dotted with volcanic rock.

I wondered if PJ's heart was pounding as much as mine at the thought of this new adventure.

Chapter 4

"Here we are," Sandy said, speaking through his headset, his face beaming with pride.

I stared at him in disbelief, and then at PJ who was sitting beside me, her eyes glued to the view unfolding beneath the helicopter.

Four or five acres—approximately twelve hectares of open ground—had been turned into a bustling tent city.

"Sandy, when... how did all this happen?"

"It was fast, Doc. When I got those aerial pictures back and worked up some charts, I flew to Boston. My purpose was to talk to you guys, but Frederick said you were away on a fishing holiday. I briefed him a little on what I thought I'd discovered and told him that I wanted you and PJ to join me, if that was at all possible." He fingered his mustache. "After looking over the pictures and charts, he asked me if I had done anything about funding for the project. I told him, truthfully, that I hadn't gotten that far along yet. The next thing I knew, he was wining and dining me in true Curtis fashion."

I knew how persuasive her father could be and was not surprised to hear PJ laughing.

"My dad didn't amass his wealth by making bad decisions," she said. "So, if he's backing your project, he must think it's worth the risk."

The chopper made a circular descent in preparation for landing, so I saved further questions for later and took another look out of the window. The tent city was right beneath us as we dropped slowly toward the ground and a large X marking the spot of the landing pad. I glimpsed the Aegean in the distance, just before the helicopter's rotors raised a swirling mass of dust and small debris into the air and cut off our visibility. We remained in our seats, keeping Pup in his crate until the motors were shut down and the dust settled. When we stepped outside, a light, warm breeze and the unmistakable scent of the not-too-distant sea greeted us.

"What do you make of all this?" PJ asked quietly.

"For the moment, I'm stunned."

"Come on," Sandy said, "let me take you to your tent and get you settled. We can meet later to go over the charts, and I'll bring you up to speed."

A delicious aroma drifted from the cooking tent.

"We have two of the best chefs in Greece to make sure we're well nourished," Sandy said, looking pleased with himself.

He showed us into a spacious blue tent furnished with a double bed mattress and two brand new sleeping bags still wrapped in plastic. I figured we'd zip those together in no time. When I glanced at PJ, she nodded her head, as if she'd arrived at the same solution.

In addition to the sleeping arrangements, the tent contained a large folding table for computers and such, and a small table with a single burner and a teakettle. Half a dozen boxes of Earl Grey tea were stacked beside the kettle, tied with a festive red ribbon. In another corner of the tent, a small refrigerator was stocked with soft drinks and snacks.

"You've thought of everything," PJ said to Sandy. "The ribbon was a nice touch."

His expression revealed a complex picture of the shy young man and the seasoned scientist.

We placed our laptops on the table and our personal baggage on the mattress. Sandy had assured us that our tools and research materials would be deposited in one corner once the cargo chopper was unloaded. "We have electricity, at least, for the computers," I said, flipping the switch and watching the table-mounted surge protector power up.

"Yep," Sandy said, "that trailer by the helipad generates all the power we need, and if that's not enough, later on, when we really get down to business, we have another one on stand-by."

"What about showers and other necessities?" PJ asked, looking around.

"Over there, in that building." He pointed across the compound. "Showers and toilets. Men on the left and women on the right. By the way, as you may have already discovered, Grecian plumbing is temperamental. Small diameter pipes and low flushing pressure. Throw all your paper into the receptacle provided."

"Oh, yuck. You're kidding, aren't you?" PJ screwed up her nose.

"I'm afraid not."

"How come we even have flushing toilets out here?" I asked.

"This used to be a park of some kind, so that was here waiting for us. It needed a bit of work, but it's okay now."

Pup, meanwhile, had staked out his corner of our cheerful abode and lay with his head on his front paws watching us.

"Sandy, my man," I said, "this beats the hell of what we had in the Superstitions."

*   *   *

After he left, we started unpacking. Kim noticed several new things in my daypack, among them, a book on yoga. "I didn't know you were into that."

"Susanna suggested I try some asanas and meditation to relieve stress. She told me that massage is also good for relaxation." I searched her face for disapproval or concern. Her expression was merely thoughtful, and she took time to study and touch a few of the items I had laid out.

"Scented candles. Lotion. A spiral college-rule notebook with a red cover."

"Not just a notebook, that's my discovery journal."

"Sorry, discovery journal. What will you do with that?"

"Now, don't laugh. I'm supposed to write in it every day and even try some poetry."

Kim's face softened. "I don't think it's funny, though it sounds difficult. If Dr. Armstrong thinks it will help you, I'm all for it." She put her arm around my waist and drew me close. "And you know how I love massages."

"I don't suppose you'd try some yoga with me? Right now, I can't decide if the best time would be first thing in the morning or last thing at night."

"First thing in the morning, I should think." She loosened her grip, and I turned to face her. "I'd be happy to try any of it with you. It never hurts to improve one's flexibility."

I gave her a hug. Thanks to my therapy sessions with Dr. Fleming, I could now welcome Kim's closeness without fear or panic. After what had been a frustratingly long time, we'd become intimate again, and while it wasn't quite our usual, passionate liaison, it had been enjoyable for me and, I hoped for Kim, too. She had assured me that we would be fine with practice. I knew that her continued gentle support would make it so. I believed in her, and she made it clear she believed in me.

As I gazed into her eyes, I noticed that the tiny lines at the corners seemed more pronounced today, or maybe I was just now noticing them. I reached up and stroked her cheek. "You look tired."

She took my hand and kissed my palm. "So do you."

"This has been a long and exciting journey," I said, "and coming so soon after our return from Wales... I guess we haven't regained our stamina yet."

"And it's only just beginning. From his initial data, it appears that Sandy has a major project on his hands."

I detected a gleam in Kim's dark eyes. She was as eager as I was to learn the details of the expedition.

"What do you think of the photos? It could be as big as the Palace at Knossos on Crete."

"It's too soon to tell, and we shouldn't jump the gun. However, there have been rumors of major ruins near Eresos. And it's possible that Skala Eresou is built over ancient Eresos."

"That's exciting."

"There are rumors, too, of other ruins in the area. Maybe Sandy has stumbled onto one of those."

"What do you think, Kimmy?"

"I think we shouldn't get carried away. We don't know anything yet."

"But Sandy thinks he knows."

Still embracing me, Kim rested her chin on top of my head. "It's going to take time, with a little luck and lots of hard work thrown in." She tightened her grip. "In the meantime, we have this cheerful place in which to make ourselves at home."

I looked around and failed to visualize it in such a positive light. Though comfortable about recapturing so much of our relationship, I was not as enthusiastic about our temporary home. "Kimmy, get real. It's a tent."

"Ah, but it's a lovely, big blue tent."

"Isn't that peachy?"

She kissed the top of my head as I leaned my cheek against her chest. Her shirt held the faint scent of fabric softener and spices, so familiar and so comforting. I inhaled her essence, and my anxiety eased, replaced by an overpowering love for this woman who enfolded me in her protective embrace.

"What is it?" She tilted my chin upward, flicking a stray tear from my cheek.

"It's not important." I sniffed, feeling like an ingrate. "I guess I had visions of a secluded villa with a balcony overlooking the

Aegean, that's all. Oh yes, and with bathroom facilities on the premises."

Kim's fingers massaged my back and neck, and I felt the stirring of arousal. It probably wasn't the best time for that.

"Skala Eresou isn't that far away, my love," Kim said. Her hands ventured under my shirt and continued roaming across my lower back. "I'm sure Sandy will allow us a weekend off now and again, for exploring."

"He'd better." I leaned into her, relishing her soothing touch. "That's where Sappho was born. Did you know that?"

"Mmm."

Right now, an ancient poet was the farthest thing from my mind. My hands got busy under her shirt, tickling the sensitive skin just under her bra. I heard her quick intake of breath. "But what do we do when we need to be close before the weekend?" I unhooked her bra, and our breathing grew more labored.

"Sandy has placed his tent and ours a bit farther way from the rest of the camp."

"How perceptive of you to have noticed that."

She gave my neck several kisses. Nimble fingers made short work of the hooks on my bra. I was breathing through my mouth now, pulling her down onto the bed. We let our tongues tease and tangle freely as our desire mounted.

My hands cupped her breasts, and her mouth opened wider, allowing for deeper kissing. She gasped in delight and slid her hands to my chest. Liquid fire filled my lower abdomen.

"It may be a tent," she whispered against my ear, "but it's all ours." We sank back on the mattress. "And what we do in the privacy of our own place..."

"Hey, Doc! PJ!" The cry came from outside the tent. "You in there?"

"...can be interrupted in a heartbeat," I finished as we hastily broke apart and rearranged our clothing.

"Just a second," I called out. From past experience, Sandy knew better than to enter uninvited.

"We'll be right there." Kim lowered her voice to a husky whisper. "Just as soon as we get our breathing back to normal."

I fanned my flushed face. "He'll never know."

"Right. Your face is red, your eyes are still smoldering, and you're breathing rapidly. He won't have a clue."

"It's your fault." I'd been trying unsuccessfully to fasten my bra. I stopped wriggling and turned my back to Kim. "Hook this, please. And hurry."

"Hold still, you're all twisted." She had just pulled my shirt back down when Sandy poked his head through the tent flap.

*   *   *

In the few seconds it took Sandy to call to us from outside the tent and then enter when we gave the all clear, PJ and I had a chance to take a deep breath or two and quiet our libidos.

"Are you two busy?" Sandy asked.

"Not any more," PJ said, keeping her head down, avoiding eye contact.

"Not really," I assured him and then tried to explain the delay in letting him enter the tent. "We were just taking a short nap after the trip. We were in our undies and had to get dressed. What can we do for you?"

"I'd like for you to meet some of the crew." Sandy glanced at his watch. "How about we meet in my tent in an hour? Irini will be here, too, and I'd like you to join us for lunch."

"Sounds great." I glanced at PJ.

"You're getting ahead of me," she said. "Who's Irini?"

"A special friend," I told her.

"Oh." She shot me a questioning look before turning to stare at him, watching his cheeks redden. "Ohhh."

I leaned closer to PJ and whispered, "I'll explain everything soon."

She put her hands on her hips. "Seems to me, there's a whole lot of explaining to be done. For instance, how come Dad knew all about this, but didn't let us in on what you were doing?"

I motioned for Sandy to sit down on one of the folding chairs. I flopped down cross-legged onto the bed, and PJ joined me there, her face still flushed. I wondered if mine, too, showed the remnants of passion.

"He swore me to secrecy," Sandy said. "I had no choice."

"Why, for goodness sake?" PJ looked at me, her eyes spitting sparks. "He's going to get a piece of my mind."

"Don't be too hard on him," I told her. "I'm sure your father had a good reason."

"He wanted to surprise you," Sandy said. "He wanted you to see for yourselves how big a discovery this is. He's funding the whole operation, at least the Curtis Foundation is. What's more, he's so excited about it that he's going to take over as project manager."

"He's what?"

"Easy, honey. Let him explain."

"What it means is that I'm not going to have to worry about the Greek government or local authorities. We won't have to worry about the political aspects of the operation." He stroked his mustache. "We're not going to want for supplies or financial help, either. All we have to do is the archeological work we were trained to do and uncover what's hidden beneath our feet."

"I love my father," PJ said, folding her arms across her chest, "but I'm not sure I want him hovering over me while I'm working."

"That's just it, he won't be doing that. He'll have his job, and we'll have ours. We're a team, working together in this operation. It's as simple as that."

"I guess—if you say so."

"Okay, Sandy," I said, getting up off the bed. "Let's go meet your people and find out what's going on around here."

Chapter 5

Half a dozen Greek graduate students were assembled in Sandy's tent when we arrived there. The tent was as big as ours and furnished in much the same manner, with a double sleeping pad rolled up neatly in one corner. What looked like two sleeping bags zipped together were rolled up on top of it.

Sandy gave us a quick tour, pointing out charts neatly displayed on a lightweight, folding easel, a table with a desktop computer which was for project use only, a laptop for his use, and stacks of project-related papers, sketches, and photographs.

I noted that all the students spoke perfect English. There were four men and two women. Dorian, Tiffany, and Gregor were archaeologists, Alexander specialized in Ancient Forensic studies, Niklas was the team photographer, and Selena was a paleo-archaeologist. From their enthusiastic greetings and specific questions, I learned that they were all familiar with our Amazon work.

Even though they set up chairs for PJ and me, the students seemed to prefer sitting on the floor.

"It's time," Sandy said, "to bring you up to speed on what's happening here."

"You'd think it was a big state secret or something," PJ said.

"Settle down," I whispered.

"But I can't stand all this mystery."

Ever since her experiences in Wales, PJ had been short of patience, especially with herself. I learned rather quickly to ignore her outbursts, because she soon got over them. I didn't really see the point of all the secrecy either, though Frederick must have had his reasons, and Sandy, dependent on the foundation for funding, went along with his wishes. I would have done the same. I had in Arizona, when I learned I had to take his daughter on as my assistant. Thinking back to those tumultuous first days brought happy memories. Breaking PJ in to the expedition's routine was rather like taming a tiger. Sandy's voice penetrated my thoughts, bringing me back to the present.

"Okay. Here's the story," Sandy said. "Kim, PJ, I know you're familiar with the Myth of the Minotaur—the Cretan Labyrinth, because you've sent me links and information whenever I've asked for data."

We nodded.

"What we have here is something far greater than all the myths or factual sites, greater even than Knossos. We think that beneath our feet is a labyrinth of gigantic proportions. We have reason to believe that it was at one time hidden under a fortress or palace."

PJ gasped.

I held my breath.

He looked at each one of us in turn. "History does not tell us that there ever was such a structure on this spot, but my research, the photographs, and everything else points to a labyrinth buried beneath the rubble of another structure or structures. It could be an ancient village or a palace that was built on top of an even older ruin. The labyrinth might possibly have been a buried fortification. We don't know yet what we're going to find."

I stood up. "You're sure of what you're seeing in those aerial photos?"

"I am."

"Is it possible that the impressions shown in the pictures could be misinterpreted?" He opened his mouth to speak, but I cut him off with one more question. "Could they be of natural origin?"

"Yes," PJ added, "how can you be so sure?"

"Look at the charts." Sandy stepped over to the easel. "If you look at the circular design of the impressions, you'll see that there's nothing in the natural world that would be so precise. It has to be a man-made structure. It just has to be."

"What about water run-off, old stream beds, or ditches?"

"Dr. Blair," he said, addressing me formally, "streams meander according to the lay of the land. The pattern here is not random. It's too even, too orderly."

"You mentioned when you met us at the airport," PJ said gently, "that you always felt there was something here, but you admit that there isn't a lot of factual research to back you up."

"I know, but I've been reading some of Lester Malloy's book on Sappho."

"Malloy's book is hardly scientific," PJ said. "He's been known to take liberties with data in the past."

Sandy pushed some papers to one side and perched himself precariously on the corner of the table, keeping one foot firmly on the floor. "He's collected as much real data as anyone can on the subject of Sappho. We know she was born near here, at ancient Eresos. From piecing together scraps of her life story, Malloy determined that she lived quite well. Possibly in a palace, or at least in the home of a wealthy merchant."

"But did Malloy's book convince you beyond any doubt?" I worried that he had ventured too far from scientific principles, but there were those enticing photographs, as well as Frederick's enthusiasm.

"Her ultimate joy was here. This is the place. I know it in my heart. Malloy quoted Sappho as referring to beautiful gardens and a citadel."

"I can't believe that you've based your thoughts and theories on such incomplete information." I regretted the words as soon as they left my mouth, but he appeared to take no offense at my comment.

"And you think she lived right here, on this very spot." I felt that PJ's words were more statement than question.

He turned to her, shaking his head. "No. What I'm saying is that she *could* have lived here, in a place like this. Not enough of her life is known for us to be specific."

But is it specific enough to risk your professional reputation? What are you thinking? I was afraid he was making a big mistake. He shouldn't gamble his future on fragmentary data. That sort of speculation had ruined the careers of many respected scientists, and made crackpots of otherwise intelligent archaeologists, some whom I knew personally. Before the women were discovered in those caves in Arizona, many of my contemporaries scoffed at my ideas, too. I didn't want that to happen to him.

But what about Frederick? Sandy must have convinced him that this was no ordinary project. He said it was Frederick who had suggested the partnership. Frederick was an extremely wealthy man, an astute business tycoon. He would not back a project without a thorough investigation. Sandy couldn't have convinced him just by quoting Malloy, so I had to trust Sandy's belief in the project and Frederick's intuition.

"Our teams of local laborers and students have been working around the clock and are this close." Sandy gestured with forefinger and thumb. "When we break through, and that will be any day now, we'll make our discovery… at least, I hope we will. Then, it'll be pure archaeology from then on, and it will be big."

Sandy was enthusiastically convincing. I gave him that. I could tell he totally believed in the project.

* * *

When the meeting broke up, Kim and I shook hands with each of the students, assuring them that we'd meet later for some informal discussions. While Kim and Sandy discussed further proton magnetometer probing of the area in question, I took a moment to survey the private corners of the huge tent. It was bigger than ours because it doubled as the expedition's office. Sandy's private quarters were toward the back and were furnished like ours with a double bed pad and two sleeping bags zipped together. He was sleeping with someone. I couldn't wait to tell Kim. Maybe it was this Irini person.

Pup stood up and wandered over to the tent entrance and sniffed the air, giving a soft whine and a whimper.

"What's the matter, fella?" I bent down to scratch behind his ears. The most divine scent of baked goods wafted through the opening, and a beautiful, dark-haired young woman appeared, dressed in jeans and a colorful T-shirt. The fabulous aroma came from the large basket of breads and pastries that she carried.

"Hello." I pulled Pup to one side so she could enter the tent.

She looked confused until she saw Sandy talking with Kim and she relaxed. "Kherete, hello," she said, extending her hand to me. "And welcome to Greece. You must be Dr. Curtis."

"Yes."

"Sandy has told me so much about you and Dr. Blair."

"And you must be?"

"I am Irini."

I shook her hand formally. "Sandy has not told us nearly enough about you, but then, we haven't been in touch until the past week or so. Please call me PJ."

Sandy had turned at the sound of her voice. A delighted expression spread across his face, and my heart gave a little thump. Whether he knew it or not, it looked as though he'd met that special someone.

"Doctors," he said, with a wave of his hand, "may I present Irini Thanos. Irini, this is Dr. Kimberly Blair, the best archaeology professor I ever had, as well as my mentor, and very good friend."

Kim asked to be called by her first name also, and soon we were chatting away like old friends. I watched Sandy relieve Irini of the basket and slide his free arm around her waist. They made a handsome couple: her olive skin, flashing dark eyes, and waist-length, shiny black hair complemented his blonde hair and blue eyes.

They led the way toward the mess tent for our first lunch on site.

I elbowed Kim. "Looks like our cowboy has found himself a woman."

She poked me back. "Think she'll stunt his growth?"

Her teasing comment brought a pang of regret at losing my number one spot in Sandy's affections. "Hey, I found my true love. Why shouldn't he?"

We watched him snatch a pastry out of the basket he was carrying and stuff it into his mouth as they walked.

"I think she'll be perfect for him," I said. "She's already found a way into his heart."

"Men are so easily led."

"Says someone who can't wait to get to the food tent."

"Can you blame me? The aromas coming from that place are incredible."

* * *

I don't know what Kim was expecting lunch to be like, but it certainly didn't disappoint me. Sandy assured us that it wasn't an affair of festive proportions every day. Thank goodness for that. If it were so, we'd be the heaviest archaeologists on the planet. We suspected that this feast was in honor of our joining the expedition.

We were introduced to the chefs, Demetri and his son Pietro. Both men were big and unmistakably Greek, with dark curly hair. Demetri sported a full handlebar mustache and spoke in loud bursts of Greek-accented English. His son was more reserved and spoke English with very little accent. Sandy told us that Pietro had attended culinary schools in France and England before returning to his native Greece, and both men had worked in Athens at one of the more fashionable restaurants. Sandy was able to hire them for as long as they were needed.

They greeted us with effusive hugs, kissed our hands, and asked a multitude of rather personal questions. We weren't too surprised because the guidebooks we had hastily consulted prior to our trip had warned that many Greeks were friendly and inquisitive.

"Ah, pretty lady," Demetri tapped his large, surprisingly soft palm against my cheek. "Dr. PJ, you are American?"

"I am."

"Are you married?"

That caught me off-guard. "Um, no."

"Ela! Impossible. How old are you?"

I was not prepared for such a thorough grilling and cast a quick glance at Kim who seemed to be enjoying my predicament. "Thirty-six."

He turned and dragged Pietro to his side, giving his son's back a solid thump. "You like my boy, my Pietro?"

"We just met, but—"

"He will make a good husband, no?"

My face burned from this scrutiny. Sandy and Irini, trying to keep from laughing, found seats along one long table. I tried to join them, but Demetri was waiting for my response, and his large frame blocked my escape route. "Yes, I'm sure he will. I'm… um… not married, but I have someone very special in my life. Thank you, though, for thinking of me. I'm flattered."

"Ah, so." He shoved Pietro back toward the serving trays and wiped his hands on his snowy white apron. "The pretty lady has someone special. He is a lucky man."

I didn't know how to respond at first, but when I looked over at Kim, the right words came easily. "No, I'm the lucky one."

Demetri marched me to a seat and then focused on Kim. "Are you American, too, beautiful lady? Dr. Kim?"

"Uh-huh."

"Married?"

She shook her head.

It was my turn to watch her squirm.

He made sympathetic noises, then thought for a moment. "Special someone for you?"

"Yes, as a matter of fact, there is." Kim glanced quickly in my direction. "But before you ask how old I am, let me ask you a question."

Demetri pressed his palms together and bowed. "For you, Dr. Kim, anything."

"What are we having for lunch that smells so good?"

Demetri beamed. From my vantage point, it appeared Kim had made a good friend. Lunch began with salads of olives, tomatoes, feta cheese, mushrooms, and some dry, crisp bread. That was followed by lamb souvlaki with warm pita bread and a medley of vegetables, all presented with a flourish.

Pietro watched while we ate and enjoyed the feast, giving us a shy nod when we offered our praise. Demetri, on the other hand, seemed to take our compliments in stride, acting as though he expected them.

Sandy requested a simple dessert of fruit. "We don't usually have this sumptuous a lunch," he admitted. "I guess our chefs heard about our illustrious guests and whipped up a banquet."

"I'm certainly glad to hear that." I patted my stuffed belly. "I read that Greek suppers were usually the biggest meal of the day."

"Oh, they are," Irini said. "We often take a rest in the afternoon and don't start dinner until later in the evening. "But Sandy has his workers on a more American schedule." Her eyes glittered as he squeezed her hand, and she blushed when he kissed her check.

We made a few toasts to the project and to our good health. Some of the crew drank a small glass of wine. Kim and I had bottled water. I looked around at the assembled staff. Quite a congenial group.

Irini's voice brought me out of my reverie. "Kim, PJ, I have brought you both small gifts from my village." She offered Kim a lovely pendant of blue and white beads. "This will ward off the Mati, the evil eye," she said. "Superstitious, I know, but a wish for good fortune, just in case."

"Thank you, Irini. It's lovely." Kim held up the amulet so we could all see it.

"And for you," she said, handing me a string of wooden beads, "I offer Komboloi. Greek worry beads. Traditionally, only for men, but lately it has been most fashionable for women to use them." She held them up to show us how the string was held with most of the beads hanging over the middle finger, then flicked up onto the palm so the index finger and thumb could rub each bead individually. "They are made of olive wood from very old groves. Sandy told me of your recent troubles, PJ, and I wish to take some of the stress out of your life."

My eyes stung with tears. I took the beads and practiced the maneuver she had demonstrated. "Thank you so much. I will treasure them always, along with your kind thoughts."

We offered our thanks to Demetri and his son, praising them for their culinary efforts, vowing to return for dinner with appetites worthy of the occasion.

Apparently Sandy had declared our arrival some kind of a holiday. He and Irini left the group to stroll around the compound. Kim and I returned to our tent.

Neither of us noticed that Pup was missing until he padded into the tent with a large bone clenched between his teeth. He flopped down on his bedding with a throaty whine.

"It seems our Pup has found a kindly benefactor," I said, as Kim and I stretched out alongside each other on the air mattress.

"Mmm," she whispered in my ear before nibbling on the lobe. "I'll bet he didn't have to go through any third degree to get it either."

"Yeah, wasn't that something?" I remembered the look on Pietro's face. "I think the son is kind of shy. I was embarrassed for him."

"He's probably used to it," Kim said. "I think Demetri is eager to push poor Pietro to the altar." She slid her hand under my shirt and traced lazy circles around my bellybutton, making me giggle.

"But enough about them. We have a whole afternoon to pleasure ourselves."

When she lifted my shirt and kissed my belly, the giggles turned to moans.

Chapter 6

"This is the hardest part." PJ and I stood watching the laborers going about their work. "The waiting, the anticipation, and the inability to do much. It's tough."

She glanced in Sandy's direction. "And it looks like it's really getting to him."

We were standing beside a makeshift table composed of a faded green door that a local worker had found and placed on top of a couple of sawhorses. On it, Sandy's charts lay open, anchored at the corners with four rocks. The sound of shovels sliding into the dirt was mesmerizing. Whenever metal clanked against stone, everyone stopped, picked up less damaging tools, and scraped or brushed the area at a slower, more cautious pace.

"This is wearing on anyone," I said, "especially Sandy. He's put his heart and soul into this project, and it's taking longer than he thought to uncover anything of value."

"Tell me about it," PJ said. "I can remember the frustration a certain archaeologist suffered when she bet her whole life on a lost tribe of Amazons."

"Point taken." I hoped my look conveyed all the love I felt for her. Thinking of our love brought something else to mind. "It's not true, you know, that his heart is one hundred percent into the project. A good part of it belongs to a certain Greek beauty."

PJ narrowed her eyes and cocked her head. "It is possible to fall in love and devote most of your time and energy to a major archaeological project."

I gave her hip a nudge. "You're sure about that?"

"Uh-huh. I heard of a rare case in Arizona awhile back, but I forget the details."

"Don't worry, I'll refresh your memory." I lowered my voice to a whisper. "Later, when we're alone."

"Mmm. I think I'd like comparing notes with you on that subject, Dr. Blair."

* * *

It was disappointing and tiring when days passed with nothing but dirt and rock to show for our work. PJ and I joined the crew, sifting loads of soil for signs of ancient habitation, but so far, we'd found nothing. Sunshine beat down on our heads, and we were often distracted by curious visitors who stopped on the outskirts of the compound to see what was going on. Sandy had signs posted around the area indicating that this was an archaeologically-sensitive site. Security personnel would remove any trespassers.

One morning, during our digging and sifting, I noticed Sandy standing apart from the project, hat off, scratching his wispy mustache, talking to himself. I wiped my hands and walked over to him. "Don't sweat it, buddy."

"What? Oh, sorry. I didn't hear you, Kim." He replaced his hat.

"I've been over and over those aerial photographs, and I believe that you're on to something. Just what, remains to be seen."

"Yeah, that's what worries me. Suppose I overestimated the historical value of the site?"

My attempts at reassuring him didn't appear to be working. Perhaps he needed a more professional approach. "You were smart having your photographer take overlapping vertical and oblique shots, so they could be viewed stereoscopically. That, in itself, tells us a whole lot."

"I did everything I could, Doc. Shortchanging the initial investigation was something I wasn't about to do. I needed to be as sure-as-damn-is-to-swearing that I was right, before I put other people's money into the cause. I don't understand why we haven't broken through. According to my calculations...."

This was Sandy's first major discovery. It was his baby. I could understand the pressure, the second-guessing; I'd been there myself, often.

"Incorporating the digitized and mapped information within the Geographical Information System plots was a smart move," I said, mainly to underscore the fact that so far, he had done everything right. "You have a three dimensional image of something, be it a labyrinth or the remains of an ancient village—either will be important."

He nodded slowly and thoughtfully, as if mentally reviewing the steps he had taken and the comments I'd made. "The GIS plotting zeroed me into this spot. It's one reason I'm so sure—"

PJ squealed, and the laborers chattered excitedly. Sandy and I rushed to their location. A dirt-filled wheelbarrow stood in our path, but Sandy vaulted it easily. I went around it. One of the laborers had struck stone. PJ, Dorian, and Tifani were on their knees, trowels in hand.

"I think we're onto something," PJ called over her shoulder, as she and the others continued to scrape and scratch with careful urgency.

I felt that familiar thrill of discovery building inside me. This was not an odd rock blocking the path of progress; this object was tall and rounded. As fast as PJ and the others worked, dirt fell about them, the dust coating them in a tan-colored cloud. After carefully brushing the dirt away, they uncovered the base of a broken column. The diggers backed off to allow Niklas to photograph each piece, while Gregor took measurements and charted the find.

"Your calculations are off by about two meters." Gregor looked at Sandy as he spoke. "That's pretty darn close, boss."

Sandy was speechless. He stood staring at the broken column.

"I knew it," he managed to utter in a hoarse whisper.

I felt that one word from any of us just then would probably reduce him to tears.

PJ stood up, dusted herself off, and gave him a kiss on the cheek. "Nice going, fella."

He pulled her into a clumsy embrace. "Thanks."

"Congratulations, Dr. Arnold." I shook his hand, as tears smudged both his cheeks and mine.

"Congratulations to all of us," he said.

We allowed the laborers to take over, carefully, but swiftly moving the dirt from the center of the excavation to the entrance, using gentle strokes to scrape the surface with their shovels before digging deeper into the dirt.

It was a slow process, taking several days, as more pieces of the collapsed column were unearthed, measured, and photographed. Through it all, the workers maintained a quiet, almost reverent demeanor, never losing their patience or their interest in reclaiming some of their heritage.

A few weeks after the initial discovery, one of the laborers, a grizzled villager by the name of Eugenio, slid his shovel into a void. He shouted as the dirt gave in around him, revealing a half dozen crumbling stone steps and a passageway.

"The sun shines on my past," he said, in excited, halting English.

Although the light was bright outside, we could see only a little way into the passage. It appeared to be accessible.

Sandy released the laborers for lunch while we, together with the excited students, continued to probe first the opening with trowels and brooms, and then the interior of the passage with strong flashlights. Two columns flanked the entrance. The first one was fragmented; the second one had survived in somewhat better shape, though it, too, was broken in half. We studied the spiral scrolls on what remained of the capitals and determined them to be of Ionic design. We worked until darkness forced us to stop.

"Loukas did the electrical hookups for the generators. I'll have him run some power in there so we can see what we're doing," Sandy said, after thoroughly examining the immediate area of the entrance and pronouncing it safe. "Let's get cleaned up and break for a meal. After that, we'll rest a bit and make some plans for further work shifts."

* * *

That evening, the moon illuminated our tent village in a pearl-white, shadow-casting glow.

"The light of the Gods," PJ said, as we walked with Pup close on our heels. Although we were bone tired, we couldn't sleep. The events of the past days, the opening of the entrance and all that it implied, had left us with too much on our minds.

At the top of the ancient stone steps, staring downward into the dark unknown, I put my arm around PJ. She was trembling.

"What is it?" I glanced sideways, but her face was in shadow, so I couldn't read her expression.

She leaned into me. "I don't know. I've been having a weird feeling that there's more down there than we expect." Pup sat at her feet, looking up at her as if he, in his own canine way, was trying to put her at ease.

"You're still on edge, after what happened in Wales." I brushed my lips against her sweet-smelling hair. "Dr. Armstrong told us it would take time, so don't be impatient with yourself. Try not to read more into this excavation than is really here."

"I'm not, am I?"

"You tell me."

She took a step downward. "Let's take a look."

"Now?"

"There's nothing here but empty passages and, if we're lucky, some artifacts that will date the structure. Isn't that what you meant, when you told me not to read anything more into it?"

"That's what I said, but I hardly think that one in the morning, when no one else is around, is the time to go exploring."

PJ shone her flashlight into the depths. "So you're reluctant, too?"

I added my light to hers. "I prefer to call it prudent. All we know for sure is that these steps lead into what appears to be a fairly well-preserved passage. We don't know where it goes from there or what condition it's in beyond the entrance, and we have to make sure it's safe. That'll take time."

PJ exhaled and climbed back to my level. "You're right, of course. I wasn't thinking."

I couldn't blame her for being impatient. The Ionic columns marked the entrance to a potential blockbuster of a find, but much work had to be done before we could continue.

"We'll be in there soon enough," I said, taking her hand.

On the return loop to our tent, we passed Sandy's tent. We could see a light glowing inside.

"Insomnia must be contagious tonight," I whispered.

He stepped out, wearing only a pair of boxer shorts. "I thought I heard you guys. What are you doing up so late?"

"Too much on our minds," PJ said. "We couldn't sleep."

"Me neither. The promise of what we might find in that passage makes it hard to sleep."

"Where's Irini?"

"Oh, she had to go into Athens. Some family thing."

"Since you're all alone, how about a cup of Earl Grey?" I asked. "Considering the hour, we'll make it decaf."

"Sure. Your place or mine?"

"Ours," I told him, "since our project leader left us a huge supply."

"Geez, what a thoughtful guy."

PJ snickered. "We think so, even if he doesn't get enough sleep."

"Okay, I'll get some cookies and… um…" He hugged his bare chest. "I'll be there as soon as I get into a shirt and pants."

"No need. You can see we're pretty casual."

She was in old cut-off jeans and a blue sports bra, and I wore my standard sleepwear while away from home—a pair of well-worn scrubs.

Sandy joined us in our tent, and after an hour of socializing, he yawned a few times. PJ and I agreed that we were relaxed enough to get some sleep. Before parting, however, all three of us vowed to continue such impromptu gatherings whenever necessary.

* * *

"Ommmmm, Shanti, Shanti, Shanti. Ommmmmm, Shanti, Shanti, Shanti." Two nights later, I was in our tent in the padmasana, the lotus position, determined to free my mind of the excitement surrounding us. Rest was not easy when thoughts constantly flitted in and out of my brain. I had read that Om in Sanskrit is spelled "aum," and each letter was a sacred symbol. As I attempted to balance my mind, body, and spirit, I reflected on the self in a material world, the psychic realm, and the indwelling spiritual light. I heard Kim's breath catch, and I opened my eyes in time to see her grabbing her lower back.

"What's wrong?"

"Those darn chairs in Sandy's tent. I'm stiff from sitting in them, and now I've got a major kink."

That was all I needed to hear. I popped right out of my meditative posture and kneeled at her side.

"Lie down on your stomach."

After much grimacing, she was positioned. I placed my hands on her firm, thinly-covered rear end. "Let me take care of it." Suddenly, I was meditating on a whole new subject. Kim certainly had a buff looking butt. I was reluctant to move my hands.

"PJ, the problem is in my back. You know, a little higher up."

"Sorry. I got distracted." Straddling her hips, I pushed her shirt up to expose the lower lumbar area and started massaging. "How's this?"

"Mmm. Feels much better. Keep it up."

"Hold on a second. Let me get some lotion. That'll make it feel even better." I padded over to our supplies. Pup stirred and rolled over. He snuffled softly, dreaming no doubt, of Greeks bearing gifts of large soup bones.

I squeezed a good-sized portion of mango-scented fluid into my palm and gazed at that luscious butt again. It was so hard to concentrate. She turned her head at that moment and caught my rather lecherous expression.

"Hiya, gorgeous." My voice sounded husky, even to my ears.

"Save it for when I don't hurt."

"Yes, ma'am." I resumed my massage, working all the muscles with equal attention. I finished her lower lumbar region, unhooked her bra, and worked my way upward over her exposed skin.

"Gods, that feels so good. You are wonderful with your hands. Have I ever told you that?"

"As a matter of fact, you have." I placed a kiss on the wide expanse of her back, realizing the remark could be taken several ways.

"What a dirty mind you have tonight, PJ." She turned her head toward me. "Lucky for you, I love dirty-minded blondes."

"Do you? I haven't heard you saying as much lately."

She frowned. "Is that true? Haven't I told you that I love you today?"

"Nope. But it's still early. There's time." I continued working.

"I do love you, you know."

"I know. And I love you, too… very, very much."

A contented silence followed, during which I remembered when we had first met. "Kimmy, when did you first feel attracted to me?"

"Funny, I was thinking along those same lines. I think it was when I saw that picture of you in a bikini in *People*."

I gave her back a light slap. "Go on! You didn't. You did? Really?"

"Uh-huh. And when I read your paper on tools and artifacts of the Alibates Flint Quarries."

"Oh, now I know you're joking."

"I swear it. I saw that picture and two days later read that article. I knew, then and there, you were a woman with beauty and brains."

"Geez, I'm flattered, even though I know you never read *People*. Besides, I didn't know you cared so deeply about Clovis points. And other things."

"I did, too, read *People*… as a diversion when I was standing in checkout lines."

"If you were so interested, why didn't you contact me?"

"Because I assumed you were straight."

"Mmm. Yes, there was that." I pulled her shirt back into place.

"And, we didn't exactly get off on the right foot."

"True." Kim had been convinced that I'd seduced Sandy on my first afternoon in Apache Junction, and she was understandably indignant.

"So, when did you first become attracted to me?"

I kept her waiting, but I knew. "It was when Sandy and the guys and I arrived on the site in the Superstitions that first day. I saw you working with the students, and I was so impressed with the rapport you had with them, the way they respected you."

"Interesting."

"When did you know it was love you were feeling for me, Doc?"

She exhaled. "Now that's a little harder to pin down. Was it when you threw up all over my cactus garden?"

"Oh, God."

"Or, was it when you told that reporter about the expedition and got it spread all over the news?"

"Geez."

"Nope. I think it was when you tried to confess your guilt to your father. I got a real shock that night, when I saw how things were between you and him. That took real courage, and I loved you for it."

"Aw. But you didn't let me take the blame."

"You were willing to, and that was enough for me. So, when did you know you were in love with me?"

I gave her butt a pat. "I'm still deciding."

She rolled her hips, nearly tossing me off our mattress.

"Hey, take it easy. You'll undo all my good massage work."

"Come on, PJ. When did you know?"

"It was a gradual thing, I guess. Let me think. I knew when I kissed you after Thanksgiving dinner and had to confront you on site about it later. Remember how you ran away from me like a big chicken?"

"Hey, I thought you were straight."

"But I wasn't. At least not where you were concerned. It just took me a while to realize it. I had spent a good deal of time trying to sleep with every male in the New England area, and for that matter, around the world. I kept wondering why I didn't feel anything significant with any one of them. I didn't know early on, like you did."

She folded her arms under her cheek, turning her head to the other side. "Let me tell you, love, knowing you're different at an early age can be a real bitch."

I slid off her hips. The discussion had just moved into uncharted territory. I had been curious about her youth, but she had never talked about it. I stretched out beside her, pulling the covers over us. "What was it like for you, growing up?"

Her eyes closed and, for a few moments, I thought she had shut me out, again. "I grew up with parents who couldn't accept me as different, as gay. My father and brother refused to have anything to do with me. My mother hoped I'd grow out of it. We lived in a small town in the Midwest. The saying, 'small towns, small minds,' fit Plainfield perfectly, at least when it came to sexual preference. I think my mother mellowed a bit, just before she died, but not Father or my brother Kurt. Eight years ago, when my father died, Kurt sent me a card, but that was to tell me I would not be welcome at the funeral."

"Jesus. I'm sorry." I stroked the side of her jaw and pulled us together for a kiss.

"Yeah, well. It's in the past now. Let's just say I didn't have a very loving childhood and let it go at that."

"Wasn't there anyone you could talk to?"

"No people. Only Rusty, my cocker spaniel. He was my constant companion. I used to talk to him when things got too bad. We'd hide out in the shed or go fishing in the creek. Rusty never let me down. He didn't care if I was straight, gay, or alien."

"You've always loved dogs?"

"Yes. They don't judge you. They just try to please you and love you, no matter what." Her voice softened. "That's what got Rusty killed."

"Oh, Geez. I didn't mean for this to bring back painful memories."

"What it brings back is disgust and anger when I think of those punks." Her jaw tightened. So much for the gentle massage and the warm thoughts of love I had hoped to instill. "Four jerks from junior high school used to tease me. I never went to dances or made goo-goo eyes over them when they played football. I wasn't the least bit interested in them, and they knew it. One day, they followed me home from town. It was just before the Fourth of July. A couple of the guys had the little snapping firecrackers that come joined together in a string. They shut me up in the shed and tossed a lit string of them inside. Rusty tried to defend me and got badly burned. I was so enraged that, when I got out of the shed, I beat all four of them to a pulp and sent them racing home with bloody noses." Tears welled up and she swiped them away.

"Oh, God." I fought off my own tears, thinking of her pain. If Kim had been able to consult Susanna then, Susanna might have suggested anger management. But hell, that was a time when anger was appropriate and justified, at least in my opinion.

"I wish I could tell you Rusty recovered—that I got him to the vet in time—but he was in too much pain." Kim's eyes burned with intensity. Pup stood up and came over to lick her face. She hugged his neck.

A wave of anxiety hit me, and I fought to control it. "I have to wash this lotion off my hands, honey." I planted a kiss on her cheek. "You know if I could make it all better, I would."

"I know. Thanks."

"I can't bear to see you in pain. It tears me up inside."

She nodded her head. It was obvious to me she was still shaken. "I feel the same way about you. Seeing you hurt makes me go crazy. I felt that way when I wanted to kill Terry for what she did to you."

I paused at the tent flap and turned. "Kimmy, please. Can we not talk about that right now?" I tried to find a calm image to concentrate on. "This'll just take a moment. Okay?"

"Sure thing."

"Save me a spot?"

She rubbed her chest. "Right here next to my heart."

"Love you."

"Me too. I'm sorry you're upset right now, but I'm here for you."

"Always?"

"Forever, PJ."

* * *

When I returned to our tent about twenty minutes later, I felt calmer, and Kim was nearly asleep. She pulled me close when I slid onto the mattress facing her. Pup shook himself and settled into a contented comma on his bed.

"Feeling better now?" Kim's hands made light feathery strokes across my back.

"Much. How about you?"

"I'm good, but I think we both needed a time out. Things got a little too intense."

"My fault. I made you relive some bad times and when you got upset, it sent my anxiety meter soaring."

"You didn't mean to, honey. I was surprised to have such strong feelings surface after all these years."

"One thing I've learned from my weeks in therapy: You just never know when something painful is going to surface. I guess we're both sensitive to certain memories."

Kim kissed me gently. "We're still learning about each other. I think after a few decades we'll have it all worked out."

I returned her kiss. "You're willing to stick with me for that long, then?"

"Absolutely. One thing I've learned by having you in my life is that love makes all the difference."

"I couldn't agree more." I rested my head against her chest. "Will you hold me until I fall asleep?"

She wrapped me in her arms and touched her lips to my forehead. "Always."

Chapter 7

Days turned into weeks, with the labyrinth slowly revealing bits and pieces of its secrets. PJ and I joined the crew in exploring numerous side passages and niches. It was slow, painstaking work. Using the electrical facilities near the entrance and linking power cords together, we were able to explore over nine hundred meters, counting the numerous side passages and rooms. Beyond that distance, we relied on powerful flashlights, lanterns, and spelunker style headlamps attached to our hardhats.

The structure so far was in remarkably good condition and had been pronounced safe, with only two places requiring reinforcement. Forty meters from the entrance, the initial passage curved to the right where two side passages veered away from the main one. The first dead-ended at twenty-five meters. PJ, Gregor, Niklas, and I proceeded slowly, aware that one misstep could destroy something of vital importance. Because we were forced to progress deliberately, we had not yet ventured to the end of the second passage, nor had we followed the main one.

PJ and I stood peering into what looked like an entrance to a low-ceilinged storage room, no larger than five by three meters. "What do you think?"

She pointed. "There are some jars in there, against the back wall. Let's check them out."

Before I could suggest she wait for a safety inspection, she crawled into the narrow passage. "Come on. It's okay."

"Wait!" I handed her a pair of lightweight covers for her shoes. "I don't see any prints, but we don't want to disturb the floor too much." I put some on and gave a pair to Niklas and Gregor.

Dust filtered downward from the ceiling as we maneuvered laboriously within the tight space. I followed PJ to the back wall. "Being short has certain advantages right about now," I said, when forced to bend my head in order to stand upright. The room was no more than a niche in the wall of the main passageway, a cache for whatever was stored in the vessels, two rows of which stood just as they could have quite easily been placed many centuries before. A third row had been started. Two of those vessels lay tipped over, but undamaged. Another one, possibly two, had broken, and the shattered pieces were scattered about the floor.

I motioned to Niklas and Gregor to join us in the alcove. We moved to the side, allowing them space to take pictures, measure, and chart the location and position of the jars and shards. They were both slight of build and maneuvered easily in cramped quarters.

"Can we peek inside?" PJ was eager to see what was in the vessels.

"I wouldn't disturb anything until Sandy has had a chance to examine everything."

"I suppose."

We concentrated our light near the mouth of one of the tipped over jars.

I lightly touched my fingers to the dirt. "Looks like some kind of grain."

PJ tapped a couple of the standing vessels with her fingers. "Metal and pottery both." She turned to me. "Isn't that strange?"

"Unusual, but not necessarily strange." Careful to hold it only by the edges, I picked up a shard of the broken jar and blew off the loose dust. "This appears older than I would have expected. Minoan perhaps."

"How did it get here?"

"Probably passed down through the generations. Hard to tell anything until we investigate further."

"Maybe someone got them at a local flea market," she said.

The ceiling appeared stable despite the occasional dust sifting down on top of us. We examined the floor for ancient footprints. If there were any, centuries of fine dust had long since covered them. The hair peeking out from under our hard hats was matted with it, and it coated our faces, hands, and clothing.

We waited in silence for Gregor to finish up. It was so quiet in the alcove that we could hear each other's breathing and the scratching of Gregor's pen on paper. PJ moved closer to me.

"Do you feel anything?"

"Like what?"

"I don't know. It's silly, but it's as if we're being watched."

"Ghosts. They don't like us messing with their grain," I said, making light of her remark.

"No, it's something else."

Glancing sideways at her, I realized that she had been serious, and I regretted my flippant remark.

"I'm finished for now," Gregor told me.

"Then let's get out of here and call it a day," I said.

* * *

Once outside in the sunshine, we dared to take deep breaths. "You okay?" I asked PJ.

"Yeah. Why?"

"I don't know. You were quiet on the way out."

"Must have been a touch of claustrophobia." She wrinkled her nose. "Isn't that something for the books, an archaeologist with claustrophobia?"

"That's something all right." I was relieved to see the return of her normal lighthearted demeanor.

We entered our tent, where Pup greeted us in his typical boisterous fashion.

PJ dropped to her knees to give him hugs and belly rubs. Then she looked up at me. "Kim?"

"Yeah."

"Do you think we could take Pup with us into the labyrinth?"

Obviously, she wasn't as fine as she'd have me believe. I thought for a moment. "I don't see why not, as long as he's on a tight leash. We don't want him bounding about in there."

"He won't be a problem."

"Fine, then." I was going to talk with Sandy about Frederick's arrival date. Maybe he could get here a little sooner and be a comfort to PJ. Now, though, it was time to change the subject. "Cup of Earl Grey?"

"I'd love one." Her hand was still buried in Pup's ruff.

* * *

The smell of dust in the dead air and the sheer mystery of it all drew us deeper into the labyrinth each day. As a safety precaution and to avoid getting lost in some of the side passages, we strung a line out behind us.

I could tell that something was bothering PJ, but I didn't know what, and when I asked her, she was unable to explain her uneasy feelings. She held Pup close to her and appeared more comfortable having him along.

Testing revealed that the vessels we found in the alcove had once contained grain, fruit, honey, and wine. Like finding isolated pieces of a jigsaw puzzle, we saved the information, storing it with other bits of data, until we could construct a complete picture of what we had discovered, and why it would be significant in our present-day lives.

* * *

"What do we do now?" Sandy asked, as we assembled at the entrance to one of the many side tunnels.

Looking from him to PJ, and then at the broken ceiling and the pile of dirt and rubble on the floor, I stated the obvious. "It looks as if significant repairs will be needed before we proceed." Rudimentary repairs had been made to this section sometime in the past. We could see where wooden planks had been placed over the unstable ceiling area and were now covered with dirt. It continued to sift downward into the passage through the gaps.

We retreated, deciding to wait for the completion of repairs before making any further inroads. From the outside, the area looked like nothing more than a mound overgrown with grass and weeds.

Several of our colleagues had theories about what had caused the interior damage.

PJ glanced at Sandy. "Vandals?"

"Possibly," he said.

"More than likely earthquake activity," I said.

PJ pursed her lips. "Shades of the Superstitions."

* * *

Several days later we were back at the damaged section, which had been expertly reinforced. As we passed beyond the repair, we found piles of broken pottery. Studying, photographing, and cataloguing each shard was tedious, backbreaking work, which took an interminable amount of time.

"I'm going to check over here," PJ said, after finishing her assigned tasks. She took Pup with her.

At approximately ten meters beyond where we were sifting through the rubble, the passage curved again to the right, and we lost sight of her, although we could still see her headlamp casting its eerie beam into the long-undisturbed darkness.

"Oh, my God!" We heard the urgency in PJ's voice. Pup's long, low growl showed he was also distressed by whatever PJ was seeing.

Taking care to avoid any broken pottery, I ran to where she was and pulled her close. "Are you okay?" She was shaking and clinging to Pup who remained concerned about something in the shadows.

"Yeah, I just… I wasn't expecting—that." She pointed into the dark corner.

"That was a person at one time."

"I know it was. It's just..." She put her hand to her forehead. "Shit! What the hell is wrong with me?"

Sandy joined us, dropping to his knees for a closer look. While I supported PJ, he studied the skeleton. It sat in the corner, knees drawn up, head to the side, as if napping.

Niklas and Gregor started photographing, measuring, and charting his position. "This is pretty close to the cave-in," Gregor said, looking toward the shored up passage.

"Are you thinking what I'm thinking? That he was a vandal?" Niklas asked.

I looked around. "Can't know that for sure. He could have been a worker who somehow got caught inside when they sealed the cave-in. We'll know more after we do some tests."

PJ found her voice. "Do you really suppose it was someone who couldn't find his way out?"

"Possibly." I left her side and stepped closer, peering over Gregor's shoulder.

"Are you okay?" I heard Sandy ask and turned in time to see PJ slide down the wall into a sitting position, burying her head in Pup's fur.

I returned to her and leaned down, hand extended. "Come on you, let's get some fresh air."

She brushed my hand aside. "No, I'm okay. It's just the thought of being trapped in here, dying like that." She closed her eyes and shuddered.

Sandy ordered us out. "I think we're done here anyway, for the moment."

I turned to him. "Perhaps we should have Alexander come take a look since he specializes in forensics."

"Good idea. I'd like his opinion on this guy." He looked at his watch. "But it's almost lunchtime."

"Oh, Sandy. You and your stomach." PJ joked, probably trying to regain her composure, but I could tell she wasn't up to it.

Apparently, the discovery of the skeleton had really unnerved her. It puzzled me. I knew she had dealt with remains before; we'd found some recently in the Superstitions.

Once outside, I confronted her. "We're archaeologists. Remains like that are part of our world. What's going on with you?"

"Be patient, Kim, please." Tears glistened as she looked toward the entrance to the labyrinth. "It's as if I understand some things with more clarity since being a prisoner myself. I feel his pain and the panic of being lost in there, his sheer despair when he curled up in the corner, knowing he'd never again see the light of day."

I took her hand. "You'll feel better after lunch."

"No, you go eat. I'm going to lie down."

"Then I'll come with you."

"If you don't mind, I'd like to be by myself." She put her hand on top of mine. "Don't worry, I'll be okay."

"I'll bring you something." I watched her walk toward our tent. Pup stayed at her side, choosing, I thought, to protect her instead of checking on soup bones and other treats.

* * *

As I stretched out on our mattress, I was comforted by those familiar yellow eyes watching me. Pup put a tentative paw on Kim's side of the bed and, when I didn't say anything, clambered up beside me. I stroked his head and ruffled his furry neck.

"What's happening to me?"

He made a snuffling sound and shook himself.

"Is it the labyrinth?"

His head angled as if he had absorbed my question, while his eyes remained focused on me. They seemed to burn into my soul.

"Maybe I'm just losing my mind. Finding remains has never scared me before." I tried taking deep, slow breaths, extending them to my belly to achieve maximum volume—all the techniques Susanna had suggested. In with the good air, out with the bad. Concentrate on inner peace, not chaos. Tears coursed down my cheeks.

"Jesus, Pup. What if I can't get over this? I can't give up archaeology. I love it too much. What if Kim gets fed up with me? How can I expect her to stay with me if I've flipped out?"

Fear and sadness threatened to overwhelm me. Pup whimpered and rubbed his nose against my chin. I gripped the long hairs of his neck, hugging him like a drowning victim clutches a life preserver. He licked my face, cheering me up.

"Good boy, Pup. You're my buddy, aren't you?" I rolled onto my side. "Come on, big guy. I'll be okay. Let's try to get some rest." With Pup pressed up against me, I stretched out on our low bed, feeling his protective warmth throughout my body. He couldn't see my enemy any more than I could, but he somehow sensed I was fighting something.

* * *

Like the shower of dust from the ceiling of the passage, hot water sprayed over my body. The narrow stall seemed to close in on me from all sides, but I was determined to wash all of the dirt from my hair and skin. Soapy water slid from my neck, flowing between my breasts and down to the drain at my feet. The water was hot, but I couldn't stop shivering. I gave up and wrapped myself in a thick towel. Tiny tendrils of fear spread to every nerve in my body.

As I turned to collect my underwear, I picked up a pair of bronze-colored briefs. The initials TS were embroidered on one leg. I dropped them as if scalded and tried to exit the shower facilities. One wall gave way to a long, winding passage.

"No!" I shouted. "It's not real. Don't make me go there."

It was the only way out.

As I turned a corner in the passage, a pair of hands grabbed the towel, stripping it away. The tendrils of fear became thick vines that tried to envelop me.

"PJ, talk to me," begged a female voice from the shadows.

I cowered in the corner, desperately trying to cover myself. "Go away, Terry. Leave me alone."

She shook me gently. I turned away and heard Pup barking and snarling nearby. As he advanced on Terry, I crawled in the opposite direction. It was dark. I couldn't find my way out of the maze. The thick branches of my fear immobilized me.

"PJ, look at me!"

"No! Go away!"

A light flared, and I could see further into the shadows. Someone else was there. Someone to offer me help? I crawled toward the shadowy figure, scraping my knees and arms on the rough ground.

"Please, help me." I grabbed the person's arm, but the skeletal bones came away in my hand.

Screams tore at my throat and echoed in my ears.

* * *

I stood in the midday sunshine, worried about PJ's obviously fragile mental state. She had been doing so well, or so I thought. Dr. Fleming had released her to travel to Greece, providing her with exercises for mind and body. PJ had been faithful in her activities and appeared to be improving.

With my mind so much on the project, had I neglected her? Had I failed to support her while she was still in need?

The hum of voices from the mess tent reminded me of where I was headed.

As I drew closer, the hum became conversations mixing together in a potpourri of Greek and English. Looking neither right nor left, I entered the mess tent and was surprised to hear Frederick's booming voice calling to me.

"Kim, join us, over here."

He was seated at a small table with Sandy and Dr. Susanna Armstrong.

What was she doing here? Maybe I could talk to her about PJ's strange behavior.

Frederick rose from his chair and enveloped me in a bear hug. This man whom I had at first disliked, had become all things to me: friend, older brother, father, and father-in-law. He was gruff at times, but as gentle as a doe at others. The difficulties he and PJ had experienced for so long stemmed from the great love he had shared with his deceased wife and the love he had for his daughter, but didn't know how to express. PJ's difficulties with him had arisen from the same source—the grief she had suffered when her mother was killed. The inability to resolve their grief had resulted in years of misunderstanding.

"We weren't expecting you for another week or so," I told him.

"I know, but Sandy said it would be a big help to PJ if I could get here sooner. Since I was eager to get here, I managed to wrap things up a little early."

"It's good to see you." I kissed him on the cheek. "And you, Dr. Armstrong. What a pleasant surprise."

Her expression held a hint of merriment. "I wasn't expecting to be here, but Frederick suggested I come see how PJ was doing, and he can be very persuasive."

Sandy stood up. "Doc, what would you like for lunch? I'll get it for you."

"Thanks. A salad would be nice. Horiatiki salata, and some rizogalo for dessert."

"How is PJ?" Susanna asked.

"Not too well, right now." When Frederick grew pale, I added hastily, "Nothing serious. Physically, she's fine, and she's been doing really well mentally. At least I thought she was, but I'm really glad you're both here."

"There are always setbacks as we work through the painful memories," Dr. Armstrong said. "I'm sure Dr. Fleming has discussed that with PJ, and I think he'd expect me to help her right now. Tell me what happened."

Sandy arrived with my lunch, but didn't sit down. "You folks have stuff to talk about, and I have to speak to some of my people. So, if you'll excuse me, I'll leave you to talk."

Frederick stood and shook Sandy's hand. "We'll discuss the project a little later on, okay?"

"Of course," Sandy said, and exited the mess tent.

"Now, tell me everything," Susanna said, when Frederick resumed his seat.

"We found some remains this morning, a full skeleton. It unnerved her, sending her over the edge for a few moments. That's why she didn't come to lunch. She said she needed to rest." I shook my head and took a few bites of salad.

"She's an archaeologist, for God's sake." Frederick frowned. "She's seen remains before."

Susanna reached for his hand, squeezing it. He covered hers with his. To my eye, it was an act that spoke of mutual affection. "You must understand that she's not looking at it rationally. The obstacles she's facing color her real-life view of things."

"That's serious."

"Yes, Kim, but nothing that can't be cured."

"She won't go down in the labyrinth without Pup. It's as if she thinks he'll protect her from whatever is in there."

"He's her anchor, her hold on real life. When she's down there, it's another world. Isn't that what archaeology is? Other worlds that we, in this one, are investigating and, some might say, disturbing?"

"What about me? Can't I be her anchor?"

"Of course you can, and most of the time, you are. But when you're down there, you're building that other world around you, as she does, when she's well. For now, Pup is only interested in her world and her well-being. He's the perfect anchor because he doesn't expect anything from her, and he isn't looking at her as though she's crazy."

"I don't think she's crazy." My tone was snappish.

"I know you don't, and she doesn't think so either, but there are moments when the troubles overwhelm her and block all logical thought."

"I want to see her," Frederick said, standing up.

"Wait. Kim hasn't finished her lunch."

"It's okay, I'm not really hungry." I had picked a bit on the salad and had eaten half of the rizogalo. It was good, but I wasn't in the mood for food. "Wait, though, I promised to take something back to the tent for PJ." I ordered a salad and for her dessert, loukoumi. Turkish Delight for the delight of my life, who, right now, was in pain. The kind of pain that doesn't respond to an aspirin.

We left the mess tent and were halfway across the compound when we heard PJ's screams. We rushed inside to find her sitting up, tears rolling down her face, hugging Pup for dear life. He turned on me, showing his fangs.

"Easy, boy. We're not going to hurt her." I dropped the food containers on the table and took hold of his collar, while gently unclenching PJ's fingers. "There you go," I said, hoping my words were reaching her. "It's okay. I'm here, and Susanna's here to help you... your dad, too." I started to back away with Pup.

PJ's expression held so much pain and shock. When she spoke, it was to whimper, "I'm in trouble, Kimmy."

"I'm here, sweetheart," I whispered, putting one arm around her while holding Pup with the other.

Susanna politely ordered us to leave, saying, "I need to have some time alone with PJ."

* * *

Susanna sat beside me on the mattress, offering tissues when needed. It took us almost two hours to get through all the stuff leading up to and including my horrendous nightmare, but by the time I had recounted the last detail, I was feeling stronger and more confident. I was grateful that she was a compassionate and patient woman, who didn't seem to mind how soggy I made her expensive linen jacket.

"This is just one little pothole on your road to recovery. We talked about how it would be a day-by-day effort, and that you shouldn't be afraid to ask for help from your friends and loved ones."

"I know, but it was so sudden and so scary. Maybe it was some sort of claustrophobia. Do you think it could have been just that?"

"Possibly." She gently took my wrist and checked my pulse. "I wasn't there to see it happen. It sounds more like a panic attack, though, that Kim managed to avert by getting you outside and away from the stimulus. She loves you very much, you know."

"I know. I'm so lucky to have her in my life." I sniffed and blew my nose. "Susanna, help me. I don't want to be sick any more. It freaks me out to think that I might scare Kim away with this craziness."

"From what I've observed, I doubt that will happen. But let's focus on coping with any recurring episodes, okay?"

I took an uneasy breath. "Okay."

"Good. I know from your e-mails that you've been doing meditation and the Sun Salutations I gave you. What other exercise do you get?"

"I walk Pup either in the morning or evening. Kim and I trade off. I do some running."

"Good. That will get the endorphins flowing. Your dad told me you ran a few marathons."

"Oh, years ago, when I was just out of college."

"Perhaps you can do some distance training to help get your stamina back."

"Maybe."

"I have a booklet of exercises to give you, and perhaps you can try some self-hypnosis." She paused. "If insomnia is still a problem, I can also give you a supply of mild sedatives."

I shook my head. "I hope it won't come to that."

"Okay, I know you don't like the idea of pills."

"I was medicated when Mom died, and it nearly became an addiction. I don't ever want to feel that way again."

"You make a good point. Medication will be a last resort."

Susanna spent a few moments reading my journal while I fixed two cups of Earl Grey and added some pastries that Irini had brought. I hadn't touched the lunch Kim had left for me, but when I was on edge, a cup of hot tea always seemed to work wonders.

"You've written an unusual poem about the ocean," Susanna said, after leafing through my journal. "I see a lot of humor and cockiness in it. You wrote it before you left for Greece, though, didn't you?"

I took a swallow of tea. "Yeah, I did it one day when we were in Newport. I don't think I'm cut out to be a poet, though."

"But you do think you're cut out to be an archaeologist?" Susanna's tone was gentle, yet firm.

"Yes, I hope so. I want it to be my profession. I hope to make contributions in this field because it's very important to me. I don't want to be known as Frederick Curtis's daughter for the rest of my life."

Susanna studied her tea before taking a sip. "I'd like to ask Kim to join us, if you'll allow it."

* * *

When Kim came into the tent with Pup, I was shocked. I had never seen her so pale and her eyes so full of pain. It made my heart ache. "I'm so sorry." I hugged her close and cried again, dampening her shirt collar. "It'll be okay, really it will."

"I think…" Her voice cracked. "I'm supposed to be saying that to you."

"Here." Susanna sighed, took a tissue and passed the box to us. "I sure wish I had stock in one of these companies. With the amount of tissues I dole out in my profession, I could be a wealthy woman."

That bit of humor broke the tension. I left Kim just long enough to fix her a cup of tea. We sat side by side on the mattress watching Susanna, who had moved to the table.

"Relax, this isn't the Inquisition. I wanted to talk to both of you as part of my usual counseling with couples, but the trip came up, and off you flew."

"That's often the way our life goes," Kim said.

"So I hear from PJ's father."

"Susanna, there's something I've been wondering about. Is your trip purely recreational, or were you concerned about my health?"

Her expression softened. "I must admit that I was wondering how you were managing, but no, it's mostly vacation and a little curiosity about this amazing discovery your father keeps talking about."

We chatted a bit about the underground passage and what it might become, but using generalities. It was Sandy's project, after all, and we weren't at liberty to reveal any secrets. Susanna seemed to realize this and did not press us for details. Instead, she spoke to Kim.

"PJ tells me you have joined her in doing some of the yoga asanas. I'd like to give you a book that has several partner exercises. You may find them useful."

Kim glanced sideways at me and took the book from Susanna. "Thanks, we'll try some, even though I'm not really into that sort of thing."

"You just might find them beneficial. Also, I'll be happy to counsel you individually or together while I'm here." She stood up. "For now, though, I'm going to leave you with a prescription."

"But—"

"I promise you'll like this, PJ. Both of you are to take the afternoon off and get some rest. I'll tell Sandy that it's doctor's orders."

We thanked her and watched her walk through the tent flap.

I looked at Kim. "Resting for the afternoon with my favorite woman. I think I can manage that."

"Depends on what you mean by 'resting.'" She pulled me close and we shared a tender kiss.

"Oh, my." I took a moment to catch my breath.

We stretched out on the mattress, trading kisses until we fell asleep. We didn't awaken until the afternoon sun had faded, sending shadows into the corners of our tent.

"Mmm," I moaned, when her lips found the hollow of my neck. "I'd like to rest in a more undressed and comfortable state. How do you feel about the idea?"

Kim unbuttoned my shirt with practiced ease. "Whatever you say. We are, after all, following doctor's orders."

Chapter 8

I was sitting in our tent the next evening, meditating, when Kim returned from her shower. The scent of her shampoo interfered with my focus so much I was forced to open my eyes.

"Geez, you smell good."

"And you're supposed to be concentrating on your therapy, if I'm not mistaken."

"It's all your fault. Coming in here, fresh from the shower, smelling so sexy." I sniffed the air. "So distracting."

"Sorry."

"What is it, anyway?"

"Um…" She rummaged through her bag to locate the bottle. "Strawberry-Kiwi-Passion Fruit Delight."

"They got the passion and delight part right."

"I got it because it was on sale, but I'm glad you like it."

I watched her put away her shower supplies and apply a towel to her damp hair. "I love how your hair curls at the ends when it gets wet. Makes me want to twirl it up on my tongue and slurp it dry."

"Is that a fact? I'm definitely not getting near you now, no matter how much you pout."

"I am not pouting. Merely feeling hurt at your rejection."

The towel stopped in mid-fluff. "Rejection? You're kidding me, right?"

"Gotcha!"

The damp towel sailed into my lap. "Hey!" I wadded it up and threw it back in her direction. "This has thoroughly disrupted my meditation time. I hope you're satisfied."

Kim hung the towel over a chair back and sat down beside me on the mattress. "It was never my intension to disturb you while you were doing your therapy." She heaved an exaggerated sigh. "If you'll forgive me this time, I promise to use axle grease on my hair from now on."

"Don't you dare." I pulled her into a fierce hug.

After a quick kiss, she moved away. "Okay, but no sucking on hair. I have to draw the line on that."

I looked at her until she leaned in for another kiss.

"Party pooper," I said, as our noses rubbed together.

"Shampoo sucker."

Pup chose that moment to approach and whine.

"Perfect timing." She broke away to look for his leash. "Now, you can get back to your yoga without having me to bother you."

When he saw the leash, Pup went into a frenzied doggie dance.

"Geez," I said, "you'd think we never walk the poor animal."

Kim calmed him and perched on the edge of our bed. "I'm trying to support you while you do what you have to do. I don't want to be in your way."

"You're not in my way." I patted her knee. "And I'm sorry if I gave you that impression."

"I'm so new to this therapy stuff."

"It's okay."

"No, PJ. I want you to have your private time. I want mine, too, for that matter. That's what makes for a healthy relationship."

"Are you suggesting that I'm crowding you?"

"No, no, we're doing just fine. What I'm saying—apparently badly—is that I want you to have all the time you need for yoga and whatever other exercises, without my disturbing you. But I also want us to have the time we need for each other."

"Me, too, but it shouldn't be regimented like that, especially our time together."

With her free hand, she gripped my knee. Pup propped his muzzle on top of her hand.

"Somebody else needs our time," I said.

"Let me take him out for a while, okay?" Kim gave his ear a scratch. "It will make him happy and let you relax."

I added a few scratches to Pup's other ear. "Good idea."

When they returned, I was working on my journal entry. Pup slurped some water from his bowl and flopped onto his bed. Kim pulled a can of juice from the mini-fridge.

"Have a good walk?"

"Yeah. How about you? Feeling more relaxed now?"

I nibbled the end of my pen. "I think so."

"Good." She slipped off her shoes and stretched out on the bed. "But…"

"But what?"

"I was just wondering."

"Oh, brother. When you get that look on your face…"

"What look?"

"All innocent and sweet like that."

I put my journal aside and scooted closer to her. "I am innocent and sweet."

"And I'm the queen of Sheba."

"Okay." I held up my hand. "All teasing aside, I would like to ask you something."

Her expression softened. "What?"

"Could we do that partner asana again? The one that we liked so much from the book Susanna loaned us?"

"Double Heart something-or-other?"

"Gazing. Double Heart Gazing. Want to?"

I thought I detected a sudden gleam in her eyes. "Okay. If you're sure."

"I'm sure. Ever since Susanna explained how it combines meditation with quiet mutual communication that's meant to connect our heart chakras, I've wanted to try it again."

She took my hand. "And it felt good when we did it."

"That too." I pulled her up off the bed.

We sat cross-legged, facing each other, our knees touching. This close to me, Kim's fragrant hair proved to be an even greater distraction. We looked into each other's eyes, tentatively at first. Then, gazing beyond the surface, we let our minds probe deeper into our souls.

I placed my right hand over Kim's heart, feeling the warmth of her body beneath the thin fabric of her oversized T-shirt. My heart's rhythm quickened to match hers. Kim put her right hand on my chest, creating a heat that penetrated my shirt, spreading to my breasts.

Each of us pressed our left hand over the hand that already covered our heart. From her expression, I could tell that Kim had felt and was affected by the powerful burst of energy that flowed between us. We closed our eyes and welcomed the communion of our souls.

"Whew! That was intense," she said, stretching her legs afterwards.

"Every bit as good as the last time. Thanks, honey."

"My pleasure."

Still recovering from the intensity of the yoga session, we took a late stroll around the compound and got ready for bed. Snuggled against Kim's back, I twisted a strand of her hair around my finger, resisted the urge to taste it, and whispered loving words in her ear until we fell asleep.

* * *

We had no on-site work scheduled until late the next morning, so after breakfast Kim worked on her laptop and I made more entries in my journal. I wrote several paragraphs about the progress we had made with our therapist's help.

Kim's learning that she can suppress her anger, but certain buttons will still trigger excessive fury if she's not on guard.

I twirled my pen through my fingers, thinking. Prior to my abduction in Wales, I never knew she harbored such fury, but I realized now that it was her way of dealing with post traumatic stress. And although it was the wrong way, she was working on it. I turned again to my journal.

Unfortunately, my being threatened is one of the buttons that will ignite her simmering anger and turn it into a raging inferno. A raging Kim Blair is not a pretty sight.

I remembered something from Kim's past that connected to the present. Rusty, the dog she had loved so deeply during her youth, had given her unconditional love. Now, I offered her that same kind of love, and the situation brought all her protective instincts to the surface.

She needs assurance that what happened to Rusty was not her fault, and that she wasn't to blame for what Terry did to me. Somehow, she must learn that she's not responsible for protecting me all the time. Neither of us can live that way.

We'd managed to take several day trips away from the stress and strain of the site. On one outing, Sandy and Irini introduced us to the novelty of Greek outdoor cinema. I'd never been to a drive-in movie, but I had seen movies that included teenagers going crazy at them. The outdoor cinema was similar, except there were tables and chairs instead of cars, and local bands entertained us before the movie started. Irini assured us that most of the movies were American films, so we had no trouble following the plot, even though it was a bit unnerving to have Clint Eastwood hovering over us on a big screen while we ate. The food was excellent, and the patrons usually behaved themselves, though once the wine and ouzo started flowing, some made their own comments about the movie in all sorts of languages.

I glanced up at Kim in time to catch her frowning at her monitor. She rubbed her chin, launched a powerful burst of keystrokes, paused to reread, and pounded one final button with a terse expletive.

Kim and I both need to accept that life has its fair share of ups and downs, triumphs and tragedies. I can't always control my stress, and she can't always repress her anger, but we can reduce our problems to a manageable level. With a calm and positive attitude, everything will work out in the end.

Naturally, some days will be calmer than others.

After taking a deep breath, Kim wandered over to me. She ruffled my hair and leaned in to kiss my forehead. "You're looking mighty serious."

"Just writing some hard-earned lessons in my journal."

"I see."

"How about you? You seem a little serious, yourself."

"Oh, it's nothing. Just a bit of unfinished business. We can talk about it later."

"Okay."

Kim's lips were so invitingly close that I took advantage of them a few times.

She sat down beside me. "Oh, I almost forgot. Sandy and Irini want to take us to the outdoor theater again."

"Wonderful. When do they want to go?"

"Tonight.

"Wow. That doesn't give me much time to pull an outfit together."

"You brought suitcases full of clothes." She got to her feet, pointing to the corner of our tent where my cases were stacked and a rod held items on hangers. "What's wrong with any of those things?"

"They've seen most of that stuff." I went over, sorted through some shirts, tossed them aside, and picked through some hanging garments. "It's a work night, too. We can't let them take us to a taverna afterward." I rejected the clothing on hangers and started back to check a pile of clothing nearer our desk.

Kim grabbed my arm to keep me stationary. "Okay, no local ouzo in any form, and no filling up on those delicious appetizers."

"Mezedes."

"Right… mezedes. Our stomachs will thank us, and we'll all be clear-headed for work tomorrow."

"It's for the best. I don't ever want to replay that time in Arizona when I threw up on your cactus plant. I swore afterwards that an occasional glass of wine or beer would be my limit."

"Yeah, I remember. You were in bad shape that night." Kim grimaced. "The local ouzo though. My head throbbed for days after just two glasses of that stuff."

"Sandy said that even with water to dilute it, the anise taste is still strong. Since I've never been fond of licorice, I don't think I missed much by avoiding it."

"You didn't, but I felt that one of us should try it, just to be sociable."

"Yes," I said, "we couldn't offend anyone." Kim pulled me into an embrace, resting her chin on the top of my head. "Still, I don't want us to end up with fuzzy brains."

I felt her chest expand with laughter. "I don't either."

"I told Sandy it was probably an acquired taste. One I just didn't have."

Her lips brushed my forehead, and her hug rocked me back and forth. "Definitely one we both lacked."

After a few seconds, I sighed. "But I will miss those little stuffed mushrooms with the feta cheese."

"We all have to make sacrifices, PJ."

*　*　*

After one particularly long day of working underground, Irini took Kim and me to the sulfur baths of Loutropoli Thermis. She had relatives who managed the place. We walked all around the ancient stone buildings that housed the baths and marveled at the solid construction. The chambers had vaulted arches that dated back to 3000 BC.

"No telling how many ancient Greeks warmed their butts on these heated stones," Kim whispered as we lowered ourselves into one large bathing area, one step at a time.

"True," I said, trying to maintain my decorum.

We had discovered earlier that our voices echoed from the chamber walls and were careful to be as dignified as possible. Irini had said that the best way to benefit from the experience was to soak in the nude, so it was just the three of us in attendance. Sandy had volunteered to accompany us and scrub our backs, but we declined his generous offer.

I'd tried a topless beach or two in Brazil during my travels, but a nude bath in a public place—albeit an ancient stone facility—was a first for me. Having Kim beside me for the venture made it all the more exciting. Irini promised that we would have the place to ourselves, and we did. Once we stopped acting like a trio of giggling schoolgirls, we relaxed and thoroughly enjoyed ourselves. The stiffness left our joints and the mineral salts rejuvenated our bodies and our spirits. When we begged her for a return visit, Irini readily agreed.

* * *

Dad seemed happy to be part of our expedition. He and Sandy had decided that Dad would run the business operation and handle all our financial and managerial details without interfering with the daily archaeological work. He joined us once a week in the labyrinth to view the progress. He was, after all, our benefactor. Besides, he looked rather cute in a hard hat. I guess he was trying to make up for our lost years together, but he seemed genuinely interested in how I did my job.

I realized that I was as much to blame for our alienation as he was. We'd probably need to discuss it more in the future, but we loved each other, and we'd told each other so. That was a good start.

It made me curious when I learned Susanna was staying here indefinitely. I was delighted to have her, but I wondered about her practice and her many patients. When I asked her, she assured me that a competent associate was substituting for her back home.

* * *

"I need to stop by Sandy's tent," I told Kim the next morning, as we finished dressing. He wants my comments on that revised budget he worked up for Dad."

"Okay, but I'm feeling hungry for some of those gooey pastries." She squirted some sunscreen in her palm and started applying it to her arms and face.

"Don't wait for me if you get hungry." I gave her a hug. "If I don't find you here in the tent when I return, I'll just meet you at breakfast."

"Don't be too long, or the good stuff will be gone."

"Can't you save me one?"

She paused a moment, considering my request. "Perhaps I could be persuaded."

"You drive a hard bargain." I grabbed my daypack and gave her a kiss. "Will that do for starters?"

Kim required another as a down payment before she'd release me.

"I have to go, but there's plenty more where that came from."

"Okay. I'll be happy to collect later on."

* * *

Sandy's shirt was unbuttoned and he was lacing up his work boots when I entered his tent.

"Hey, PJ. How's it going?" He secured his boots, buttoned his shirt, and tucked it into his faded jeans. Without missing a beat, he grabbed a pile of folders and rifled through them, extracting a page here and several there, intent on creating a new folder for some specific task.

"I'm fine, but you look a bit frazzled." I pulled the paperwork from my daypack. "Here's what I came up with on the budget you asked for. Anything else you and Dad need?"

"Fantastic." He took a quick glance at the bottom-line figures. "Not bad. I was afraid we'd be way over after adding all that extra lighting, but what you have here should be doable."

I took a step backward. "Good, then. I'll just be off to breakfast."

"Wait. I hate to ask, but I'm really running late this morning. Could you take all this to your dad for me?"

"Sure, no problem."

He added my page to the new folder's contents and gave it to me. "Thanks, PJ. I owe you."

"Bring me some baklava from Thanos's Bakery, and we'll be even."

"You've got a deal."

"See you at the site." I waved and started off.

My dad's tent was a little larger than ours, but it doubled as both an on-site office and living quarters.

The tent flap was closed, but not sealed, when I arrived, so I called out a cheery greeting and stuck my head inside.

Dad was still in bed, but he wasn't alone.

"Ahh!" I covered my eyes. "God. I'm... I'm... Oh, man. I'm sorry."

I hastily pulled myself back outside the tent.

"Priscilla, it's okay." Dad was clearly flustered, trying to smooth things out as if I didn't really see him together with Susanna.

I could tell that he was as embarrassed as I was. "Um... I have the budget you asked for." My face felt hot, and my tongue was glued to my teeth. "I'll just leave it here... under this rock." Like a child caught coloring on the walls, I continued to stammer my apologies. Inside the tent, Dad made soothing noises, and Susanna, to her credit, remained silent.

When Dad pulled the tent flap aside, he was dressed only in a pair of silk boxers. I looked away. "Listen, honey, we need to talk to you about this."

I guess so. But you'd better put some clothes on before I can even look at you.

"Sure, Dad. That's fine. We'll talk real soon." Staring down at his bare feet, I shoved the paperwork in the general direction of his hands. "I'll just leave this now, and you can check this over at your leisure."

That was brilliant. He had better things to do with his leisure right now.

Keeping my eyes focused on some fascinating blades of grass, I backed away. "I have to catch up with Kim and Sandy. We'll talk real soon," I repeated mindlessly.

He said something else, but by then, I was too far away to understand him.

I must have scared the crap out of Kim when I returned to the tent.

"I was just about to—What's the matter? I've never seen your face so red. Are you feeling all right?"

"I... Oh, my God. I just walked in on Dad and Susanna. Together. In bed."

The worry lines on her face relaxed. "Oh, is that all?"

"What do you mean is that all? Isn't that enough? It's my dad I'm talking about. My dad!"

She held me close, stroking my back. "Surely you could see they were romantically involved. Dr. Armstrong is a fine woman. I would think you'd be happy for both of them."

"Oh, I am. Truly, I am. It's just that..." I took a deep breath and rested my cheek against her breast.

"That what?"

"I know I'm thirty-six years old," I said, sniffing, my voice muffled against her shirt, "but I'm still his daughter, you know. And a child never considers that a parent might have a sex life."

"Well now, how do you suppose you got here?"

"That's different. He and Mom were young then."

"Contrary to what younger folks think, we don't suddenly dry up when we reach a certain age. I might serve as an example."

"You? You're not old. Besides, the issue is parents, not lovers. I just don't want to think about him in that way. He's my father, not some stud muffin."

Kim pulled me to her. "You're a treasure. You know that, don't you?"

"Yeah? Well, I'm your treasure, and you're mine. So don't you forget it."

*　*　*

"Damn and blast it!"

"Kim? What's wrong?"

She stormed around our tent, tossing papers and clothing about. I tried to take her arm, but she brushed me away.

"Remember your anger management."

"To hell with that! This is insane. I can't believe it."

"What is?" I got her to stop pacing and grabbing things to throw. "Sit," I said, "and that's an order."

She sat, surprising me.

"Now, what's this all about?"

"You remember when you were writing in your journal, and I was working on my laptop?"

"Um..."

"You said that I looked serious and—"

"Oh, yeah, now I remember."

She balled her hands into fists. "I was answering an e-mail from that crazy photographer—the one who insisted on getting in my face with his camera the day we flew here from Logan."

"Uh-oh."

"'Uh-oh' is right. Your father just told me that the little worm is suing all of us and Curtis Enterprises for intent to cause bodily injury."

"What? That's absurd."

"Exactly. I was merely protecting us from his verbal abuse and harassment."

"And I appreciated it, believe me." I sat on her lap and hugged her neck. "Though you do know that I can take care of myself without your using force to protect me." I kissed her cheek and tried rubbing the tension out of her shoulders. "Sometimes, you're like a wild animal about these things. That isn't good for your health." I employed some of the same soothing strokes I used to calm Pup when he grew agitated. The results were surprisingly similar.

"It's a bunch of crap. Reporters! Photographers! I've had it up to here with them." Kim sliced her finger across her throat. She stood up, barely giving me time to hop off her lap, and paced. This time she refrained from disturbing stationary objects.

"Dad will take care of it. He's used to this kind of thing. They just want money and a little free publicity." I sat her down again and kept rubbing and snuggling against her. She put her arms around me, and after a few more seconds, I felt us both relax.

"I'm sorry, PJ."

"I know you did it because you love me, and I really can't be upset with you for that."

I stood up and gathered up our hard hats and dusty daypacks. "Come on, slugger, we've got work to do while the gang is off in town celebrating some religious feast."

"I wondered where everyone was. After I talked with your father, he and Dr. Armstrong were headed to town to help Sandy and Irini deliver baked goods to some church. Meanwhile, we can keep ourselves occupied in the labyrinth, going over some of the newest areas."

"Oh, yeah. Can't wait. Let's go, Pup." He danced excitedly between us.

"Don't get carried away, PJ. We'll be in there alone, without the crew. We have to be careful, and we're not to go beyond the already-explored face, do you understand?"

"Of course I do. I'm not going to take any unnecessary chances. And we'll have Pup for protection."

She gave me a stern look, the look I called her Great Stone Face. "Next time we're in New Hampshire, I want you to see a replica of that look, on the side of a mountain."

"Very funny." Kim took her pack from me and slipped on the headgear. Our hats clinked when she kissed me.

"Whew. One more of those and I'll forget about the work entirely."

We started off hand in hand. "So what holiday is this?" she asked.

"I haven't a clue. But it requires a lot of baked goods."

* * *

"You okay?" PJ asked as she, Pup, and I started down into the labyrinth.

"No, I'm not okay. I'm still furious."

"You know Dad can take care of the legal problem for you. He'll put his attorneys on it, and if there's any settling to do, it can be done out of court."

"Yeah, he told me he'd take care of it, but that's not the point. I shouldn't have to settle anything. Damn it all, the photographer was the one who invaded our privacy." I hitched my pack up onto my shoulder. "Infernal reporters. They're nothing but trouble."

I had been fuming ever since I heard about the lawsuit. "How could he say he was injured? It was just his camera. And it was his fault, sticking it in my face that way and daring to challenge our relationship like that."

PJ paused at the bottom of the steps leading to the passage entrance. "I know I'm not a good one to speak. I certainly have enough psychological problems to go around, but you have to curb your anger. You're letting it take precedence over good sense."

"I know." I looked down at the smooth stone flooring. "It's just that when we're threatened as a couple, it unleashes something vicious inside me. It's like a primitive fury that fills me up and overflows."

She took my hand. "Try to let it go, okay? Or talk to Susanna or Scott."

"Oh, PJ. I don't think—"

"They've helped me so much. I know they can help you, too."

"I've talked to her. You know that."

"Yeah, but knowing you, I suspect that you're holding back. You need to be completely open with her."

I looked away. It wasn't easy, admitting that I couldn't always manage my anger. "I'll think about it."

"Good. Now we can get back to work."

We walked side by side down the main passage, following Pup to the end of our explored area. Once into the passage, I felt myself relaxing.

We passed the spot where, three weeks earlier, PJ had stumbled on the skeleton.

Tests carried out at the University of Athens revealed the remains that PJ had found were approximately twenty-four hundred years old. We had determined, too, that the original cave-in had been repaired within that time frame, so our unfortunate friend could very well have been a laborer, a slave laborer, helping with the repairs. Test results also indicated that he had been a young man and a hard worker who was suffering with the beginning stages of osteoarthritis. We were sure that, initially anyway, he had no idea that he was doomed to spend the next several centuries in the labyrinth.

I watched PJ closely when she hesitated at the spot where he was found. "May you rest in peace," she said to the now empty space.

We continued along the passage in silence. When we weren't chatting, we couldn't hear anything except the sound of our footsteps crunching and Pup's toenails scratching, albeit muffled, through the rubble and debris of time. The smell of dust was always noticeable. Fresh outside air, trapped as it was by so many twists and turns, did not penetrate this far into the labyrinth.

By the time we arrived at the end of the already-explored sections, I had forgotten about my problems and was focused entirely on archaeology. We were almost a kilometer-and-a-half into the labyrinth, a maze of narrow winding corridors, mostly dead ends. Ironically, as the crow flies, we were only a few meters from the entrance.

PJ peered into what seemed to be little more than a crack in the rock wall, a crack easily overlooked because it had been concealed, perhaps deliberately, by a natural notch in the wall itself. The opening was just wide enough for a slim person to slip through.

"I wonder where this goes."

"We'll find out soon enough." I was ready to move on, but she was too intrigued with what lay behind the mysterious crevice.

"Just a quick peek? It won't take a minute."

"I don't think so. Not until the crew has been down here to check things over."

"I mean just inside, to see what's there."

"Not yet, PJ."

Too late. Acting like her old self, she turned sideways and slid into the crack.

"Looks like an empty room. Not even that. An alcove." Her voice was muffled, as if she spoke from a long way off.

"Stay, Pup."

The light from the lamp on my hard hat reflected in his yellow canine eyes. He crouched obediently several feet from me, but he was not relaxed. I had a gut feeling the room was off-limits and we shouldn't go in there, but PJ, in her usual enthusiasm, was not to be deterred. And really, what could be the harm? I swept my fear aside, took a deep breath of stale air, and squeezed through the crack in the rock.

When I reached PJ's side, she was exploring a faded fresco of a panther on the far wall of what looked like a rounded, naturally-carved room. She had pulled a soft-bristled brush from her daypack and was gently removing a gritty layer of the past from the animal's eyes. They glowed like burnished gold. It was an unnerving sight, raising the hairs on the back of my neck and setting Pup on edge. Even though he couldn't see me behind the rock wall that separated us, he must have sensed some supernatural vibrations, because he was showing his displeasure with alternating whines and yelps.

"It's all right," I called back to him. "You stay out there. We won't be long." My voice was not as firm and confident as I would have liked, but he settled into infrequent whimpers.

My nerves were on alert. I turned to PJ. "Did you hear that?"

"It's just Pup." She finished cleaning the fresco's surface, replaced her tool, and wiped her hands on her cargo pants. "What's gotten into him, anyway?"

"No, something else, muffled and far away. Do you hear anything?"

She shook her head. "Like what?"

"Thunder."

"The sky was cloudless when we left the surface, and even if it were thundering, we wouldn't hear it in here."

A strange sensation struck me, and I didn't feel right. Not sick exactly, but not well. It began with my head and moved downward through my body, leaving me paralyzed.

"Are you all right?" PJ's voice sounded close, yet far away. As if I were having an out-of-body experience, I saw her guide me to the stone wall for support, but couldn't feel anything solid at my back. "Are you feeling okay? You're scaring me."

I was scaring myself. What was happening? I was so hot and dizzy. "I don't know, honey. I just don't know." My mind refused to focus on anything.

"Kim, please, what's the matter? Are you sick?"

Unable to answer, I reached out for her, but something pulled me away, catching me up in a whirlwind. I could only watch as PJ grew more and more distant, eventually becoming just a blurred speck. Though I couldn't hear her voice, I could feel her panic.

I held my hand out to her, but she was out of reach, and then, out of sight.

A whirling kaleidoscope of color blurred my vision. Rainbow waves and shooting stars appeared as everything swirled around me, and my mind shut down.

When I came to, I was sitting on the ground in the middle of a strange and beautifully pristine meadow. It was peppered with hundreds of yellow, red, and white wildflowers. Fighting a bout of vertigo and ignoring the churning of my stomach from what I could only describe as a weightless journey, I attempted to stand, and promptly sat down again.

I heard a roaring sound like heavy surf crashing onto a beach, but as far as I could see there was no beach, no surf. The roar grew louder until—as mysteriously as I had lost her—PJ appeared on her knees beside me.

"What the hell happened?" she asked. I noticed her eyes were wide with fear. "God, I feel so sick. Where are we, anyway?"

"I don't know where we are or how we got here, but here we are." I looked at the abundant flowers surrounding us. "You have to admit, it's beautiful."

"That's what worries me. Are we dead?"

I shook my head. "Hardly." I felt at peace and yet I was troubled, as if by guilt, for putting us both in this predicament.

"Then, how did we get here?" PJ brushed some soil from her arms and clothing. She sat back on her heels, frowning at me. "Where is this place? And how do we get back to where we were?"

"Why would you think I'd know that?"

"Kim, you know I have absolutely no sense of direction, so give me a hint."

"I've no idea. And thinking about it makes my head hurt." Still feeling slightly dizzy, I staggered to my feet and offered PJ my hand. "Up you go."

She gripped my hand and accepted my support. "I wonder what Dr. Fleming will have to say about this dream."

"You're sure it's a dream?"

"Of course. What else could it be?" As she turned to face me, her gaze drifted to something over my left shoulder. Her face paled. "Don't look now, but we have company."

I turned and studied them. From this distance, they appeared to be ancient warriors, about a dozen or so in number.

So, this was a dream after all. Or was it?

"Who are they?" PJ tightened her grip on my arm.

"I don't know. They're too far away to tell, exactly."

"Do you think they're friendly?"

I swallowed hard. "Possibly, but I have my doubts."

She took a deep, tremulous breath. "Kimmy, I'm afraid."

"So am I, darling. So am I."

Chapter 9

Kim used her body to shield me from the approaching strangers. She put her hand behind her back, and I gripped it hard, hoping the gesture conveyed my support as well as my fear.

It was now apparent that the strangers were women. "Who the hell are they?"

"Some sort of warrior band, it would seem." Her voice was filled with awe. "They might even be Amazons."

"Oh, come on, Kim." I leaned against her, my arm tightly circling her waist, as we watched the women draw nearer. "This is all so crazy. It's a dream—no, a nightmare. Tell me we're going to wake up any minute and find ourselves back at the site." I put both arms around her and pressed my forehead against her firm back, feeling her muscles tense. "We'd better be waking up, and soon."

"Meanwhile, we need to appear harmless. Those crossbows are notched with very real looking arrows."

"It just keeps getting better and better."

At some silent command, the six heavily armed warriors surrounded us. The two carrying loaded crossbows pointed them at our chests. One woman, apparently the leader, brandished a sword, and the rest held staffs at the ready. The daggers, sheathed at their waists, did not appear to be fashion accessories.

All of them were dark-skinned and muscular. Judging by the scent of damp leather and sweat that filled the air, they hadn't showered or changed clothes in quite some time. Deodorant obviously wasn't considered a necessity in this dream. I took a quick glance around the circle and noted that all of them were of medium height, taller than me, certainly, but shorter than Kim. The leader wore a buff-colored tunic, belted at the waist, and leather breeches. Silver arm bands encircled her beefy biceps and some sort of metal chain hung around her neck. If it had a pendant attached, it was hidden beneath her tunic.

The rest of her associates preferred the nearly-naked look, proudly sporting red and black tattoos along their arms and across their rippling abdomens.

Who the hell were these women? How did we end up eyeball to eyeball with them? Talk about the wrong place at the wrong time.

"Kim," I said in a voice barely above a whisper.

"Easy, love, just relax. Show them that we mean no harm."

Most of the women's legs were bare and well muscled. Their boots, though crudely-made, had apparently tramped many miles without the aid of rejuvenating polish or oil. Clad in an assortment of halter tops, they displayed a variety of bust sizes, but all of them could have benefited from some quality under-wire bras. Despite their dirty and disheveled appearances, I was impressed with, and a little jealous of, their obvious self-assurance, as well as the feathers, beads, and metal doodads that adorned their hair and clothing.

Kim and I stood silently watching them until the boldest of the lot, probably the leader, stepped forward, drawing her dagger. Her buddies bounced on the balls of their feet, looking like they anticipated a brief, but bloody rumble.

I had an urgent need of a bathroom.

"We mean you no harm," Kim said in a strong, even voice, though I could feel her body trembling.

That sounds good. Makes no difference that they outnumber us three to one, and they're armed to the teeth.

"This is so ridiculous," I said, unable to suppress my irritation. Apparently my remark was interpreted as rude; I felt the end of a staff poke me in the back. *Hey, watch it, woman. You're dealing with the daughter of Frederick Lane Curtis, and this woman is Kimberly Blair. She's an Amazon, too, and isn't to be trifled with.*

The leader spoke. Although her speech was unfamiliar to me, I understood by her body language the gist of her remark. They were where they should be, but we weren't. She leveled her sword at Kim and flicked the weapon as she barked her questions. I sensed she wanted some sort of explanation for disturbing their progress to wherever they were going.

"Stay calm," Kim said to me, "and for goodness sake don't antagonize them. I'm going to try and reason with them."

"How, when you don't speak their language?"

I stared in disbelief when she turned to the leader and spoke some sort of gibberish at them. Her voice held no hint of fear. "We are sorry for the intrusion, but we seem to be lost," she added for my benefit.

The warrior ignored Kim and grunted at a couple of her sturdier warriors.

The command must have been to search us for goodness knows what, because two of the more scantily dressed young women pushed us apart and grabbed our daypacks.

"Hey, easy with those," I said, when our tools and log books clattered to the ground. "You can't just toss those things around."

"Easy, PJ, let them look. They need to make sure we're not here to harm them."

"Harm them? That's rich. In case you haven't noticed, those weapons are the real thing."

The leader stepped forward and, shouting something, backhanded me across the mouth. I lost my balance and fell to one knee, my head ringing from the blow. Jesus, that was a bit excessive.

"Stop that!" Kim advanced on the leader with clenched fists.

"Honey, wait. I'm okay." I rotated my jaw and spat out some blood. "Keep cool. It's my fault. I shouldn't have mouthed off like that."

Kim hesitated. She stepped back, appearing to pick discretion over valor. The leader lowered her sword, but kept it handy. She stood by while the rest of the band picked through our belongings. Apparently finding nothing of value, they kicked our packs to the side and stood, watching us with cold, dark eyes. The leader glanced at our stuff, and then nodded to one of the women.

The woman I presumed to be her second in command motioned us downward.

"You've got to be kid—" Two of the warriors pushed me to my knees and from there, flat on my face. "Ow! Cripes. You want me to smell the grass? Okay, I'm doing it. Just take it easy."

Kim lowered herself beside me, putting her hand on the small of my back. "Don't rile them. They don't know who we are or why we're here. We're like aliens to them."

She turned to the leader. In a steely tone, she spoke to them again in that same strange language.

"What the heck are you saying?"

"You hurt her again and you'll have me to deal with. Got that?"

"Thanks for the translation, Kimmy, but that sounded antagonizing, in any language."

Methodically, they patted us down, moving along our pant legs, turning our pockets inside-out, poking and prodding us in sensitive and private parts of our anatomy. Had it been gentler, it would have tickled. As it was, a couple of the leather-clad ladies had a lot of fun checking out our bodies while their leader examined the contents of our pockets.

I could sense Kim's fury mounting. One of the gang acted a little too friendly while running her hand over Kim's firm buttocks, and the maneuver raised my hackles as well.

"Watch it, sister." I glared at the offender. "Keep your filthy paws off her."

Smirking, the warrior rolled me onto my back and touched me in several personal places. The others stood by, laughing and pointing, probably critiquing her technique.

Kim, though, didn't miss a trick. While still on the ground, she lashed out and kicked the smirking warrior right behind the knees. Taken off-guard, the woman yelped and fell face first across my chest. I shoved her away, but caught the blur of a swinging staff out of the corner of my eye.

"Look out!" My warning came too late. The staff wielder clipped the side of Kim's jaw, spinning her around. Two other warriors piled on with flailing fists, punching and jabbing her midsection, driving her into the ground.

"Stop that! Damn it!" I leaped to my feet, pulled one of the women off, wrestled her down, and kneed her in the groin. When I glanced at their leader, I saw a bemused expression on her face. She looked like someone who knew the inevitable outcome, but wanted the futility to continue for a few more seconds, while the outnumbered were pounded senseless. Kim and I never had a chance, but we refused to give in.

Boss lady made a grunt of some kind, and her assistant drew a sword. In one swift movement, she pressed her blade against my chest, forcing me into submission. Kim kicked and punched her way out of the heap and paused for breath. Seeing me held at sword-point, she gave a ferocious roar, took one step toward my captor, and was promptly smacked on the back of her head with the stock of a crossbow.

I fell to my knees beside her, cradling her. "Kim! Oh, God! Wake up, please. This dream's over. Scott's going to get a piece of my mind for all those wasted therapy sessions."

Sounding bored and a little disappointed, the leader said something, and I was yanked upright, my arms pulled behind my back.

"Wait, she's bleeding. Please let me help her." They tied my wrists so tightly the leather strips cut off the circulation to my fingers.

The leader shot me another dirty look and spat out a command. One of her posse forced a dirty piece of cloth between my teeth and secured it. Two of the women seized Kim under both arms and hauled her along behind us. We were dragged and shoved the entire mile or so to a camp.

If this was what Kim called Amazon hospitality, she could have it.

Once in camp, they dropped her on a mat in the corner of a small hut. She was still unconscious. When they tried to move me to another location, I lowered my head and butted my nearest captor. She shoved me backwards and something heavy came down hard against the left side of my head.

* * *

"Kimmy? Wake up. Please."

PJ's voice seemed far off. I managed to open my eyes despite a warrior-size headache. She was leaning over me, tears trickling down her cheeks. I reached for her, but even that little activity caused my body to scream in pain. "Where are we?"

"We're still in dreamland. Only now it's a full-blown nightmare."

"It doesn't feel like a dream."

She ignored me and unleashed all her pent up fears. "These women, Kim. They're wild warriors. Amazons or something. Like your Marna."

"Marna wouldn't do this to us."

"You don't know what Marna would do. When you met up with her she was just a bunch of bones."

I tried to shift my body only to hear myself whimper. "God, I hurt."

PJ stroked my forehead and sniffed. "We were both unconscious for a time. The only good thing is that now our hands are untied." She paused to wipe her nose with the back of her hand. "What are we going to do?"

Her touch was soothing, but the side of my head felt like it had connected with a freight train. "Wake up soon, I hope."

"Sweetheart, this is a nightmare of the worst kind."

"Must have been some of that Greek food we've been eating lately," I said. Maybe a joke here and there would keep her from panicking.

I tried to recall what had hit me and remembered the meadow, though how we came to be there was lost in a haze. I remembered fighting with a roving band of warrior women. They were treating PJ with disrespect. Nobody would get away with that kind of behavior, not as long as I had a fighting breath in my body. I remembered the side of my face being smashed and a thudding blow to the back of my head. That's when everything went black. I guess I remained unconscious until I woke up here on the floor of a hut.

PJ curled up alongside me. Her face was streaked with tears, her hair matted with dried blood.

"You're hurt." I tried to examine her for a wound, but she shook her head.

"It's nothing to worry about." Her eyes filled with fresh tears. "But we need to do something, Kim. What should we do?"

"Wake up, that's what." I managed to get my arms around her, holding her tightly. She tucked her head under my chin. The closeness made me feel a little better, but nothing could ease the throbbing inside my head. We clung together, unmoving.

Sunlight, shining through the chinks in the hut, partially illuminated its interior. Gradually, as time passed, what little light it offered disappeared, leaving us in total darkness.

Still holding each other, we slept fitfully, awaking now and then to the sound of drumming and chanting.

"I thought a dream lasted only a few minutes in real time," PJ whispered, her anxiety escalating. "Why aren't we waking up? We should be waking up."

"Dream time is longer than real time," I said, trying to calm her. I had no idea why I said that, but I tried to be positive for her sake.

"Kim, you were speaking their language. How did you do that?"

"Huh? I've no idea."

"You expect me to believe that? You just don't suddenly speak a strange language."

"I told you, I don't know. I wasn't even aware that I was doing that. How could I have?"

"Jesus, forget it." PJ huffed and turned over, away from me.

I was sorry she was upset, but I couldn't give her an explanation. I was probably as scared as she was, though I tried not to show it.

We slept again, awakening only when the skin flap that served as a door was thrown open, and the bright morning sunlight struck us full in the eyes. Two ferocious looking warriors stood in the doorway. They approached warily, one setting down a ceramic pitcher of water and an empty bowl. "Clean yourselves, then eat," the taller of the two said, taking a basket of fruit from her companion. They spoke in that same strange tongue, and although I had no idea what language it was, I understood every word.

"I want to pee," PJ said in clear, unadulterated English, and in a tone that was far too demanding for the precarious situation we were in.

"Shush, don't upset them," I whispered.

She shot me a withering look. "It'll upset them more if I pee right here."

The taller warrior gave her a quick nod.

"Come," said the shorter one, and then looked at me. "You, too."

PJ helped me to my feet, but I was too dizzy to stand on my own. With the taller warrior supporting me, we walked out behind the hut and into the bushes. PJ helped me unbuckle my belt and loosen my pants. The warriors stood and stared at us.

"No, don't." I was too late again. PJ had advanced on our guards.

"What's the matter with you? Are you so uncivilized that you've never heard of privacy?"

While I stood, holding my pants up, she grabbed the guards and turned them around. "Stand there, if you must, but keep your eyes on some other prize." Strangely enough, they seemed to understand her, though her hostile body language probably made words unnecessary.

The warriors must have been too astonished to do anything. They waited for us to relieve ourselves and helped us back to the hut. Though they looked intimidating, their gentle touch surprised me. Their kinder treatment was lost on PJ, however.

"Such manners. I can't believe your behavior." She scowled at them and shook her head several times while we were marched back to the hut. "We really must speak to your superior."

The guards looked at each other, ignoring her comments, but I thought I saw their lips twitch with amusement. Through signs and demonstrations, the women told us to wash ourselves, eat, and rest.

"Yeah," PJ said. "They want us clean before they drop us in the cooking pot."

* * *

It helped PJ's disposition to be able to clean up. We hadn't thought about food since this whole adventure began, but once we tasted the delicious figs, peaches, grapes, and apples, we realized just how hungry we were.

At the conclusion of our meal, a masked woman shuffled into the hut. She lit a small fire and boiled some water, all the time chanting and adding what appeared to be herbs and crushed flowers to the bubbling pot. Barely acknowledging our presence, she took a wad of moss, dipped it into the hot liquid, and after letting it cool slightly, dabbed it over our injuries.

"Who are you?" I asked. "What do you want with us?"

"There you go again, spouting their gibberish."

"Be still," the woman said.

"Yeah," PJ added, turning to the woman, "how about letting us wake up. Better yet, how about letting us go?" Her disposition had turned sour again.

The woman rocked back on her heels, peering at PJ intently through the slits in her mask. "Be still, child."

PJ folded her arms. "Stop calling me a child."

Now how did you know that she referred to you that way?

I would figure that out later. Right now, it was more important to calm PJ down.

"Honey, please, she's trying to help us."

PJ made a face. "Yeah, like she's dressing the pig for roasting over a spit."

* * *

Something seemed familiar about the way the masked woman touched me and acted around Kim. She didn't resemble the Amazon spirit who had visited me in Arizona and in Wales, but I felt as though I knew her from some place. My anxiety increased with each minute she remained in the hut. I couldn't demand that she leave because she was trying to soothe Kim's painful wounds.

Kim was in a great deal of discomfort, but when I made suggestions, the so-called healer dismissed me like some irritating brat. I pinched the bridge of my nose and closed my eyes. A monster headache threatened to take off the top of my head.

Jesus. Why wouldn't we just wake up from this nightmare? Why couldn't we return with no injuries and no worries to our normal lives in that ugly blue tent?

I watched the woman place a poultice over Kim's ribs and cover her body with a thin animal skin. Tears of hopeless frustration slid down my cheeks.

Chanting something soothing, the healer moved toward me. Gentle, gnarled hands wiped my face and dabbed once more at my various scrapes and bruises. She patted my belly and her words seemed to form a question about my health.

I sniffed and touched the side of my head. The wound there had been especially painful, but no blood stained my fingers. "I'm okay, I guess. Nothing a return to reality wouldn't cure."

The old woman looked puzzled. I figured she thought I was a few eggs short of a dozen and that a conk on the head hadn't helped matters.

She and I sat and stared at each other while Kim drifted off to sleep. I took a deep breath. "Listen, I appreciate the fact that we've been untied and that we were allowed to clean ourselves and eat some food. I don't suppose we could wash our clothing, too. We managed to get pretty dirty when the village Welcome Wagon greeted us earlier."

She shook her head as if not understanding my comments, and stood up.

"Wait, I still have questions." But she ignored me and left the hut.

"Shit." I kneeled beside Kim, touching her forehead with the back of my hand. As gently as possible, I kissed her cheek and was relieved to find no fever present. She reached for my hand, but her eyes remained closed.

"Kimberly Elizabeth Blair," I whispered.

"Mmm?"

"Don't you ever let me eat kalamari and octapothi for lunch again."

* * *

Later in the day, after I'd slept for a while beside Kim, the healer returned. Without her mask, she looked older, but much less intimidating. Two young women trotted behind her and carried clothing.

She did understand. But how? This got crazier by the minute.

I caught the old woman's arm. She stepped back as though she had been burned, and I released her. I tried again to approach her, standing so close that I could smell her breath. It was not unpleasant, rather like a mixture of herbs and spices. "Tell me please, how Kim can speak your language when she has no knowledge of it?"

I thought the old woman's features softened a bit. She reached forward, pulled my medallion up from inside my shirt, and spoke one unmistakably English word. "This."

"Holy cow! Now I can understand you." I put shaky fingers to my lips and a shiver raced along my spine. My words were not English. "This is insane." I took a deep breath. "You've got to tell me more. 'This,' just doesn't cut it. I need an in-depth explanation."

She shook her head at me, and I felt like a child again.

The old woman raised the medallion until it was right in front of my eyes. I could see kaleidoscopic colors pulsing with life inside it. When she replaced it under my shirt, its heat warmed my skin.

While I was interacting with the healer, I watched her two assistants remove the poultice from Kim's body and bind her ribs with long strips of clean cloth. One of the women dropped a tunic of soft deerskin beside her mat. Kim thanked her for the gift.

I was given what could only be described as a leather hand towel and a few thin leather straps. Kim fingered her tunic and her mood seemed to brighten. When she saw me holding up the pieces of leather, her mood brightened even more.

After leaving the scanty items of clothing with us, the healer and her companions turned to depart.

"Wait a minute," I called. "I'm missing most of my wardrobe. And you never explained how a piece of jewelry can act as a translator." Since the healer had left the hut, further questions were pointless.

One of her assistants turned back, took the leather towel, and held it to my waist. "This goes here."

I sucked on my lower lip. "Okay, I'll pretend it's a miniskirt. But what do I wear on top?" I pointed to the area of my breasts.

She raised the two braided strips.

I took a step back. "They're no more than belts, and not very wide ones at that. There's no way I'm wearing those."

She reached to pull up my shirt.

"Hold it, sister." I grasped her wrist. "I can dress myself, thank you. That is, if you'd just give me the rest of the costume."

The second of the healer's assistants paused at the tent entrance. She returned to assist her cohort in tugging down my pants, both of them.

"What the hell are you doing?"

I snatched back my underpants which had been the object of much curiosity. It must have been the lace that fascinated them. They watched with interest as I pulled them back on.

Enthusiastically, the two women wrapped the leather skirt around my waist, where it hung just below my navel, and then they rid me of my shirt and bra.

They examined my bra, too, giggling as they held it up to the light, pulling it this way and that, measuring the cups to their own breasts. Almost as an afterthought, they took the belt-like strips, crisscrossed them several times around my chest, and tied them in the back with what I hoped was a square knot. I felt my face and a good portion of my upper body turn crimson from their scrutiny. Like a second heartbeat, the medallion, nestled comfortably between my breasts, continued its warm steady pulse.

The women stood back, apparently happy with my transformation. I couldn't bring myself to see how much they left exposed, but judging by the chill on my skin, it was significant.

When Kim struggled to stand up, the women helped her into her tunic. I kept my arms folded over my breasts and my back turned away from her for as long as possible.

"PJ, turn around. Let me look at you in your new duds."

I moved just my head, twisting it enough to appreciate her form-fitting, one piece ensemble. "Wow! You look sensational!" I admired the deep V-neckline and how it enhanced her cleavage.

"Come on. Now you."

"Oh, geez." I turned toward her and lowered my arms.

"Ooo-la-la. I'm feeling better already." The expression on Kim's face was positively lecherous.

"If I as much as breathe the wrong way, I'll pop out of this crazy harness. I can't possibly go anywhere dressed like this."

"Oh, but you must," the healer said, rejoining her assistants. They stood by, watching as we exchanged compliments, until chanting and drumming sounds came from someplace in the village.

As if heeding a message in the various drumbeats, the old woman and her assistants took our hands. "You are to be taken to our largest visitor's residence," the old woman told us. "Later, there will be a feast in your honor. The queen has commanded."

"Isn't that just peachy," I said.

I dropped the old woman's hand and turned to face her. "I'm not going anywhere until I know about this language thing. How is it that we can communicate with you? We've never been here before."

The healer shook her head and pointed to my glowing medallion. "All in good time."

I noted for the first time how gnarly her hands were and how claw-like her fingers. She appeared older than time itself.

I turned to Kim when the old woman and her assistants had left. "How old do you suppose she is?"

"Ancient. And I bet you our freedom that she's a shape changer."

I shook my head. "Aren't we in enough trouble without you suggesting more?"

* * *

A young woman came to escort us across the clearing and into a larger hut that sat among other large huts, each with a fire pit in front.

"Ah, the Ritz." PJ couldn't resist the sarcasm.

"Shush. Like it or not, we're guests here. Let's act graciously."

She nudged me as we surveyed our new, larger quarters. "You're taking this all very seriously, aren't you?"

"You bet I am."

"Okay, to humor you, I'll be on my best behavior, though I must tell you, in this dreamland, you're a bore."

It hurt to laugh, so I had to be content with a snicker. "You're not such a scintillating conversationalist yourself. But that outfit makes up for all sorts of shortcomings."

Hands on hips, she gave me a withering look. "One more crack about this costume and injuries or no—"

"You may rest now," our guide said. "The festivities will begin at sundown. Someone will come to escort you."

"Festivities? What festivities? Are we to be the sacrificial lambs?"

The word festivities had evidently rung alarm bells with PJ. "It's all right." I moved closer and put my arm around her to allay her trembling. "They're not going to hurt us."

I turned to our guide. "Thank you, uh… what is your name?"

"Sheena."

PJ coughed. "Sounds like something out of Lion King."

"What is this Lion King?" Sheena asked.

I answered before PJ could utter another smart remark. "It's a movie, but you don't know what that is, do you?"

"Moo-vee?" Sheena repeated the word slowly, but was visibly puzzled.

"It's a story about a brave lion who became king."

Sheena threw her shoulders back and stood proudly at attention. "I will do brave things some day." Her smooth skin, almond-shaped eyes, and long, black hair offered us a preview of the beautiful woman she would become.

"You are a warrior?"

"An apprentice warrior, but some day I will be like this Lion King."

"You will indeed," I said, having witnessed the earnestness of her demeanor.

PJ had listened to the exchange in silence, but she confronted me after Sheena left. "Lion King? For Pete's sake. You've lost it, you know. Gone completely 'round the bend. Bonkers. Daft." She paused in her tirade. "And just for kicks, will you tell me what this language is that we can now understand?"

"I think it's some form of ancient Greek. And you understand it, too. You'll be speaking it fluently in a few days."

"A few days, my ass. We aren't going to be here a few days."

"Don't be too sure."

"Scott Fleming isn't going to get another dime until he can explain this." She paced and waved her hands with vehemence. "This is on his head. Therapy indeed." PJ spat out the words and poked her finger in my direction. "Before he started analyzing me, I had fun dreams. Now look where I am. Wandering around, lost in nightmare alley."

"Haven't you wondered why our captors didn't take our medallions when they took everything else we had with us?"

"Actually, no. I've been a little busy taking care of you, making sure my boobs were covered, and wondering if we'd ever get back to reality."

"It's just kind of strange, that's all."

"This whole trip to Amazon Land is strange, if you ask me."

* * *

The interior of the hut was bright with late afternoon sunlight streaming through the doorway. On one side, an inviting bedroll awaited, beside it, a large basket of fruit and assorted sweetmeats, a pitcher of water, and goblets.

I pulled PJ down onto the bedroll which was piled high with soft animal skins. "Bonkers I may be, but Sheena suggested we rest in preparation for the big doings tonight. Let's make the best of it and do what they say."

"Scott's going to have a field day deciphering this dream," she whispered, snuggling against me, and I'm thinking that you're going to need his services more than I am."

"I thought you had decided to dismiss him."

"Probably. But first I'll enjoy hearing his reaction to all of this."

I wrapped her in my arms and kissed her, gently at first, then greedily as passion consumed my whole being. "I love you so much. You're part of me, what I do, and who I am."

PJ's breath was warm against my neck. "I love you, too, and though I may be a little crazy at times, when it comes to you, I know exactly where I belong." She nibbled my earlobe, causing electric currents to race through me.

"That's the perfect place. Belong there as much as you like." My lips sought the soft spot under her chin.

"Are you sure?" She tried to raise herself up to look at me, but I was too absorbed in kissing and caressing her exposed skin. I had plenty to attack thanks to the Amazon clothiers.

"Of course I'm sure." I buried my head between her breasts and inhaled her familiar fragrance, now enhanced with moist, salty leather.

She gasped at the boldness of my passionate tongue.

"Kim."

"Yes?"

"I—just thought. Whew! Down, woman."

I paused. "You don't like?"

"Oh, I like. I like a lot. But I'm worried about your wounds."

"What wounds?"

My teeth nipped at the underside of her breasts and she gasped, breathing from her mouth, making little mewing sounds, slipping into the familiar rhythm of arousal.

"The... oh, you know... I thought you might not feel up to this right now." She groaned as I slid the straps from her heaving chest. "But obviously I was wrong."

"Obviously. Help me get my tunic off, will you?"

"With pleasure." PJ lifted the garment carefully and draped it beside our bed. She kissed each and every bruise on my body. It took a long time, but I felt no pain at all for the next several hours.

Afterwards, I gazed at PJ as she slept, happy that she was at peace and that I had contributed to the lingering smile on her lips. But sleep would not come as easily for me. I was vaguely aware of camp sounds: women's voices, laughter, the metallic sound of practice swordplay, and cheering bystanders. The sounds and the smells were vaguely familiar. I wondered if this was, as PJ had said, a dream, or if we had somehow been transported back in time.

No way. PJ was right. It had to be a dream.

A tiny part of me wished it was real and that we really were here with the Amazons, but common sense told me it was not possible.

I dropped off and awoke just as it was getting dark.

Chapter 10

Two young women escorted us into a clearing.

"Who do they think they are?" PJ asked when they twirled their weapons and saluted several of the older women.

"Apprentices," I whispered.

"Gee. No kidding."

"Come on, you were young once, looking to impress people."

"I guess it's not too far from wearing tight leather pants and riding Harleys, hoping to get my father's attention."

They seated us near the front where we would have a good view of the festivities, then took their places, one on either side of us.

I gave PJ a nudge. "You rode motorcycles? You never told me about that."

"Once or twice. The chauffeur we had before Mitch owned one. Let's just say that I've grown up a bit since those days, though riding would still be a kick."

"A Vespa was the biggest two-wheeler I ever rode."

"They're fun, too."

Our companions frowned and made shushing noises. PJ stared straight ahead, arms folded across her chest. I took a longer look at our storybook surroundings, soaking up the atmosphere. Many campfires burned in a bright circle, casting an orange glow over the assembled crowd of scantily-clad warriors. A slight breeze ruffled the thin plumes of smoke rising amidst the flames. Whenever a log was tossed onto one of the fires, sparks rose in an upward shower of stars that disappeared into the night.

Beneath a brilliant moon, older women chatted excitedly among themselves. Others stood about, tapping their feet, keeping time to the drumbeats that echoed and re-echoed around the clearing. My heart picked up the beat. I felt strangely exhilarated and aware of the anticipation building toward the queen's arrival. I wanted so much to share my feelings with PJ, but I knew that she was not ready yet to accept our situation.

She edged closer to me, her eyes darting from one warrior to another. I could tell the pounding drums were unsettling her.

"Relax, honey." I gave her thigh a rub. "They're just showing their pride. Queen Elizabeth and her entourage couldn't have a better build up."

"Yeah, but it's my sanity that's at stake here."

"There's nothing wrong with you, other than what's to be expected after the trouble in Wales. You're going to be okay."

"And what about this charade we're playing? It's all some sort of game, and I haven't a clue how it works."

"Shush. Something's happening."

The drums quickened their tempo, forcing my heartbeat to keep time. A group of young bare-breasted women saluted the full moon, before throwing themselves into a frenzy of movement.

"Oh, goodie. We get a floor show."

"PJ, please. Just go with the flow, okay?"

"If you're expecting me to take off this top and join the rave, you've got another think coming."

"Hmm. I hadn't considered it, but if you feel the urge, I won't object."

"At least this hideously skimpy series of straps covers my boobs, and I intend to keep it that way."

I kept my voice as low as possible. "Whatever you say, sweetheart, but you have nothing to be ashamed of in that regard."

She was silent, but I think her lips twitched.

Fresh participants arrived periodically to replace tired, sweating dancers. As the drumming intensified, my head throbbed. The feeling wasn't unpleasant; it allowed for the release of the primitive me, calling from deep within my soul. That essence had survived despite the centuries separating the original Marna and myself.

I knew she was here, but where? Would I recognize her?

I glanced at PJ and viewed her through a veil of lifetimes. What was she thinking? Had she discovered her past self? Or did she think this was caused by illusions, dreams, or even demons?

She had a strange expression on her face when she looked at me.

"PJ? You okay?"

"I can't figure out if I'm behaving badly in your dream, or if you're being anal-retentive in mine."

Biting back a laugh, I took her hand and squeezed it. "Did it ever occur to you that it might not be a dream?"

"Yes, but that's not what really scares me."

"What then?"

"The expression on your face is a cross between rapture and remembrance. You're so totally into all of this." PJ encompassed the clearing with a wave of her arm.

"Don't you find it spell-binding?"

She watched in silence with me for several seconds. "I find it bizarre."

A few seconds later, she tugged my shirtsleeve. "This part's fun, though. All these dancing girls and food. Just look at all that food."

A dressed pig roasted slowly on a spit, the grease spluttering into coals, creating jets of orange flame. The aroma of pungent herbs filled the clearing, mixing with the scent of pine trees and wood smoke. There were wooden platters of fowl and fish, baskets of fruit, cakes, breads, cheeses, and other assorted edibles. Pitchers of rich brown ale and wines lined several tables, waiting to quench thirsts. Tankards filled to the brim overflowed onto the ground creating dark, frothy puddles.

"I wonder if our taste buds work as well in Dreamland."

"PJ?"

"Hmm?" She was still gazing at the roasting meat.

"Marna's here," I whispered.

"Oh, come off it." PJ pushed against my chest. "You're taking this dream stuff way too seriously."

I gripped her hands, stilling them. "No, she is here. I was worried that I wouldn't recognize her, but I have."

"Where?" PJ scanned the crowd. "Point her out to me."

I pulled her hands to my chest, gently this time. "Inside me. Somehow, we're one. Since I'm here, she is, too."

PJ's eyes glistened and she bit her lower lip. "Are you sure that clunk on the head didn't affect you just a little bit?"

"I'm sure." For just a second, I saw fear in her eyes. Over the past few months, that haunted look had periodically appeared and muted the gleam in them. I put my arm around her and held her close to me. "Don't be afraid. I'm here for you, and I always will be. No matter what or who I am, you can count on me."

"Hold me?" she asked, voice trembling.

"Forever." We drew into each other, absorbing comfort and warmth from our loving relationship.

The dancing and chanting grew more frenzied and then stopped. The vibrations from the drums continued to reverberate in the ground beneath our feet and in the still air all around us. It was accompanied by the crackling of the many fires. Oiled bodies dropped to one knee, heads bowed, and arms reached out and down as if to grasp the earth and become one with it. Skin glistened in the moonlight as dancers curved their spines and lowered their heads between outstretched arms.

A single drummer started to beat, then another, and another.

With small gasps, our escorts dropped to one knee.

"Look," PJ pointed off to her left. "Who do you suppose—?"

"Our queen has arrived," one of our escorts whispered. "On your knee, head bowed."

It felt perfectly natural to do as she bid, and I scrambled into position.

"If you think I'm going to—"

"Down, for me, please?"

PJ shot me an irritated look, but dropped into position beside me. "I feel ridiculous."

"Silence. You must pay your respect."

PJ threw an exasperated look at the woman who had spoken. "All right, I'll play along, for now."

The queen, a personage whose features were hidden behind the ornate carving of a heavy mask, carried weapons: a sword at one side of her waist, a dagger on the other. Dried grasses adorned her mask, making it difficult in the darkness to see the detail of the carving. A warrior walked at her right side. Her features were also hidden behind a mask, but her arsenal of weapons was evident. She held herself erect and was attentive to her queen.

Only a single, slow drumbeat broke the silence that had fallen over the camp. Three heavily armed women followed the two and took their places behind the seats of honor.

"I'm dying to see their faces," PJ whispered into my ear, nibbling on my earlobe as she did.

We didn't have to wait long. As if answering PJ's request, the queen removed her mask. My heart thudded in my chest. "My God. It's Leeja." I turned to PJ, looking for confirmation.

She swallowed. "She's the spitting image of the model Dr. Westermeyer made of her."

"Then we know who the other one is." The queen's consort removed her mask and took her place at the queen's right hand.

"Marna," PJ said in a harsh whisper. "You and she could be sisters. Oh, God, this gets worse."

The royal couple sat on their fur-covered thrones and the drums pounded. Dancers lithely contorted before their monarch.

"Kim, are you all right?"

"I guess so, though I'm not sure I know at this point what is going on."

"Join the club."

I inclined my head toward the queen and her consort. "It's so strange. Am I here? Or there in a younger version, beside my queen?"

"Yeah, your queen who is also your lover."

I failed to recognize the sarcasm in PJ's statement as I continued to stare at the two Amazons. Months ago, we had found bones in the Superstition Mountains of Arizona that when reconstructed through forensics, resembled these two. But these women were very much alive, and judging from the way they touched and spoke to each other, very much in love.

The feasting, the drumming, and the dancing continued long into the night. We remained seated among the group, almost unnoticed. The experience provided us with the chance to observe the rulers and their subjects. PJ and I ate, drank, and joined the dancing in a subdued manner.

The queen glanced in our direction once or twice during the festivities, but made no move to talk with us. After she and her party departed, some of the women scattered to their respective huts, but the majority remained to feast and dance, probably until daylight.

Exhausted and stuffed with food and ale, PJ and I ambled toward our hut, intending to call it a night. We were intercepted by a heavily armed warrior. "Our queen will see you in the morning. Be ready by two candlemarks after sunrise. Someone will come for you."

"We'll be ready," I told her.

"Why us?" PJ gripped my arm. "Why does she want to see us?"

I hugged her and ruffled her hair. "I don't know, sweetheart, but now maybe we can get some answers to our questions."

* * *

I awoke to feel warm sunlight on my face, filtering in through the cracks in the walls of the hut. Not wanting to disturb Kim, I stretched my body slowly and gently under our thick fur covering. She and I had made the most of our free time, making slow, sweet love and then drifting off to sleep. I felt mild aches from the exertion of the evening, and my head still buzzed from the effects of too much ale and frenzied dancing. Me? Dancing? In that skimpy costume? Oh, God.

Kim stirred, and drew a long, steady breath. We had settled into one of my favorite positions, with Kim on her back and me snuggled against her side, a leg over hers, one arm across her stomach, my chin resting on her collarbone. She made a delicious body pillow.

"Mmm," we sighed in unison. Our fingers intertwined across her taut abdomen.

"Some party, huh?"

I groaned. "Is it possible to dream you got drunk, made love, and fell asleep?"

"I don't know, but I think we did. At least the last three parts of that. I know I'm satisfied in all the right places."

"Is it time to see the queen? My watch seems to have stopped. I'd sure like to wash and find my cargo pants and T-shirt before we have to march out in front of those people again."

"Oh, PJ. Don't give up those leather thingies."

"Sorry, hotshot. I have to get some underwear on before I see the queen again. Walking around half-naked might be de rigueur in this village, but I find it drafty and very hard to concentrate."

"Spoilsport." She pulled my chin closer and planted a kiss on my lips.

"Ugh, please Kimmy. Let me brush my teeth first. My breath could probably stop a charging rhino."

"Yeah, me too. Wonder what these folks use for dental hygiene?"

I kissed her cheek and threw back our covers, chilling our bare skin. On hands and knees, I crawled in the direction of the basin and water container.

Someone had started a small fire and warmed the water for our use. I thought it had been a very considerate gesture, until I realized it meant that same someone had intruded on our privacy while we slept.

I discovered a soft scrap of cloth and some herbal oil beside the basin, and wasted no time washing my face and upper body. Kim joined me in a quick cleaning. We used cold water and mint leaves to freshen our breath.

"Not exactly our usual routine, is it?" She tickled my neck with a sprig of mint.

I ducked away from her assault. "Oh, look! Someone has washed and dried our stuff. Bless their hearts." I dashed to the pile of familiar clothing in the corner of our hut and hastily dressed in my usual work clothes.

Kim pouted. "I'm going to miss seeing so much of you."

"You can stay in that soft tunic, if you want." I rubbed my face against the deerskin and handed it to her.

"Perhaps I will." Her eyes glazed a bit. "Wearing it gives me a strong feeling of kinship with these women, especially Marna."

She pulled the tunic over her head and cinched it with a strip of leather. I felt a warm glow when I saw her in that outfit. "You look like you belong here—wherever here is—a dreamscape or something."

"It's strange, but I do feel somewhat at home here." She wrapped her arms around me and pulled me close. "I sure wish you had stayed in that skirt and those leather strips. All that exposed skin gave me all sorts of warm feelings."

"Yeah." I snickered. "Right between your legs."

"That wasn't what I meant. If you'd stay in that new outfit, I bet you'd feel more at home in this village, too."

"The only place I'm going to feel at home is at home, or back on site."

The door to the hut opened, and two well-endowed warriors beckoned us.

"Come, the queen awaits."

Kim straightened her tunic. "We're all yours, ladies."

The two women gave us frank, appraising looks before exchanging amused glances.

"Jesus, I don't think that's quite what you meant," I said as we were escorted out.

* * *

"This is just too weird," PJ said, as we made our way toward the queen's hut.

Our final escort was a beautiful, young, olive-skinned woman with dark eyes. She wore a short skirt of soft doeskin and a fringed band around her breasts. Her leg, arm, and shoulder muscles rippled as she moved gracefully across the clearing.

I took PJ's arm and we fell into line with our guides. "Try to relax. Accept what is happening as an experience you won't soon forget."

"I'm sorry. I can't accept it so calmly." She stopped walking and turned to face me.

"We're trapped in a dreamscape, on our way to meet two characters who coincidentally happen to look like the embodiment of remains we found on our excavations in Arizona." Her index finger jabbed me in the stomach. "You say you are Marna, her descendent, or some sort of reincarnation. We have to be dreaming, but we can't seem to wake up." She threw up her hands. "What's wrong with this scenario? What's right about it? And you wonder why I'm apprehensive?"

"Reality as we know it is nothing more than our acceptance of it. Who's to say that our dreams are not reality? I can't be absolutely sure that our life in the twenty-first century is absolute reality. There's so much we don't know, PJ, so much yet to learn about dimensions way beyond those we routinely accept."

We stopped outside the queen's hut while one of our escorts announced our arrival. Then she stood to the side and motioned us inside.

"Thank you, Petrina, you may leave us."

"You're sure, My Queen?"

"Yes, we are perfectly safe with our guests."

The queen examined us closely. Her gaze bared my soul, and I'm sure it did something to PJ, too, because she edged closer to me.

"Be seated." Leeja's command was forceful, but cordial.

"Thank you," I bowed my head and dropped to the floor, seating myself comfortably on soft animal skins.

PJ remained upright, feet wide apart, arms folded across her chest. "I'll stand, thank you."

"As you please."

The queen was a strong woman, clearly equal to the task of dealing with PJ's defiance. She glanced at Marna who nodded some sort of unspoken agreement.

"First, I must apologize for the rough treatment you received when you arrived."

"I should hope so," PJ said.

I gave her a stern look. "Not now."

The queen ignored us. "Unfortunately, you encountered a scouting party that has been away for a while. They had no idea you were coming for a visit."

"Apology accepted," I said.

"A likely story," PJ countered.

"PJ." I tried my stoniest expression on her, but she kept her eyes focused on the queen and her consort.

Marna stepped forward, looking both dangerous and beautiful, and directed her comments to PJ. "You may remain standing if you like, but we have much to talk about, and you will surely be more comfortable sitting."

I watched, fascinated as they held a staring contest, each refusing to back down.

"Relax, you two." Queen Leeja turned to Marna. "Sit here beside me, and we will see how long our friend wants to stand so rigidly at attention."

When Marna smiled, the gleam of her perfectly white teeth softened her features. PJ didn't move.

"You're Dr. Kimberly Blair," Leeja said, looking at me, "a noted archaeologist in your world. In this one, you're recognized as an equally noted Amazon warrior. You are courageous, independent, loyal, and—best of all—you share the soul of my beloved consort." She gave Marna a look that left no doubt about their devotion to each other.

A movement at the door heralded the arrival of a young woman bearing herbal tea and a basket of fresh fruit. She went quietly about pouring and serving the tea, a strong mixture of ginger and other herbs.

"Thank you, but no thank you," PJ said, when offered a cup.

Excusing myself to Leeja and Marna, I took PJ's hand and pulled her down beside me. "You will sit, you will relax, and you will drink the tea." I ignored PJ's scowl and turned to the queen, "Your Majesty, I—"

"We don't stand on ceremony here. I may be the queen, but I'm also a woman who likes to chat, to laugh, and to love." She glanced again at her consort. "You may call me Leeja, and of course, you are well acquainted with Marna, my protector, advisor, companion, and the love of my life."

"Thank you. I am deeply honored to be in your presence."

"Come off it, Kimmy. This is completely crazy. These people only exist—"

"PJ, watch your tongue."

She turned to me. "Can't we stop this charade and get on with our lives?"

"Don't blame her for not believing," Marna said. "It's quite a step from your world to ours. But you're here for a reason. We know who you are. We know all about both of you."

"So, who am I?" PJ demanded.

"PJ!" I could have strangled her right there on the spot.

"No. She knows so much. Let her tell me who I am. We'll get to the bottom of all this."

Marna folded her muscular arms under her full breasts. "You are Dr. Priscilla Josephine Curtis, daughter of the wealthy and well-respected Frederick Curtis. You have a doctorate from Boston University and you are an archaeologist of some renown, though much of your early professional years were spent... jet-setting. I think that's the word you use. You met Dr. Blair while she was still searching for the Lost Tribe. You two fell in love, and your life changed forever. Not long ago, you traveled together to what is now called Wales."

"Stop. That's enough." PJ took a deep breath. "So you know a few facts. It doesn't prove anything."

"What can we say to gain your trust and your undivided attention?"

PJ glanced in my direction. I felt she was blaming me for all that was happening to us. "If you love me, Kim—really love me—you'll ask these two to wave their magic wands and return us immediately to reality."

"I'm sorry, PJ, I can't do that. I need to find out more about these women and what our destiny is with them. This is a chance to know Marna on a—"

"Marna, Marna!" She tapped her chest. "What about me, huh? The woman you profess to love? Can you answer that?"

So that's it. PJ felt threatened. She was jealous of Marna and my closeness with this group of Amazons.

I spoke against the lump that grew in my throat. "I'm asking you to go along with me. Listen to what Leeja and Marna have to say. Learn why they brought us here."

Tears welled in PJ's eyes. "I'm afraid I'll lose you if I do that."

"You're not going to lose me. All I'm asking is for you to trust me and go along with me this once."

She looked up at the hut's matted ceiling, blinked back tears, and took a long, shaky breath. "All right, I'll do it for you, but we're going to have a serious talk when we get back to reality. We need to take stock of our relationship in light of your fantasies. Life is not an illusion, Kim. It's real." She turned to Leeja and Marna. "You have my attention. What is it you want?"

"You talk to them," Leeja said to Marna, "since you probably know more of their situation than I do."

"You're here for several reasons. There are things you must know about us and about your destiny, but before we can go into that, you both need to work out the demons that afflict you. We want to help you both." Marna stopped and watched us. I sat quietly waiting for her to continue, but PJ's face was a mask of discontent.

"Speak for yourself, or for my friend here, but don't go putting any demons on me."

"Your demons are quite obvious, PJ, and understandable, considering what you went through in the place called Wales. Kim's are not as obvious, but they're just as deep and just as debilitating."

"And why would you want to help us?"

Showing a great deal of patience, Marna refused to react to PJ's hostile attitude. She sat beside Leeja, her hand resting on the queen's thigh. "We've told you that Kim shares my soul. What we haven't told you is that she was selected for that honor because of her unique abilities."

"Yeah, right. Kimmy the Warrior." I could hear the bitterness in her words and knew she was upset with me, with them, and with herself. "Just because you think you're acting all noble, and that Kim has swallowed your story hook, line, and block of concrete, don't expect me to be as gullible. I was doing just fine back in my real life."

"Are you sure?" Leeja entered the discussion, speaking to PJ in a low, non-threatening voice. "Think about the nightmares and waking in the middle of the night in a cold sweat. Think about the labyrinth, about how you reacted when you saw the bones. Your business often deals with bones. Why did they affect you so?"

I watched PJ squirm at the queen's probing questions and felt compelled to try to rescue her. "PJ won't like me telling you this, but she's willingly going through therapy with a doctor in our time.

"Ah yes, Dr. Armstrong and Dr. Fleming."

PJ stared at Leeja. "How do you know about them?"

"There are dimensions far beyond the obvious," Leeja said, "where everything that has ever happened and everything that is happening, as it is happening, is laid out for all to see. The future, too, is there in what you might call a Book of Ages. We are all mentioned within its covers."

"Hmph!" PJ's snort echoed around the room.

"I had thought she was doing rather well," I said, ignoring PJ's tight-lipped expression. "But now, I'm not so sure."

"The Book of Ages is there for all to see, but only when we are ready." The queen's expression was one of understanding and patience.

Marna turned her attention to me. "And you have seen Dr. Armstrong, too, but you're not convinced she can help you. Am I right?"

"Yes. But what does that have to do with our being here?"

"You're here because we care about you, and we want to help." Leeja poured us each some more tea from the earth colored pitcher. The container's design depicted women warrior figures in black, battling to the death. "We can help destroy your demons."

"'Destroy' being the operative word. And in practicing your mumbo jumbo, you'll probably destroy us as well."

"PJ!"

"You need to willingly give yourselves to us before we can help you."

"Do we have a choice, Your Majesty?" PJ's expression was decidedly unfriendly. "Will we be shot full of arrows or sliced and diced with Marna's sword, if we refuse?"

"I only do that in life and death situations," Marna said, her eyes dancing in amusement.

I looked at PJ. "What do we have to lose?"

"A whole hell of a lot." Her bottom lip quivered.

"For me, please."

PJ's hands fisted. She closed her eyes and took a deep breath. "I know I'm going to regret this."

I focused first on Marna and then, Leeja. "Okay, what do you want us to do?"

"You will come with me," Marna said. "We'll be gone for several days, during which time you will learn the art of managing your anger."

"You know about that?"

"Ah, yes I do. And you, Dr. Curtis, will spend time with Leeja expanding on what your healers have already taught you. She has much to tell you about your soul and will ask a couple of other women to assist her. You will learn a lot from them."

"We'll be separated?" Fresh tears welled in PJ's eyes.

"Yes, but it will not be for long."

"No. I can't."

"I know." I pulled her into my arms. "I don't want to leave you either, but something good may come from this."

"That's easy for you to say. You already have the heart of an Amazon." PJ buried her face in my tunic. "You're leaving me in Fiction Land while you go off with someone you've been in love with for centuries in your imagination." She swallowed. "And now that she's with us in the flesh, beautiful flesh, I might add, you expect me to go along with it."

"You know me well enough to know that I wouldn't leave you anywhere unless you were perfectly safe."

"I'm beginning to wonder."

"You'll be with Leeja, and I'll be with Marna. Working separately, we may actually get some answers to our questions."

PJ stroked the soft deer hide covering my stomach. "Only for you," she murmured, "and only because I love you more than anything in the world."

I kissed her again with all the love I possessed.

Marna spoke a few words to Leeja, kissed her tenderly, and stood to exit the hut. "Kim and I will leave right away. I have everything you'll need for the journey."

"And our group," Leeja said, "will move up to a grotto in the hills. We will work there in peace." She stood and took PJ's hand. "I promise you will have no regrets."

"I already have a ton of them."

"Your Majesty, before we go, I have to ask, why was it that the scouting party that captured us didn't take our medallions when they searched us?"

"They recognized the medallions as those belonging to certain members of the tribe, but weren't certain they were real. Their leader told me they were afraid to take them from you."

"Amazons afraid of something? Hard to imagine."

"PJ, please."

"Thank you, Your Majesty. I was curious about that."

"I know you both have questions. We will try to answer them for you during the days ahead."

PJ was silent, but her facial expression revealed her dissatisfaction with this whole scenario.

Marna and Leeja left to allow us to say goodbye. We hugged each other closely, sharing a kiss meant to last several days. We voiced apologies for words spoken during the emotional confrontation with Marna and Leeja. Neither one of us wanted to part on angry terms.

"Please don't think that I'm letting you down," I told her. "I'll show you that's not the case. We'll find out what all this means, and we'll be stronger after our separation. You'll see."

"Just come back to me in one piece, or I'll never forgive you."

"Absolutely. I promise."

Chapter 11

Movement outside the hut meant that Marna had arrived with the horses. "I'll be right there," I called. Already feeling the pain of separation, I pulled PJ into my arms, kissed her gently, and whispered my love. It wasn't easy leaving her here alone, but I trusted Leeja to take good care of her.

"When were you last on a horse?" PJ asked me.

"About seven years ago. I'll probably be stiff as all get out when we arrive where we're going."

"Do you know where you're going?" She was trying to be brave, but I could see the anxiety building in her eyes. The tears would come after my departure.

"No. How about you?"

"I heard the word grotto, but other than that, I've no idea."

We embraced again knowing the physical contact would probably have to last us for several days. While I was reasonably comfortable with our situation, I could sense she was totally terrified.

"Isn't it time for us to wake up?"

"I wish we could," I said, going along with her theory that this was nothing more than a dream. I didn't believe it, but this was not the time to force my thinking on her.

"Why can't we all go someplace together?"

"I think they have reasons for doing it this way. We just have to wait and see what they are."

"You still don't believe that this is a dream, do you?"

"I didn't say that. Whatever's happening to us, there's a purpose. Until we find out what that purpose is, we won't know what to think of it."

She hugged my waist. "I don't want you to go."

"I don't want to go, but it's something we have to do. I have a feeling it'll affect the rest of our lives."

"I was happy with our lives the way they were."

"We have a long ride ahead of us," Marna said, from outside our tent flap. "It's time we were on our way."

"Coming." I grasped PJ again, holding her tightly against me, imprinting every luscious curve of her body into my memory. "Don't be afraid. Leeja is a good person. You'll be safe with her, as I will be with Marna. We have lessons to learn from these two." I released her and turned quickly away. I didn't dare look back.

* * *

We had been riding for several hours. Marna was ahead of me, astride a beautiful tawny-colored mare. She led a short, stocky packhorse loaded with furs and other supplies. My mount, also a mare, was black as midnight with a coat that gleamed in the morning sunshine.

After leaving the clearing, we had ridden through the forest, weaving our way through the trees. The dappled effect of the sunlight reaching the forest floor was mesmerizing. Marna, every inch a warrior, was attired in a shirt of soft material—silk I think, from what I could see of it.

Over that, she wore a black sleeveless tunic made of leather, and wide leather straps crisscrossed her chest. Metal medallions, carved with intricate designs, studded both the straps and also a wide belt cinched around her narrow waist. Below the tunic was a short, leather skirt cut into narrow slits, presumably for ease of motion, and to protect her lower legs from brush and thorns she had on leg covers that reminded me of modern-day cowboy chaps. Matching hammered bracelets accentuated her muscular arms. A wicked looking sword nestled in a scabbard across her back, another was fastened to her saddle, and a dagger was secured in a sturdy, but worn sheath at her waist.

We rode side-by-side through a narrow valley; we spoke little, except when we stopped to water the horses and ourselves. I could feel Marna's eyes measuring my progress. "You're already missing PJ," she said, breaking the silence.

"And how would you know that?"

"You forget that I have love in my life, too, one that consumes my very being."

I turned my attention from the trail to her. "So you understand how I feel. I do miss her, and I worry about her when I'm not around, especially now when she is so vulnerable. She just doesn't understand what is happening."

"Have no fear. Leeja will take good care of her."

We climbed steadily into the hills and then up a mountainside. Because the trail was so steep in places, I leaned over my mount's neck, placing my weight forward while the animal scrambled upwards over loose rock. I soon realized that these animals were surefooted and accustomed to such terrain, so the nervousness I felt when we started the climb dissipated.

It was almost nightfall when we came to a cave high on the mountainside. Though it had been warm down below, it was bitterly cold up there.

"Here, let me help you with those." I reached for the heavy furs and skins that Marna was unloading from the pack animal.

"Put them in the back of the cave, close to the wall," she said, as I struggled under the heavy load. I recognized the remnants of a campfire close to the entrance.

"I'm going to light the fire so that the heat is directed into the cave and towards us," Marna said, as if reading my mind. It took her no time at all to gather some of the already blackened rocks and arrange them into a three-tiered semicircle behind the rudimentary hearth. In a short time, she had a good fire going, its orange flames warming as well as comforting us. With my imagination in cruise control, I visualized the flickering firelight painting animated pictures on the back wall of our cave.

When we first arrived, my legs and lower back ached from the cold and the long ride, but in no time at all, the fire had me feeling cozy and relaxed. It's hell to get old, I thought, as we devoured bread and cheese and chased it down with wine.

Marna was the strong quiet type, but the strength she exuded as a warrior and a woman was palpable. It was hard to believe that this warrior and I were connected in a very special way. Looking at her now, in the flickering orange glow, I had difficulty visualizing the bones we had unearthed in Arizona. The story was on-going. My search for the lost tribe was a long way from being over. I hoped PJ would accept that fact.

I was so tired after a long day on horseback that I fell asleep as soon as I had crawled under my fur covers. Marna lay a few feet away. When I awoke, sometime in the night, I could tell from her heavy breathing that she was deeply asleep. It was in this primitive setting that my thoughts turned to PJ. I wondered where she was and what she was doing. I was comfortable with her being part of Leeja's entourage, and I knew she was safe. That helped ease the loneliness and the longing I felt for her.

* * *

Snow had fallen during the night, obliterating our tracks to the cave, but painting a wonderland of white, punctuated with the darkened shapes of snow-crowned rocks and tree trunks. The slightest whisper of a breeze filled the air with tiny, glistening particles, reminding me of a Christmas paperweight that, when shook, created a snowstorm within its tiny, plastic dome.

"So, we're here," I said, as we ate our breakfast of fruit and sipped mugs of hot tea. "Now what?"

"All in good time."

After banking the fire, we left to gather wood—windfall that would continue to keep our cave warm.

"Have you ever hunted?" Marna asked.

"As a youngster, but I can't stand to kill anything now."

"You'd better get over that in a hurry. That is, if you want to eat."

After tidying up our bedrolls and clearing up our breakfast things, we put on our robes and prepared the horses for the hunt. It was a cold, crisp morning and the thought of sitting on a horse for I don't know how long was hardly an inviting prospect.

As soon as I was comfortably settled in the saddle, I urged my horse forward, allowing it to follow Marna's. I admired the ease with which she rode while leading a packhorse.

After what seemed like an hour or so, we arrived at a small mountain meadow that was serene and undisturbed. Apart from the occasional snuffling of the horses, we were surrounded by silence so pure that I found myself holding my breath. Marna dismounted gracefully and dropped to one knee. She first studied the ground, and then squinted into the shadows of the forest.

"What are you doing?" I asked.

"Scouting a game trail."

"How can you track anything with all this snow on the ground?"

"There are signs. There are always signs."

"You're really going to kill something for us to eat?"

"Of course."

"What about the food we brought with us? Isn't that sufficient?"

Marna stood up and turned to look at me. "We have no meat."

"Can't we make do with what we already have?"

"Not when it's this cold. We need the fat to keep us warm."

"Warrior dietician," I said, but Marna ignored my facetious comment. Her knowing look annoyed me.

We sat behind a snow-covered rock looking across at the tree line. I grumbled about the prospect of killing anything, fat or not. Marna wrapped herself in a fur robe, large enough for both of us, but she did not offer to share.

The cold gnawed at my bones. In no time at all I was shivering. I could see that Marna was comfortably wrapped in the heavy robe, and I worried about my own impending hypothermia.

"Hey, I'm freezing. Is there another robe that I can use?"

"Not one that isn't the result of a kill."

I gritted my teeth and said nothing, but I began to doubt my feeling of security. I was out here, alone in the wilderness with this warrior. As a person from a more modern and civilized era, I was not as equipped as she was to survive on my own. And at the moment, Marna didn't seem to care about my welfare.

She stiffened and stared across the meadow to the tree line. I couldn't see anything, but she was already notching an arrow into her bow. A moment later, she laid it down. "A doe," she said. "One that will live and produce again."

"Is that all she is to you, something that exists merely to procreate?" I met her cold eyes with anger.

"You need to remember where you are and in what time frame you now exist."

"It's all the same, your time or mine. There are too many who would have the female in the kitchen and continually pregnant. That goes for humans in future times, too."

"You are angry."

"You're damned right I am." The rage I was feeling provided enough internal fuel to keep me warm.

Marna sat perfectly still, staring forward, weapon ready.

This time I, too, saw the slight movement. Marna notched the arrow, sighted, and released it all in one smooth operation. She jumped up, threw the robe in my direction, and ran across the clearing to where the stilled body of a buck lay in the snow.

"Here's your damned robe," I said, when I caught up to her. Disgusted, I threw it down on the ground and stared at the once magnificent buck. The eyes were now sightless and dull, its blood seeping into the snow. Tears froze on my cheek. Marna knelt beside the animal and intoned what sounded like a prayer before rising. She bled him out and cleaned him, leaving a feast of steaming entrails for the scavengers. After stuffing the cavity with snow, she stood and let out a shrill whistle. Her mare trotted over, pulling the pack animal still tethered to her saddle. Marna lifted the buck and hoisted him effortlessly onto the pack horse. Although skittish with the carcass on his back, he settled down when she whispered soothing words into his ear.

Back at the cave, Marna dressed her kill, ignoring my smoldering anger. She wrapped the hide to be worked later, and cut the meat into manageable pieces.

* * *

The aroma of fresh meat sizzling over the flame played havoc with my gastric juices, but I was determined to hold on to the anger I felt at seeing such a noble animal slaughtered. "What were you saying back there?"

"I was thanking the buck for allowing us to kill him and get enough food for several days."

"What do you know about how he felt? I'm sure he didn't awaken this morning with the idea of allowing himself to be killed."

"I know more than you think I do." With that, she curled up and fell asleep, leaving me gnashing my teeth in frustration. I wanted a confrontation. I wanted her to fight back, to feed the rage that was churning within me.

I sat for the longest time, staring into the flames, listening to Marna's even breathing, and growing angrier by the moment until I fell asleep from pure exhaustion. When I awoke, the sun was high in the sky. Sometime during the night, Marna had covered me with a robe.

When I stepped out to relieve myself, Marna was nowhere to be seen. The sunshine, sparkling on yesterday's snow, created a jeweled wonderland. I thought it looked beautiful, until the vision of that recent and bloody death appeared in front of my eyes.

I turned to go back inside the cave, but stopped when a sound signaled Marna's presence. She stood, feet wide apart, with her sword drawn, looking fearsome with blood marking her cheeks and forehead. Her eyes were as cold as steel.

"What's this about?" I asked, unnerved by her appearance.

She came at me with the sword, missing me by a fraction of an inch when I reacted with a quick side-step.

"There's a sword behind you. Pick it up."

"Why should I?"

"You either pick it up, or I kill you right here."

Fear turned in my stomach. "What are you talking about? Why would you want to kill me, or for that matter, I you?"

"I don't want to kill you, but I do want to kill the anger that rots your soul."

I stood unmoving, staring at her, trying to fathom her next move.

"Pick up the sword."

I did as she bid. The weapon felt good in my hand, perfectly balanced. I waited until she lunged and sensed my Amazon spirit springing into action, directing my arm, blocking her blade. "What the hell are we doing? If you kill me, what are you going to tell PJ and Leeja?"

Marna lunged, and again, I parried; the sound of clashing metal echoed back and forth across the mountain. Sweat coated my body; my grip weakened. I turned away and splintered a small log with the sword before throwing the weapon into the snow. "I don't want to kill you. I just want to get back to PJ and live my life out with her in a civilized manner."

"Pick up the sword."

My throat was dry, my chest heaving. "I will not."

"Pick it up." She advanced, but I stood my ground. The tip of her blade bit into my neck, and I felt a trickle of blood. A vision of PJ flashed into my head. I imagined her holding me, weeping, as my life's blood stained the snow.

Marna stepped back and her expression softened. "You have passed your first test. You laid your anger aside to think about PJ."

"How do you know what I was thinking?"

"Because I love, too, and I know the way a strong mind works. Mortal danger always triggers thoughts of a loved one." After wiping the tip of the blade, Marna sheathed her sword. "Now I shall prepare some herbal tea for us."

I followed her into the cave, wondering what other tests the warrior had in mind, and if I would be up to the challenge.

* * *

That night, the snow continued to fall until every single rock was covered and the branches of the nearby trees bowed low with their burden. Snow had drifted up to the cave entrance forcing us to dig our way out. With each step, we sank up to our thighs. I longed for the sun, the warmth of Lesvos, but mostly I longed to be with PJ in our tent on the island or in my, no, our home in New Mexico. I wanted it to be her home, too. I didn't care where it was, as long as I was with my beloved.

"Conditions won't allow us to do much today," Marna said, after scouting the vicinity of the cave and bringing the horses inside. "Might as well rest up."

She cooked some of the venison, using a stick for a spit. It smelled so good, but for the longest time, I refused to eat. When I could no longer stand it, I reached for a piece, burning my fingers in the effort. Marna tossed me her dagger and a stick so I could slice the meat and hold it over the flame, allowing it to cook slowly.

Once I had eaten, I relaxed into a dreamlike state. The cave was a pleasant temperature. The smell of the horses, the roasting meat, and the sight of the warrior, with her face fiercely chiseled in the flickering shadows, all combined to give me a feeling of well-being. If PJ could've shared such a moment, she would've understood my love of the Amazons. On second thought, maybe not. She was still fighting the idea of my being directly descended. She was just not ready yet to accept and be in a moment such as this. I thought back to the Superstition Mountains and how gentle and loving she had been with the bones of the women we found there, and yet, she harbored an unexplained hostility to this Marna and Leeja.

"Am I right in assuming that you do not eat meat on a regular basis?" Marna asked.

"I eat meat."

"Then why the fuss yesterday when I killed the buck?"

I stared at her, trying to come up with a logical answer. "I guess because he was so wild, so majestic."

"And what of the animals you eat? The cattle, the fish, and the fowl?"

"Somehow, it's not the same."

She made a derisive sound. "What is the word you use? Ah, yes. Bullshit!"

My relaxed mood changed. I glared at her, but did not respond. I was finding it difficult to relate to this Marna. She was no longer the gracious host she had been when she sat beside her queen, nor was she the Marna that I had idolized in my mind since I had felt her overwhelming presence in the Superstition Mountains of Arizona. This Marna was hard to the point of being cruel. She seemed hell bent on putting me down.

"Why are you so angry?" I asked.

"Who are you to speak of anger?" She stood and put on a long, thick fur coat.

"Wait, where are you going?"

Without another word, she picked up her weapons, took the horses, and left.

Alone in the silent cave, I heated some water and made some herbal tea. By the middle of the afternoon, I was hungry again, but Marna had taken the dagger. I tore at the slab of venison, until I had a small chunk to skewer with the now-blackened stick, and cooked it.

Later, I stood at the cave entrance, watching the night fall around me. It was black with no stars or moon to cast light over the ghostly landscape. Snow clouds sent their large, fat flakes spiraling downward. I wondered where Marna was and when she would return. How would she ever find the cave again with no tracks to follow? Would I be left here to eventually starve to death? PJ would forever wonder what had happened to me. Even if she knew where I was, she would never find my bones, scattered as they would be by wild animals. Would she think I had deserted her? I brushed my thoughts aside. "Don't panic," I said. "Stop, evaluate your situation, and think. You have food enough to last several days if you're careful. Then, when the storm lets up, head down the mountain. Down will always get you somewhere."

Shivering, I banked the fire and crawled under the robes. I was cold and miserable and unable to dispel my rising anger. I was scared, too. Panic crept into my psyche. What if something had happened to Marna? What if she'd fallen somewhere out there and couldn't move? I had no idea where she was or where I was.

After a restless attempt at sleep, I got up, walked to the cave entrance, and called her name. My response was the muffled silence that only gently falling snow can bring.

"Damn you!" Shaking my fist in the air, I returned to the warmth of the robes, and sometime during the night, I slept. The fire was almost out when I awoke, so I quickly added the last of our wood.

Being as careful as I could to keep my bearings, I gathered what little fuel I could find, pulling dead or dying branches from the trees because most of the windfall was buried in the deep snow. I returned to the cave, carrying my meager bundle with scratched and bleeding hands.

"You bitch!" I stared angrily at the neat pile of wood that had been placed beside the fire during my absence. "Marna, damn it, where are you?" I continued to curse, my shouts reaching no farther than the walls of the cave. "What the hell do you think you're doing? You bring me up here, and then play games with me. Get back in here, you overrated Amazon archetype. You have no right to treat me this way." I ranted and raved until I doubled over, clutching my stomach in pain, heart pounding, and a monster headache threatening to tear off the top of my head. I managed to stumble out of the cave before throwing up, though there wasn't much for my stomach to toss. With a sigh of resignation, I dropped to my knees in the snow.

I shook partly from the anger, partly from the cold temperature, and then I didn't care any more. The last thing I remembered was whispering PJ's name, saying that I loved her, wishing I could make love to her one last time. Then, nothing.

* * *

I awoke in the cave, wrapped in furs. Marna was holding me, sharing her body's heat. The fire crackled, and sparks flew as its healing warmth spread to all corners.

Through cold lips and chattering teeth I managed to speak. "Why?"

"I wanted you to confront your own anger and know the futility of it. To realize that it's not the answer to real problems."

"But you put my life in jeopardy, leaving me like that."

"You were in no danger. I was watching you the whole time from up on the ridge behind the cave."

I cursed, determined to punch her, but could not muster the energy required to raise my hand. When I was thoroughly warm, Marna got up and made some tea. While I sipped the hot beverage, she produced some sweet potatoes, put them in the coals to bake, and roasted a large hunk of venison. We shared a wonderful meal and emptied an entire wineskin.

More relaxed now, Marna propped herself against a mound of furs, stretched, and crossed her legs. When she looked over at me, her eyes, though still penetrating, had lost their cold, hard edge. "You have lived with anger much of your life." The words were framed as a statement rather than a question. Somehow, she seemed to have all the answers.

"I suppose I have. Being different—knowing that one is not generally accepted—is especially hard for a child." I thought of Rusty, my first real friend, and the kids at school. Kids could be so cruel. Just because I couldn't fit in, I became an object of ridicule. "It wasn't easy, but I showed them. I worked hard and excelled in my field."

Marna's eyes glinted in the firelight. "Then you met Terry."

I raised an eyebrow in surprise. "You know about her?"

"You are of Amazon blood. I know all about you."

"Yeah, Terry. The less said about her, the better."

"First, she hurt you, and then she hurt PJ."

The thought of PJ's ordeal brought tears to my eyes. "Terry got away. You know, skipped bail and disappeared."

"She will be punished, sooner or later."

"I hope you're right." When I threw another piece of wood on the fire, sparks danced upward into the air like startled fireflies.

Marna stared into the flames. I imagined she was thinking of Leeja, though I had no proof.

"You have learned your lessons well," she said, after a long silence. "You have experienced the futility of holding on to your anger. When faced with a crisis, you have assessed your situation with a cool head and have formed a plan. That is how it should be. You have learned that a hot head and lack of thought can lead you into trouble. Yes, you have learned your lessons well. As soon as the weather allows and the snow melts a bit, we'll return to the encampment and to our loved ones."

Mellowed by the food and wine, I relaxed, delighted at the prospect of being with PJ again.

Chapter 12

Queen Leeja told me that we would travel to a grotto for discussion and meditation. I soon learned, however, that when an Amazon queen travels, she takes an entourage.

At least a dozen heavily armed women from the main camp joined us on our ride into the hills.

We stayed on horseback until the ground grew too steep; then we hiked, leading the horses the rest of the way. My legs were accustomed to long walks, but my shoulders, arms, and back soon protested the extreme exertion required to reach this hidden retreat.

And my butt. Jesus, I couldn't even begin to think about how I'd sit down again. My thoughts drifted to Kim and the journey she was taking. She hadn't been on a horse in years. We were both going to have sore bodies when we got to our destinations.

All the physical effort was worth it, though. The grotto must have been the equivalent of an Amazon day spa. It was a collection of small caves and stone corridors that wound labyrinth-like through one side of a mountain. Thermal pools sparkled in the available light as though they were festooned with stars from the Milky Way. Vent holes in the ceiling brought in fresh air and expelled the smoke of fires, maintaining a nearly constant temperature throughout the stone facility.

When we arrived, half of our contingent remained with the queen and me to unload supplies and walk through the rooms, while the other half threw down their supplies, ripped off their clothing, and dashed naked and frolicking down some stone steps to a partially-hidden lagoon.

Queen Leeja noticed my astonishment at the noisy, off-duty crew. "You may swim down there at any time, Dr. Curtis."

"Thank you, but the absence of swimming attire has me a little concerned."

Leeja seemed amused by my comment. "You don't need to be shy around us. We are all women, are we not?"

"I'm just not quite as uninhibited as I once was, Your Majesty. And I'm still wondering why I'm here cavorting with Amazons in the first place, though you've been most gracious to me so far."

"Ah, yes. You have questions and uncertainties about your role in all of this." Her dark eyes focused on me with what appeared to be a hint of mirth. "Why don't we relax and enjoy some of the comforts of this tranquil place before we get into such deep discussion. The water in the lagoon is cool, but exceedingly invigorating."

"Maybe I can manage that a bit later." I looked around for a diversion. "Didn't you say the private pools down those corridors are heated by warm springs?"

"Indeed." She chewed on her lower lip. "In fact, you have given me a wonderful idea. Come, we'll relocate to my favorite one and have a private soak. I imagine your muscles must ache after your trip."

I rotated my arms and shoulders and grimaced. "I'll admit to a twinge or two."

She spoke with two of her staff in whispered tones. After a quick salute, they rushed down the corridor.

I wandered over to the huge fire pit in the main room, drawn by the delicious fragrance of roasting meat and simmering side dishes. Apparently, a kitchen crew had been on duty a day or two in advance of our arrival. And judging by the amount of food already prepared, they had been busy.

"Hungry, Dr. Curtis?"

My stomach answered for me. "Sorry about that."

She waved my apology off. "We cannot help when our body speaks for us."

"Your Majesty, may I ask you a favor?"

She inclined her head. "Probably."

"Please, call me PJ, okay?"

"Of course. And you must call me Leeja."

"But you are the leader of these women. I want to show proper respect."

"Then call me Leeja in private, when we are not surrounded by my subjects."

She led me down a narrow passage, the walls of which were smooth to the touch, the result, I thought, of ancient underground rivers and streams. Soon we came to a cozy antechamber, and Leeja motioned for me to go first.

"What do you think of it?" she asked.

"It works for me, Leeja."

"Good. I know your name is Priscilla, but you want me to call you PJ. Is that a special name that Kim uses?"

"Oh, no. I prefer PJ because Priscilla sounds so formal and old-fashioned. My middle name is Josephine, so that's where the J comes from."

"I'll bet that Kim has a pet name for you, one that you care not to share."

I felt my face reddening and lowered my eyes. The conversation was getting way too personal.

Leeja gestured toward another passage where I saw shadows flickering along one wall and sniffed moist, fragrant air. "The pool is right through here."

Three torches had been lit and arranged along a curved wall, their reflected images bouncing on the water. Trays of meat, sweet potatoes, cheese, olives, and bread beckoned from a waist-high stone ledge to our left, and there were two benches along the right side of the pool, each draped with a robe and a large drying cloth.

"A hot tub, buffet spread, and massage table. You've thought of everything," I told her.

"We do our best, but I see we are missing some pillows." Before she could summon any attendants, two young women hastened in, arms laden with cushions and animal furs. Leeja nodded her approval. "Thank you, Reena, Alaina."

"You're welcome, My Queen," said the taller of the pair.

"Will there be anything else, Your Majesty?" the other asked. Both young women were dressed in white chitons and had brightly colored flowers braided into their long, dark hair.

Leeja glanced at me, but I had nothing to add. "You may prepare the wine and leave us to soak for a candlemark or so. After that, I believe Dr. Curtis and I will require massages with some of the special oil."

The young women opened wineskins and set out two drinking cups. Without a word, they approached their queen and undressed her. I was treated to the sight of Leeja's lithe, evenly tanned body before she slipped into the pool, making hardly a ripple. Displaying the grace of a dolphin, she rose again to the surface at the other end of the pool.

"What bliss. Won't you join me, PJ?"

She made a motion with her hand and the attendants stripped me naked before I could respond to her invitation. I scurried into the water, creating a huge splash, and sank onto a submerged ledge wide enough to sit on, but low enough to keep me covered up to my neck. The water temperature was perfect. It caressed my bare skin like a silken robe. I detected a mineral odor, but none of the sulfur that the grotto in Eresos contained. I leaned my head back against the edge of the pool and closed my eyes, letting my body collapse into a carefree, boneless state.

"Didn't I say that you'd find this trip pleasurable?"

The water lapped gently at our necks and breasts as we shifted our bodies into positions most comfortable for soaking.

"You forgot to mention the hand-over-hand climb to reach this Shangri-La." Keeping my eyes closed, I stretched my arms and legs.

"Reena or Alaina will take care of those aching muscles. I know you have questions for me and concerns about being here. I assure you everything will be answered in due time. Will you trust me to do that in my own way, PJ?"

My eyes remained closed, but I chuckled. "Do I have a choice?"

"Perhaps not." Leeja's voice was soothing. She moved her arms through the water and I felt something tickle my cheek. Startled, I opened my eyes to discover that Reena was sprinkling petals from a large white blossom into the pool.

"How beautiful."

"This flower is one of our queen's favorites," Reena said. "It's a white, short-tongued variety of an orchid that has an especially sweet fragrance."

I had a vision of Kim doing erotic things to me with her own sweet tongue, though hers was not short by any means. Hastily, I pushed the petal away from my heated face and took a deep breath.

Reena still hovered over me. "Would you like some food now? You have only to ask, and I will prepare a plate for you."

"I think maybe I'll wait until after soaking, but thank you."

My words appeared to have a positive effect on her.

"Why don't you and Alaina have your supper now in the main room," Leeja said, forcing Reena to redirect her attention. "When you are finished, you may prepare the benches for our massages."

"As you wish, Your Majesty," both women intoned and left us.

"That was intense." Leeja moved closer to me. "I think Reena is quite taken with you, PJ."

"Doesn't she know that I'm committed to Kim?"

"She has been working here at the grotto for nearly a moon. It's quite possible she doesn't know that you and Kim are lovers. She is rather headstrong, however, so she might not care."

"Oh, Geez. I don't want to hurt her feelings, but she has no chance at all with me."

"Don't worry. I'll see that she is informed about your unavailability. She gives a wonderful backrub, though." Leeja shook her head. "Guess, I'd better have her work on me and let Alaina give you yours."

"That would probably be better. Reena would never try anything with you. Marna would skin her alive."

"Goodness, you have such a violent image of Marna. You haven't seen her tender side."

I played with a floating petal before picking it up and inhaling its scent. "True. I saw the way she looked at you, though, and I made up my mind never to cross her."

"You are correct in that respect. Marna can get jealous easily, and before she tamed her anger, she would sooner fight than talk to any woman who so much as looked at me too warmly."

My thoughts strayed again to Kim, my own hothead, and what trials and tribulations she must be experiencing on her journey to master her own rage. I sent her loving thoughts, wishing her good health, and adding that I missed her terribly.

I felt Leeja's hand on my arm.

"They will be good for each other, you'll see. Marna and Kim share the same soul after all."

"How did you know what I was thinking?"

"Your expression gave you away. And, I must confess, my thoughts are never far from my lover, also. You must trust your soul mate as I trust mine, and know that their love, once given, lasts forever."

I blinked back sudden tears. Forever and always. That statement had already been tested.

"If you've soaked enough, let's feed ourselves."

"Sounds good to me." I stood up and joined her in exiting the pool, feeling less inhibited and more relaxed than when I went in.

*   *   *

Reena and Alaina appeared and began to work on our bodies. Alaina gave me the most incredible deep tissue massage I'd ever experienced. The warm oil she worked into my muscles gave off a rich aroma of olives and herbs. I remembered thinking I would smell like a Greek salad.

Under Alaina's deft fingers, my skin tingled and penetrating warmth spread through my entire body. When she finished, I sat next to Leeja, wearing only my medallion and a robe. We sipped mulled cider that was so strong my head no longer felt connected to my body, and my brain took a definite leave of absence.

"May I ask you a question, PJ?" Leeja finished her cider and selected a piece of cheese.

"Of course." I leaned forward and plucked a grape from our communal fruit and cheese plate.

"Where did you get that green leaf on your buttock?"

The grape stuck in my throat as I tried to swallow. After a few coughs, I regained my voice. "It's a tattoo... a shamrock. I noticed that many of your women have red and black tattoos of different symbols on their bodies."

Leeja chewed and swallowed. "Yes, but those reflect prowess in battle, and I did not think you were inclined to fight."

Now, she had me curious. "I'm not so inclined. People in my time get tattoos for all sorts of reasons. They often refer to it as body art. The shamrock symbolizes the Irish and is said to bring good luck. My mother's people were from Ireland."

"Ah, the land beyond Gaul, far to the north and west."

"Yes. You know of it?"

"I know of many things."

She chose a fig and bit into it. "Why do you have this... this shamrock where it does not show? Surely you could not hope to display it very often."

"No, I didn't plan on showing it off. I guess I was rebelling against my father, doing something I thought he might not approve of. We weren't getting along well at the time, and I was trying to get his attention."

"I see. Tell me more about your father. Have you resolved your conflict?"

I told her all about my mother's death, my father's lack of interest in me, and my subsequent acting out in various unhealthy ways. I finished by assuring her that Dad and I were back on good terms now, except for his recent shocking involvement with Susanna, whom I'd practically come to regard as my therapist.

"Therapist?" Leeja's brow furrowed. "That is like a shaman, yes? A healer?"

"I guess more like a healer, but a little bit of the wise counselor, too—a healer of the mind."

During the silence that enveloped us, I sensed Leeja was thinking and planning what to tell me next.

"I'd like us both to get a good night's rest before we get into all of this, PJ, but I have decided that you and our shaman should meet and talk. She is as old as the stones in this grotto, and as wise as all of our elders combined. I go to her whenever I have difficult problems to solve. I have consulted her about you and Kim, and she helped me arrange for an audience with the Goddess."

My jaw dropped. "The Goddess? You mean Artemis? That Goddess?"

"That's the one. Artemis is the protector of all the Amazons."

"And you actually talked to her about Kim and me?"

"Yes."

"Wow." I took a final swallow of cider.

We sat silently for another minute. Then I remembered something I wanted to ask Leeja before we got on the topic of Artemis. "I told you about my tattoo, but I'm curious about what you said earlier. The red and black tattoos have something to do with battles?"

"Yes, that's correct."

"What do they represent? The red and the black colors, I mean."

"The red ones represent wounds received in conflict. The black ones signify enemies killed during battle."

I thought about the body parts I had seen decorated this way and shuddered. These women would have many notches on their guns, if they had guns.

"It bothers you?"

"Yes. I saw so much black."

Leeja sighed. "Unfortunately, it reflects our times. The women who brought you and Kim into the village so roughly were on a scouting mission to watch for an enemy band of slavers in the area."

"So that explains the weapons you have half our group carrying at all times, even while we are here in the safety of the grotto."

"You noticed them?"

"Hard to miss."

"True. Marna would not let me take you up here without a security force. She knows, you see, that there's no place that's completely safe."

A chill slid along my well-massaged spine. Suddenly, I didn't feel quite so relaxed and mellow. I had another thought, and Leeja seemed willing to indulge me.

"So the red tattoos were for battle wounds."

"Yes, and technically, you are entitled to receive one, if you wish."

"Me?"

She gestured to my left shoulder and the pink scar tissue from a kidnapper's bullet. "You were injured in battle during your times."

I shook my head. "Thanks for the offer, but the scar is enough of a reminder."

"You have scars inside, too, but we will not go into that tonight."

"That's good. What I wanted to ask you, though, was about the medallions Kim and I found in Arizona. We thought they had been awarded for injuries or bravery or some such thing during your times."

"Not exactly." Leeja bit down on her lower lip. "They have a more powerful purpose." She stretched back on her mound of pillows. "For as long as I can remember, the medallions have been used to keep Amazon leaders connected to one another through the generations. They are given, too, to members of certain families when souls are transferred or shared. Sometimes they are bestowed when Amazons die and sometimes when women leave the tribe for one reason or another."

I leaned back on my pillows, propping my head up with one hand, and watched her. "We noticed that they get very warm."

Leeja turned her head to look at me. "Did that happen with the ones you and Kim wear?"

"Yes."

"I thought so."

Now it was my turn to stare at her. "Is that a good thing?"

"Yes, I think so. But PJ, we really should wait until morning for this discussion. We are both tired and the subject is complicated. I'm not sure how much you can absorb right now."

"You're stalling, Leeja."

"And you're not as tired as I'd hoped."

"So, start talking."

"I will explain what I was told and what I suspect, and then you must sleep. It will give you lots to ponder. Tomorrow, we will talk some more, and I will ask our shaman to help you understand better."

"Fair enough."

"The medallions are blessed by the Goddess herself. They are given to worthy Amazons for various reasons. Marna and I received ours after battles and after showing our leadership skills."

"You can wear them and give them away at the same time?"

She frowned in thought. "In a way, that is right. When an Amazon with a medallion dies, the Goddess makes it possible for her to pass it on along with her soul. This is a relatively new venture, but Artemis feels it's necessary because our tribe and our nation are in such peril right now."

"Why is that?"

"These enemies I spoke of earlier. Warlords and slavers snatch up our girls and young women. They sell them off or keep them for their own amusement. We rarely see them again unless they are able to escape, or we can rescue them. Then, we hear such tales of torture and rape." Leeja paused to take a breath and wipe her eyes. "Our numbers are dwindling, and I fear that if we don't have help, one day there will be no Amazons left."

"I'm sorry for your pain. You must feel so responsible at times."

"I do. Not everyone understands that, but you have a sympathetic heart. I know you feel what I feel."

"I wouldn't presume to say that I can know exactly how you feel."

Leeja shook her head. "You do know, PJ, because you share my soul and my medallion."

I sat up. "What?"

"Easy. I didn't mean to shock you. It's true. At least, that's what I believe has happened in your case."

"But... you're not dead."

Her laughter broke the tension of the moment for both of us. "No. I'm not. But remember, these medallions come from the Goddess and are given to many of us in the same lineage. Maybe I didn't explain myself clearly enough. Marna and I both have medallions that were meant for those of us in our given line, with our given traits. Marna's pertain to strength, ability with weapons, bravery in battle, courage, power, faithfulness. My medallion follows the line of Amazons with leadership capabilities, intelligence, compassion, negotiation and communication skills, and loyalty."

"It doesn't make sense. I'm not a warrior, and I don't have that kind of leadership ability."

"This is where it gets complicated. I believe this arrangement is temporary. I think you share my medallion because you are an Amazon, and as Kim's soul mate, you are destined to travel with her, to help her with her mission."

"Okay. I'm with you so far."

"But I think you were meant to receive another medallion."

"Whose?"

She stared at the far wall of our chamber. "I am not certain, but the Goddess knows and may, if the time is right, tell us. If I say anything now, I would only be guessing."

I shifted onto my back, feeling tired and frustrated, but full of puzzling thoughts. "Why was there a mix-up? Kim recognized her affinity with Marna right away. The medallion she kept was her rightful one, wasn't it?"

"Yes. There can be no doubt of that. When the lineage is pure and the recipient possesses all the qualities she's meant to have, then she physically resembles her benefactor. It's almost a perfect match."

"It's obvious that I don't resemble anyone in this tribe."

"You must not blame yourself or feel bad, PJ. I think this is all part of the Goddess's plan, and we must not try to second-guess her."

That was easy for her to say. She had all the right qualities, including the physical attributes. How ironic. Before Kim and I found ourselves here, I was discounting all of her interest in Amazons, trying to convince her they were myths and that we were really just dreaming. Now, my feelings were hurt because I wasn't picked to be part of the gang.

"Tomorrow, we'll talk some more," Leeja said. "And when we return to the village, we'll gather information from the shaman. Perhaps even the Goddess will speak to us. In the meantime, know this." She waited until I looked at her. "You are an Amazon. Spirit guides from the land of the dead have visited you and found you worthy. And the medallion you wear now works well enough to keep you in communication with us until you and Kim can locate your true medallion. Do not forget that."

"I won't."

"Good."

"It's just that I'd feel a lot better if a short, blonde Amazon would show up and claim me as a relative sometime soon."

"You have a wonderful sense of humor, PJ. It's one of your best qualities." She stood up and held out her hand. "Now, it's time for us to retire. We will speak further tomorrow. I'll find you a quiet chamber close to mine. All of this should make more sense after a good sleep."

I stood and gathered up my bedding. "You were right. We never should have opened up this can of worms so close to bedtime."

"'Can of worms'?"

"An expression. It means a bunch of problems."

"Ah. Unfortunately, being queen means opening up a lot of worm cans."

* * *

We spent another relaxing day, doing much the same as the first. Leeja and I ate breakfast together and swam in the lagoon with her contingent of bodyguards. She had some queen-type business to take care of, so I walked along the paths, avoided Reena as much as possible, learned special dances and songs with a few of the younger Amazons, and sampled delicious culinary masterpieces, but didn't dare ask what the contents were.

The mineral pool was a favorite place to soak and meditate. Alaina was ready to rub me with special oil afterwards. Leeja and I ate dinner together and chatted about how we had met our true loves. Of course she already knew most of how Kim and I met, but I was happy to learn that she and Marna were not very informed on the subject of my pre-Kim romantic liaisons. Leeja was also curious about our lives as archaeologists. She questioned me at length about our training, techniques, and procedures used in searching for artifacts and processing our finds.

I asked her how she and Marna had fallen in love, if they had any children, and where they would go if they were forced to leave their main village.

Her eyes lit up at the mention of children. Despite what she knew of the future, she was not informed about in vitro fertilization and other scientific breakthroughs.

"It seems like I've always known Marna," Leeja said, with a faraway look. "We grew up in the same village, but were separated when a lack of food forced us to split into three groups. She went to the mountains and was trained for warfare. She became one of the best fighters and was chosen for the queen's honor squad."

"What about you?" I asked. "Were you a fighter, too?"

"Our group of women found a quiet place nearer the sea. I guess that is why I love the water so much. I've always lived close to it. Sorry, I digress. No, I was not as good a warrior. I was a negotiator, a peacemaker for tribal disputes, and I learned the fine art of working for peace with other tribes."

"That's an attitude I can relate to," I said. "I was afraid that all the Amazons did was fight."

"We tried to live and love in harmony with the people around us. Once or twice a year our women of child-bearing age would arrange to visit certain men in a nearby town for the purpose of becoming pregnant."

Oh, so that's how the babies happened. "Were you forced to do this?"

"Absolutely not. It was done by mutual consent. Male babies were left with the men, and female offspring remained with their Amazon mothers for a period of five years. After that time, the girls could remain with their mothers, stay in the village and be cared for by lots of the older women, or choose to go back to their fathers and live as non-Amazons."

"I see."

"We have no slaves here, except those that are captured in battle, and they are, after a while, given the opportunity to assimilate into the tribe or return to their own people. Most choose to stay."

"Sounds fair."

"And to answer your other questions, Marna and I have each had three children, two boys and four girls. The boys were given up at birth, two of the girls died of fever when they were very young, and the other two are away in another village near the coast, training to be warriors. If our present village is attacked and destroyed, we will probably all go to the coastal camp and then, if necessary flee across the sea to a safer place."

My mind was processing all of this new information, trying to figure out how this group got to be connected to the group we discovered in Arizona. I couldn't reconcile the concept of time moving backwards and forwards enough to visualize it. One thing was certain: Life went on, no matter what we knew or didn't know, or how much we tried to alter it to suit our needs.

"Every Amazon has a duty to keep her nation strong," Leeja said, her voice cracking with emotion. "No matter what happens, it must survive."

"Wow. That's an awesome responsibility to be charged with."

"PJ, you need to know something. I've thought about the wisdom of telling you this for a day now, and I think it will probably help you understand your role in all of this."

I settled back against my pillows. "Go right ahead."

"From the time we were very young, Marna and I can remember our village elders telling us stories of a golden-haired bard who came into the tribe before most of them were born. She had been a slave who escaped her captors and sought sanctuary with our ancient foremothers. In gratitude for having a place to sleep and eat without fear, the bard told stories. In spite of her painful past, she had a cheery disposition and loved to tell jokes and make everyone laugh. During her lifetime, she gave birth to several children, but only one was a girl. That daughter, who was also fair-haired, grew up in the Amazon village and learned all her mother could teach her about storytelling. She became a proficient bard and a valued peacemaker when her mother passed on to be with the Goddess."

I leaned forward on my pile of furs. "Do you think I'm related to either of those women?"

Leeja gently took my hand in hers. "I believe so. The women were both named Taceesha. The older one earned a medallion for her bardly work and for her ability to seek peace and make treaties among the villages. When she died, her medallion was transferred to her daughter. Unfortunately, we have no further information about the younger Taceesha or her medallion. Marna was told that she was related somehow to her, but there is no evidence of that. We believe the young Taceesha was taught to be a warrior as well as a bard, though she disliked fighting."

"Oh, crap." I pulled away from her, rolled onto my back, and stared at the grotto ceiling. "Just when I had some hope of learning about my Amazon connection, you tell me there's nothing more about her?"

"It is disappointing, I know. But now you realize how important it is for us to find as many missing Amazon connections as we can. We need you and Kim to search for links to our past."

"You want us to use our archaeological skills to do this?"

Leeja leaned toward me. "Yes. We need all of your abilities. You would make an excellent chronicler of our stories. The Amazon history must be continued for our future and yours. Once these missing sisters of ours are found, they must be recognized as part of our heritage, and any living Amazons you encounter must know about their foremothers. This is the destiny we see for you and Kim."

I blew out a sigh. "Whew. That's a monumental task, Leeja."

"In fact," she continued, "you could keep a journal about your love for Kim and your life with her, adding how you feel about your Amazon roots."

"I don't know what Kim is going to say about all of this, but I guess I could try."

She started to respond, but stopped abruptly. Instead, she yawned and stood up, bringing me to my feet. "If your mind's as cluttered as mine right now, it's probably best that we let things go for now. You need time to think about this and talk to Kim about it. We will let the shaman help you sort it out. She and the Goddess know what is expected of all of us. We must enjoy the time we live in and make the most of it."

"Spoken like a true diplomat," I said. "Goodnight, Leeja. You've opened up a fresh can of worms for me tonight."

* * *

My sleeping chamber was located close enough to Leeja's to share the protection of a pair of muscular guards. I nodded to them when I returned from another quick dip in the private pool, an even quicker visit to the outdoor privy, and a hasty rinse of water and mint for my teeth.

"Sleep well, Dr. Curtis."

"May the Goddess bless you with pleasant dreams."

Not likely, I thought, but I thanked them both and wished them a good night.

I pulled the door covering across the threshold and, by the light of one small candle, I removed my robe, folding it carefully and placing it on the low bench near my bedding. A solitary white orchid rested on my pillow.

Now, how did that get there? Maybe Leeja still needs to give a certain Amazon a clue.

I picked up the flower, placed it on top of my robe, and extinguished the candle. Somewhere high above me, through an opening in the rock ceiling, I could see stars in a tiny corner of the night sky. Just enough light filtered down to prevent total darkness.

The flower's sweet perfume helped me drift off to sleep despite my troubled mind. I heard nothing until a noise in the predawn grayness awakened me, and I sensed a dark form hovering over me.

In a panic, I pushed against my intruder. An extremely solid, extremely naked female body resisted my efforts. An orchid petal touched my cheek.

"Reena, no," I managed to say before moist lips crushed my own, stealing my breath.

A tongue slipped between my parted lips and thoroughly plundered the interior of my mouth.

Someone—maybe both of us—moaned.

Her fingers tangled in my hair and her lips branded my jaw and chin with searing kisses. Her teeth nipped and tugged a pathway down my neck.

Fully aroused, I clutched her head, pulling her mouth to my breast. "God, I've missed you. What a wonderful surprise."

"Mmm." Her tongue teased an already taut nipple.

"When did you get here?" I asked between shuddering gasps. Her hands had begun a persistent descent down my torso, stroking, caressing, and driving me insane with desire.

"Little while ago. I cleaned myself in the pool. Didn't want to smell of horses."

"Thanks. I appreciate that."

We wrestled and groped our way at first, anxious to relieve our pent up sexual tension. Hands and fingers found a rhythm and worked in tandem, kneading and coaxing thoroughly stimulated body parts.

"Sorry if I'm too rough, but you seem to be a bit needy yourself."

I guided her fingers to a wet and waiting spot. "Needy doesn't begin to describe it. Welcome back, Kim."

Her fingers continued their masterful work, bringing me to a state of near ecstasy.

"So, who's Reena? My competition?"

"Not for you, my horny Amazon." Her fingers slid home, and I surrendered to the orgasm that rocketed through my body. When I could speak again, I reassured her. "No competition at all."

Chapter 13

We lay luxuriating in the warm aftermath of lovemaking. I had no idea how long PJ and I had slept after our exhausting reunion, but nobody came to drag us out of our room in the grotto, so I was happy to remain where I was, in the comforting embrace of the love of my life. Everything I wanted in the world was right here with me; I had no reason to move, no thoughts or desires, at least for the moment, to return to that other world.

As if reading my thoughts, the woman draped so unceremoniously across my torso opened her eyes and planted a slobbery kiss on my neck.

"I was afraid you were a figment of my sexually-starved imagination." She wrapped one arm around my chest. "God, it's so good to see you, to feel you close to me again."

"I think you mentioned that a few times during the night, but I'm just as glad to see you and to be with you. I missed you while I was on my anger management retreat to Hell."

"It doesn't sound as though it went well."

"Let's just say that Marna believes in the principle of tough love."

"That bad, huh?"

"Oh, yeah. The worst part was when she disappeared for hours on end, even overnight, and left me with nothing to eat and no firewood."

"What!" PJ pushed herself to a sitting position. "Why, that bitch. I'm—"

"No, it's not what you think. I was never in any real danger, though I didn't know that at the time. I thought I was alone against the mountain, and while I think of myself as being self-reliant, it scared the hell out of me."

PJ lowered herself and tucked her head against my neck. She was so close to me that I could feel the beating of her heart. It was steady and reassuring.

"That seems like a perfectly natural assumption to me, since you thought you were alone against the elements. I'm sure you dealt with the situation in your usual professional manner."

I massaged her hip and slid my hand across her ribcage. "I appreciate your support, but that was when I made the mistake of allowing my anger to take over. Marna taught me, very vividly, that anger doesn't solve any problems. I was my own best example."

"That may be, Kim, but Marna's methods could've been more humane."

"Mmm." In the comfort of PJ's warm embrace, it was easier to forgive and forget the trauma of the cold desperation I had experienced on the snowy mountain. I had been forced to admit that Marna knew what she was doing. "She provided the opportunity for me to face and think through the problem. By doing that, I was able to find a way to survive, an opportunity I might not have experienced otherwise."

"Oh, my poor baby." PJ clutched my roaming hand to her cheek.

"No. I needed to survive, and to do that, I had to become a thinking, planning human being. It was me against the wilderness, me all by myself, and anger was my enemy."

PJ released my hand and rested her cheek against my chest. "I'm sorry you had it so hard. And it sounds like it was a lot colder where you went."

"Yes, we rode through a long, narrow valley then climbed high into the mountains. Really high, though I had no way of knowing what the altitude was. I felt it in my breathing, though. And by the time we arrived at the cave, it was beastly cold. We were in a different zone. The snow was thick on the ground, and there was little food and almost no fuel. This place is a paradise by comparison. Have you been here since we parted?"

"Yes, we have. First Leeja and I soaked in a mineral pool, and then we were massaged with oils that I swear had magical powers. We had long discussions, during which she forced me to take a good look at myself, at what I had become after Mother's death, my relationship with my father, and the events in Wales. She said I was a scarred individual, and you know, I'm inclined to believe her."

"At least you had comfortable conditions and plenty of food here. Marna and I had a debate over killing wild game for food. We had brought some provisions along, but she wanted fresh meat, 'to give us strength,' she said, 'to combat the cold.'"

"You had to kill animals?"

"Marna did. She shot a buck and dressed it."

"Oh, Kim. How awful. There must have been some way to avoid doing that."

"You weren't there, PJ. I'll admit that I was appalled by the idea, but after going out in the cold, in a snowstorm, to gather windfall for a fire to keep me warm, I was so hungry that I literally tore meat off the carcass and cooked it on a stick over the fire. I even thanked the animal for giving its life for me, for us. Marna did that when she made the kill, and it felt right for me to do so, too."

"I can tell it was no picnic for you."

"Hardly." I propped myself up on one elbow so I could watch her expression while we talked. Much as I hated to lose her body's warmth, I wanted to see how she reacted to my experiences and to learn what she had been doing. "Okay, now it's your turn. What, beside the spa treatment, has happened to you?"

"Leeja spoke about a blonde Amazon from ancient times."

"Really? Are you related?"

"Maybe. This woman was a bard and a peace negotiator for the tribe. She told stories and taught the art of storytelling to her daughter."

"All wonderful attributes for an Amazon to contribute to her tribe."

"Yes, but that wasn't all Leeja told me. We talked about the medallions, and Leeja said I have yet to find mine. This one is more like a loaner." She fingered the medallion which nestled between her breasts. "During the time I've been here, I've been able to relax. That's been hard for me to do lately. Totally relax."

"Good. You needed that."

"Yes, I suppose I did, though I would never have admitted it. I preferred to believe that I was in sync with the world, and I really wasn't." She lapsed into silence.

"You know," she said, after a moment, "in our time, Leeja would make a top-notch psychologist. Susanna would be jealous. They both believe that facing one's demons is the first step to a full recovery. And though they came at it from different directions, the result was the same, except that with Leeja, I was able to see the bigger picture more clearly."

I stretched out to my full length, keeping my face turned toward her. "From what I've seen of Leeja, she's a wise woman and a capable queen." I tickled PJ's stomach and watched her abdominal muscles ripple. "It sounds as though your therapy was easier than mine. But then, perhaps I was more stubborn than you were."

"Possibly." She caught my fingers and warmed them against her belly. "I don't care to find out right now, however."

* * *

Little by little, we rehashed her meetings with Leeja and what she had learned about this tribe of Amazons. PJ told me that our mission might involve finding Amazon remains and trying to locate medallions to match them with their rightful owners. This sounded like a daunting task, but apparently the shaman had more ideas on the subject and would probably give us more specific data when we met with her.

PJ was curious about the red and black tattoos and how Leeja had suggested that she had earned one for the wound on her shoulder.

"I refused, of course," she told me. "I don't need anything else to remind me of that time."

I hugged her, keeping silent. I didn't want to break her train of thought now that she was willing to share her feelings. In fact, my mind was reeling from all the information PJ had gathered in her talks with Leeja.

She appeared to be honored that she wore Leeja's medallion. It had been loaned to her in the Superstition Mountains, and she was expected to wear it until her rightful medallion was found.

"What do you think of that concept?" I asked her.

"It could explain why I don't resemble any of the women in camp."

"True."

"She assured me, though, that I'm an Amazon, and more importantly, that I'm meant to be your soul mate."

I touched her cheek and gave her nose a tweak. "As if I didn't know that already."

"So it looks like we're stuck with each other for now. Maybe throughout eternity."

"Wow."

"Yeah. Do you think you can handle that?"

"Tall order, that eternity stuff." I gazed into the softness of her eyes and felt my heart melt.

"Always and forever appears to be a fact."

I pulled her face close enough to kiss with all the passion I was feeling. "I'm game if you are."

She moaned from deep in her throat and slid back on top of me. "All this talk about loving you forever has my engine racing. Are you up for another spin around the block?"

"This jalopy is ready, willing, and able."

We heard a cough outside our room and seconds later, Leeja pulled aside the skins that were hung for privacy.

PJ slipped off to one side, and we hastily pulled the animal furs up around us.

"Sorry, Your Majesty," PJ said. "Please forgive us."

"Are we late for a meeting?" I asked.

"No need to apologize. And it's Leeja. We're friends, remember. I just came in to see if you needed food. But I see the only thing you hunger for is each other. I'll request that a meal be left outside your door, and you can have it when you like."

"Thank you, Leeja. It seems Kim missed me almost as much as I missed her."

"That is how it should be." Leeja's hand moved to cover a bite mark adorning her neck. "It would appear that Marna suffered from the same affliction."

"It was a difficult separation," I added.

"Then I suggest you carry on with what you were doing." She left, pulling the privacy skins back across the opening.

PJ's body rocked with her laughter. "Our queen has a hickey. Can you believe it?"

"She's not the only one."

Her expression changed from mirth to horror, and her fingers flew to her neck. "No. God, Kim."

"Sorry, baby. These things happen."

"Where am I going to find a turtle neck in the midst of all these skimpy Amazon outfits?"

"You aren't. You'll just have to hide out with me until your neck returns to normal."

"Wonderful. What are we going to do while we wait?"

"You heard your friend. And since she's the queen, I suggest we consider it a command rather than a suggestion. We're to carry on."

"Oh, okay." PJ rolled onto her back. "Where were we?"

By way of an answer, I lowered my mouth to her breast.

* * *

Later, when we sat chatting around the fire in the queen's hut, PJ learned more about my experiences on the mountain.

"She did well," Marna said, after reciting her version of the trip. "She passed her tests and would make any Amazon proud."

"I could have told you that." Although PJ spoke softly, I could see her jaw tighten. She knew that Marna, as a warrior and the queen's consort, demanded respect, but she was probably still a little angry with her about giving me the sword scratch on my neck and leaving me alone on the mountain.

"Yes, indeed," Marna continued, "Kim's anger is now under control, especially in the area of her greatest weakness."

"Weakness?" PJ sounded confused.

Marna looked at me to supply the answer.

"She means you, sweetheart."

PJ stared at me. "I'm your greatest weakness?"

"My weakness. My passion. My love."

She put her hand to her lips, and her eyes glistened. "We'll discuss this further when we're alone."

"Whatever you say." I couldn't tell if she was pleased or displeased at the news.

Leeja rose. Taking it as a sign of dismissal, we all stood. "In the morning, we plan to return to the village," she said. "Please be packed and ready by sunrise."

"We will, Your Majesty." I lowered my head respectfully.

"If you start right away, you both should have plenty of time for your discussion."

PJ took my hand and pulled me toward the entrance. "Thank you, Leeja. You're very thoughtful."

Judging by their amused looks, it seemed that I had been the only one uncertain about how the rest of the evening would go.

Several minutes later, I got my first hint when PJ buried her face against my chest. "Oh, dear one, you're stuck with me forever, I'm afraid."

I exhaled in relief. "That's just fine with me."

* * *

The discussion about weaknesses turned into another pleasurable hour or two of rolling beneath the skins in our hut. Making love in a hut on a bed of animal skins with the soft pounding of drums as a backbeat elicited something primal within us. Who needed CDs?

The grotto, especially, enhanced our physical bond in a way no previous therapy had. I hated to leave such a magical place.

"So what time do you want to get up and pack, Kim?"

"Pack? Do we have anything to pack?"

"No, I guess not. My daypack is back at the main camp, and all I have are those flimsy leather strips the Amazons call clothing."

I trailed my fingertips across her breasts and watched her nipples tighten. Whew. What were we talking about? Oh, yes. Packing. "Then, it shouldn't take us long. I have the tunic and some weaponry that Marna gave me."

She turned onto her side, facing me. "I want to ask you something. It's been bothering me a bit, off and on."

"What?"

"How long have we been in this place, and do you think we'll ever return to our own world?"

I gave it some thought. "I guess it feels like several weeks... a month or so anyway, even longer since we woke up in that meadow. I think we'll be sent back once we know all we have to know about our mission."

"That's good to hear." She took my hand and we laced our fingers together. "When we first came, I tried to believe it was all a dream because I was afraid to think that it might be real. Logic told me it had to be a dream. But so many days have gone by, and so much has happened. It's kind of scary."

"It hasn't all been scary, though. Do you realize that our lovemaking has been better than ever? You aren't hesitant at all now."

She leaned in to kiss my neck and chin, then continued with playful nips along my jaw, cheek, and forehead. We wrestled together. "I might have known you'd notice that, but you're right. Maybe it's coincidence, but I do feel more like my old self."

I kissed her. "And that pleases me."

"And when you were gone with Marna, the absence only made my heart—and a few other body parts—grow fonder."

"You could probably tell that I felt the same way."

"Oh, yeah."

We were silent for several minutes, happy to be with each other, to be able to touch and feel each other and know that wherever we were, we were together.

"What do you think, Kim? Is this really happening, or is it a long, bizarre dream?"

I stared up at the ceiling of our hut. "As far as I'm concerned it's very real. I can't explain how it happened, but somehow we have stepped through a veil in time."

"And how do we get back?"

"Honestly, I don't know."

"Shit. I was afraid you'd say that."

*   *   *

The day after we had traveled back to the main Amazon village and Kim and I had settled into our large, comfortable hut, I sat outside in a patch of sunlight with my journal propped open in my lap. Several crumpled pages littered the ground around me. Leeja wanted me to write about living with Kim and the surprising connection we had with the Amazons.

"The truth needs to be spoken," she had said, "so that later generations know us for who we are."

It'll be easy, I thought, to write about Kim, but it'll be another thing to write about my Amazon relationship. I didn't really know what that was all about.

Kim was off somewhere with Marna, learning firsthand the ways of the warrior. I was concerned about her, hoping she wouldn't return with another "sword scratch" as she called her neck wound.

After another night of incredible lovemaking, I had trouble concentrating on my project. Write a poem about my love for Kim. Sure. How hard could that be? Hadn't I just spent hours... undercover... conducting research? Certain parts of my body throbbed pleasantly in remembrance. Ah, but it had to be about more than the physical part. I needed to write about what made me love Kim, not just the fact that she made me supremely happy in bed. I bit down on the end of my pencil, willing myself to stop thinking about how good the sex was. I had to admit that I was finding it difficult to write about Kim without revealing our most intimate activities.

"Concentrate, PJ." I took a deep breath and read over what I had written so far.

It's you I love
with all my heart.
When you are gone,
I am lost—

What else could I say about her? She had a strong, muscular body, firm breasts, and luscious lips that— Hold it right there. There were other things to mention about Kim. It wasn't just her body and the way it glistened with sweat when we made love.

"God!" I said, crumpling another piece of paper. "Why can't I focus on the deeper issues here?"

Memories of last night kept intruding. The assignment was to consider the important qualities that made me love Kim so much. There was more to it than fantastic sex, right?

"Yes, of course. But there's something to be said about multiple orgasms."

I looked around guiltily. "Did I just say that out loud?"

After a few more minutes of writing, a shadow fell across my page, and I looked up to discover Reena standing in front of me. "What's up?"

"Queen Leeja requests that you and Dr. Blair join her for a celebratory feast at sundown. She is expecting a special guest to join us then."

"Thank you. I'll alert Kim. Please tell Queen Leeja that we accept with pleasure."

"I will. Oh, and it would be preferable for you to wear Amazon attire. It is more in keeping with the event."

"Very well." I gritted my teeth at the thought of parading around in next to nothing again.

"Her Majesty requests, too, that you to spend some of your free time at archery practice before the festivities."

The journal slid off my lap. "Are you certain she said I was to do that?"

"Yes, Dr. Curtis. She told us you could give us some helpful hints. I must admit that we were surprised to learn of your prowess with any kind of weapon."

"It's been a long time since I've picked up a bow. I imagine I'm pretty rusty." How the hell had she found out about that? I don't think I ever told Kim I could shoot.

Reena folded her arms across her youthful chest. Her expression stopped short of a full-fledged smirk. "If you'd rather not attend practice, I'm sure the warriors will understand. With the threat of enemy attacks, our queen wanted everyone to keep at peak fitness, even those with limited ability. I'm on my way to sword practice now."

"Are you? Maybe you'll see Dr. Blair, then. She and Marna went off to do that sort of thing a little while ago."

The young warrior's whole demeanor changed. One hand clutched the strap holding her weapon and both knees flexed. "I'd better get going. Marna holds competitions for all her superior fighters. Dr. Blair might be too tired by now, but I'd enjoy warming up with her before the more competitive rounds."

"You would, huh?" She was so full of herself. If Kim was still down there with Marna, I hoped she'd take Reena on and mop the floor with her. Ever since Reena had found out I was off limits, she acted as if it were my loss and she was the Goddess's gift to the women in the village. Limited abilities, huh? I'd love to see Kim—or somebody—knock her on her tight little ass.

"Don't let me keep you. I guess I'll head on down to the meadow and see if I still remember how to string a bow."

"Be sure to wear Amazon clothing. You'll look and feel more like one of us that way."

She jogged off toward the practice field, and I went inside the hut to climb into my leather next-to-nothings. I couldn't explain why I resented having to wear the outfit. I was comfortable enough at the grotto, but now that Marna and Kim were back, and we were at the larger encampment, I felt self-conscious again.

And the strange visitor was arriving. Who was she? The Goddess perhaps. Leeja had talked about the Goddess Artemis. I doubted it, though. She had also spoken about sending for a Bardic Consultant. It was probably going to be some book-wormy type with a stilted imagination, shabby wardrobe, and ink-stained fingers.

Chapter 14

"Excellent job, Kim." Marna took a step back, sheathed her sword, and wiped some sweat from her forehead. "Let me see your weapon."

I handed her the sword, hilt first. "Something wrong with it?"

"No, it's acceptable." She handed it to one of the young warriors who were watching us practice. They had formed a circle around us and were very supportive and encouraging to me as we battled. "You may give me that bundle now, Carinna."

Marna held a gleaming broadsword up to the light before tossing it to me. I was pleased with its balance and design, though it was not the type of sword I was used to handling.

"It's yours. I had it crafted just for you. Keep it with you always. And when you go back to your time, I'll find a way to get it to you."

"Thank you so much, Marna." I took a few easy swings. "It's a weapon of distinction. I hope I prove worthy—"

She waved away my appreciation. "You have already proven yourself, and you should have a suitable weapon for defense. After all, if you are to continue my Amazon lineage into your time, you must be prepared for any eventuality."

"I don't know how useful it will be in my time, but I'll cherish it."

"I have no doubt that you will face the challenges ahead of you with courage and determination."

I wondered what challenges she was able to foresee in my future.

"To be honest with you, there are moments when I wish we didn't have to go back." After the words left my lips, I felt guilty about admitting such thoughts when I knew PJ couldn't wait for our return to modern day Greece.

"The time will come, Kim, when it will be right and necessary for you to return to your time."

I fingered the images carved so delicately on the hilt. It was a weapon of extraordinary beauty.

"Come along, now," Marna said, "it's time to put your new weapon to use."

I was happy to comply with her request, swinging the new sword into our mock combat with confidence. Marna had taught me so much in the past few days, and I was eager to show my mentor that I was worthy of her gift.

Several other warriors had paired off to spar with each other, and across the meadow, an archery competition was underway. Our field grew noisy with the clang of metal on metal, but in the pauses between lunges and thrusts, we could hear muffled shouts as distant arrows found their targets.

Marna and I continued to draw a small crowd as we dueled. We battled evenly for a while, sweat pouring from our bodies, with neither of us giving an inch. More by luck than any skill I possessed, I had her on the ground twice with my blade to her throat.

"Go on," she said, when I had her down for the second time, "draw blood."

I hesitated. "It's enough that I have the advantage."

"Go on, it's better that your first foe be your friend."

"I don't want to hurt a friend."

"Mark my neck, Kim, as I marked yours. That way we'll share a common scar forever."

I pressed the blade into her neck, drawing blood from the pinprick wound.

"Well done."

Shouts of praise filled the air. I helped Marna to her feet and offered her a cloth to blot her wound.

"We are true Amazon sisters now," she said, smacking me on the back.

"I hope your spouse doesn't react the way mine did to this new bonding experience."

Marna frowned. "What's one more scratch among many? Leeja understands this. Your PJ worries over such trivial things."

"Indeed. But sometimes it feels good to be cared for in such a way."

She pondered my words. "You're a wise woman, Kim, and a valiant fighter."

"Thank you." We grasped forearms in the Amazon custom of showing friendship and respect.

"Let's see what the rest of you warriors can do," Marna said, glancing around at the assembled watchers. "Stop gawking at us and pair off. Send your final champion to Kim. The two of you'll fight each other until only one is left standing, or you both collapse."

Cheers greeted her words. I took advantage of the short respite to drink deeply from one of the water skins. The liquid tasted sharp and fresh. It was intoxicating, so different from the polluted and chemically treated water of the twenty-first century.

A tall Amazon entered the competition to my left. I watched her dispatch her opponent with ease and await the winner of the match to her right. As she rested, she looked in my direction, and I saw no warmth in her expression.

What was that all about?

Marna joined me in viewing the competition.

While we focused on our combatants, we heard a burst of noise from the archery range, followed by a resounding cheer. Sword-fighting was suspended so all of us could see what was happening across the meadow.

"It appears that there is a contest going on over there, too." Marna gave my hip a nudge. "I think having you and PJ in our midst has brought out the competitive juices in our warriors."

"I'm sure it's just the chance to have a different opponent that makes your warriors want to compete and show off a bit."

"Perhaps you are right. I imagine it's the same for the archers."

"Who would be a different opponent for them?"

"If you take another look, you'll have your answer, though it might be hard to see with the crowd."

We stared at the women huddled around two contesting archers. As the group closest to us pulled back, we could see a thin, dark-haired woman, her bow at rest, watching a second archer.

"I don't recognize that one," I said, "but she did well, judging from the crowd's reaction."

"That's Jayna. She's our best archer. Keep your eye on the other one. I think you'll be surprised."

The group surrounding the second contestant broke apart at that moment, and my view cleared enough to see a short, muscular warrior draw back her bow, hold it steady for several seconds, and release it to find the target. I held my breath as a huge roar erupted at the result. Several women pounded the competitor on the back, but she ducked under the assault of well-wishers to offer her opponent a hearty forearm greeting, before the mob surrounded both of them. It didn't matter that the champion was lost from my sight. Her blonde hair was all the evidence needed to identify her.

I turned to Marna in amazement. "PJ never told me she could shoot, let alone have the skill to beat Amazon warriors at their own game. This is unbelievable."

"It would appear that both of you have hidden skills that may come in handy."

"Geez." I shook my head. "This day is full of surprises."

"And you're not finished yet, my friend." Marna produced a leather scabbard covered in carvings as delicate as those on the sword's hilt.

"Thank you again. It's beautiful." I sheathed my weapon and swung it crossways so that it hung comfortably on my back.

"Don't put that away just yet," said the tall Amazon with the unfriendly demeanor. "I believe I have earned the right to challenge you for the championship."

"Very well." I did not feel as confident as my words indicated.

The other competitors formed a circle around us in noisy anticipation. I pulled my sword from its scabbard and we touched tips. "Good luck to you... uh..."

"Reena," she said. "My name is Reena, and I won't need any luck."

* * *

I hurried to the village healer as rapidly as my weary bones would let me, hoping for a quick patch up job before PJ saw me. Despite the fact that Marna had assured her I wouldn't be hurt, she didn't approve of my sword fighting with the queen's consort or with any one of these warrior women. A few bruises and cuts were to be expected, though, and I would proudly wear every scar. In addition to the pride of accomplishment, I enjoyed the physical effort which could only strengthen my body and mindset. PJ wouldn't have understood how exhilarating it was to compete with these Amazons and hold my own. I felt younger and stronger, more able to cope with whatever trials might confront me. Perhaps the fact that my anger was now under control added to my well-being.

* * *

The old woman sat huddled with two young girls, watching and guiding them as they mixed several powders into small round bowls. She raised her head as I approached.

"What be your needs, Chosen?"

Why doesn't she call me Kim?

"Healer, can you put some salve on these injuries to make them less obvious?"

She pulled herself up. Even standing fully erect, she was not as tall as PJ. With surprisingly strong, bony fingers, she examined my arms and leg. "Your injuries are minor and easily fixed, but your garment's another matter. Unless it's cleansed, your companion will see the blood and dirt and guess what you've been up to."

"This is the only Amazon outfit I have."

"I'll give you a robe. Take off your tunic and lie down on the mat over there. One of the children will see that your garment is cleaned and mended."

"I don't think there's time for that."

She made a shushing noise and tugged at the hem of my tunic. "Hurry. I have plenty more to do before the feasting, and you're keeping us from important work."

"Sorry." Feeling thoroughly rebuked, I did what she ordered and handed everything to the young girl who rose to assist me. "Thanks."

She gave me a shy smile and hurried out of the hut.

Once on the mat, I gritted my teeth when the healer scrubbed the dirt from my cuts and abrasions. As a sponge, she used what appeared to be leaves pressed together to form a cleansing pad. It felt like I was being scoured with tree bark. The ointment she smoothed on my sore muscles smelled faintly of eucalyptus and mint. It made my skin tingle with a penetrating warmth, easing my muscle aches.

"Rest now. We'll give you some tea."

It was an offer I dared not refuse. While the old woman covered me with a soft fur, her remaining helper scattered leaves into the bottom of a thick mug and poured hot water into it. I hadn't noticed the fire before, but apparently, small as it was, it was enough to keep water and other liquids hot for emergencies. After sipping the tea and warming my insides, I drifted into a comfortable, dreamy state. I figured I'd be on my way after resting a few minutes.

The healer touched my forehead and began to chant something I couldn't decipher. She waited for several seconds and then spoke.

"Chosen, you are well-suited to your task. The Goddess is pleased with your progress, but you and your companion must be strong when you return to your world. You both face many dangers and challenges."

I tried to say something, but my voice wouldn't cooperate. The old woman put two fingers to my lips. "Just listen. I know what is in your mind and heart. Your companion will be at your side as you face the challenges that will come your way, even though she has her own tasks to perform. She will always be loyal to you and your work. Your mission is to travel in search of our Amazon sisters, for they are your sisters, too, and you represent our connection to them. We have lost touch with so many through the ages. You will seek their remains, their medallions, whatever you can find. Their remains will lead you into the future. Some, you will discover, are alive and well in your time. You will come to know them. We need every one you can locate and identify. The continuation of the Amazon Nation depends upon you."

Talk about an impossible mission.

The old woman's gnarled hand patted my cheek. "You are an Amazon. Nothing is impossible for you. Some things though, will be a little difficult."

My vocal chords permitted a bark of laughter. "Thanks for your faith in me."

Her hand dropped to my shoulder. "We will talk again soon, Chosen. But, for now, rest."

* * *

Later, as I neared our hut, I saw that Queen Leeja, Marna, and half a dozen warriors were leaving camp.

"We are on our way to meet and escort our special guest into the village," Leeja told me. "She'll be the guest of honor at tonight's feast, and I believe PJ will be pleased and honored to meet her."

"Who, may I ask, is this special guest?"

"I dare not tell you because I know PJ will wheedle it out of you. Besides, you'll find out soon enough."

Before going to our hut, I watched the party leave. Keeping the mystery guest a secret from me was smart on Leeja's part, but she didn't realize how difficult it would be for me to fend off an inquisitive spouse, even for just a few hours.

* * *

"I don't know why you're so concerned about the attire," Kim said, when I told her that we were expected to wear our Amazon garb to the festivities. "You'll blend in more easily and will be less conspicuous than if you insist on wearing your shirt and khakis."

"I suppose so." I nestled into Kim's firm hug, sniffing an unfamiliar scent on her body.

"What are you wearing?"

"My tunic."

"I know that, silly. I mean the fragrance. It has a medicinal smell."

"Oh, that. It's nothing really."

I pushed against her arm and felt her wince. "Have you been fighting again?"

"Now, PJ."

"You have, haven't you?"

She took a deep breath and nodded.

"You know how I feel about that. You could get hurt. These women do it every day and you're not—"

"I can hold my own. Besides, you're a fine one to talk. Who was over on the archery range today playing Robin Hood?"

My face heated, and I must have registered surprise, because she shot me one of those supercilious looks that infuriated me. I could almost hear her thinking, "Gotcha!"

"That's different, Kim."

"How so?"

"We were shooting at targets, not people. When you poke around with those swords, there's a person on the other end, and somebody could get hurt. I don't want it to be you, okay?"

She took my hand, pulling me down to our bedding and onto her lap. "PJ, we need to discuss a few things."

"That sounds ominous." I settled myself and hugged her waist. "But this is a nice position to be in, if things get ominous."

Her fingertips brushed my cheek. "I don't mean it to sound that way. I just think there're a few things we don't know about each other, and it's time to clear the air."

"Okay. You go first."

"It's the swordplay. I must confess that I'm not a novice."

"Oh?"

"No. I was on the fencing team during my undergraduate years in California."

"Why didn't you tell me this before?"

"The subject never came up."

"That explains one thing."

When she didn't respond, I continued. "I've read that fencers have the tightest butts from all that lunging and squatting, and you have a mighty firm ass, my dear." I moved my hand to the focus of my commentary and gave it a pinch.

"Ouch. Thank you, I think."

"No. Thank you."

"We don't have time right now to pursue that line of discussion further."

"Damn."

"Don't pout. I'm sure there'll be time later on. Besides, you seem to possess a talent that I was unaware of until this afternoon, and I'd like to hear more about it."

"What do you want to know?"

"How long have you been an archer?"

"Oh, that." I took a deep breath. "Summer camps have tons of archery facilities. I got bored with braiding lanyards one day and thought I'd give it a try. Since I didn't suck at it, I kept it up for a while."

"You won the contest today."

"Yeah. So?"

"You haven't practiced as long as we've known each other."

"True."

Kim's hand came around my upper arms and it was my turn to wince. "A bit sore there in the shoulders and pecs?" Her hand gently probed my chest.

"Hey, okay. I'll admit I'm a tad sore from the effort. And yes, I was good at it, once upon a time, long, long ago. Today, I just got lucky."

"Uh-huh." Kim continued to massage my upper body. "I remember reading that archery develops your chest muscles."

I felt my face flush again. "I suppose that's possible."

She leaned in and kissed my neck and trailed several feathery kisses downward to the tops of my breasts. "Mmm. I've always admired the firmness of your chest."

"Glad to hear that, tiger, but we don't have time to pursue that line of discussion any further, either. We've a feast to attend."

Kim pulled her head up. "You're right. I'll have to save the chat I had about our mission for later."

I grabbed a fist full of her tunic. "Kimberly Elizabeth Blair. You heard something more about our reason for being here, and you're just now mentioning it?"

"Easy." She put her hand over mine. "I'll confess all, if you stop wrinkling my one and only good Amazon outfit."

"Sorry." I smoothed the top of her garment, giving her chest a little extra attention. "All better. Now, talk."

"I dropped into the healer's hut on my way back from sword practice."

"Uh-huh. I knew it. You got hurt and you needed first aid."

"A few scratches, here and there."

"I'll examine you later. Thoroughly."

"I'll look forward to it."

"So what did the healer have to say? She's also the shaman. Did you know that?"

"Yes, I became aware of her dual role once we got talking. Actually she talked, and I listened. You were mentioned, too."

"I should hope so."

"She called you my companion and said you'd be a big help to me on my mission."

"Which is?"

"We have to find missing Amazons, medallions, artifacts, remains, and the like. It seems that it's up to us to preserve the Amazon Nation."

"Oh, is that all? I was afraid it was going to be something hard."

* * *

We remained silent for several seconds, pondering the colossal task ahead of us. I recalled the talks that Leeja and I had about my part in the scheme of things, but it didn't seem to fit together. Kim's mission would be necessary before my job could kick in. I slid off Kim's lap so we could face each other as we talked.

"In light of what you just said, I don't understand Leeja's plans for me to chronicle the Amazons' history. She seems to think it's my destiny to teach the world, our world, that the Amazons are not a myth. They're still with us, not as a single nation, but as individuals scattered across the globe, trying to correct the wrongs of modern civilization. How can I do that unless you find the missing links first?"

"Good question."

"And why me? I'm not the one who has studied and followed the Amazons for all those years. That would be you."

I hated the expression of patience on Kim's face. She exhibited it sometimes, and it made me feel patronized.

"Leeja must think you qualify, or she wouldn't have chosen you and brought us here."

"Are you saying that it's because of me that we're here?" I felt some anxiety threaten to break through my self-control.

Kim's shrug was her only response.

"You know how unsettled I feel about this whole thing. I have to believe that we're in some sort of dream state, and the sooner we get back to where we belong, the better for both of us."

"I thought by now you were getting with the program, that you were starting to believe we're in a time warp for a reason. I doubt we're here just to mollify my anger or to bring you to terms with what's happened in your life. These things are important, certainly, but they aren't enough to warrant the energy it's taken to bring us here to this place and in this time. There has to be more to it than that." She put her hand on my arm. "Maybe you're the chosen one."

I pushed her hand away. "No, I'm not the one they need for their future. That's you, Kim. They can't prove I'm anybody special. They don't know what to do with me, so they've made up a job. I'm supposed to be a reporter. You know how I hate those vermin. Shit, I might as well be your body slave for all the importance I am."

Kim held up her hands. "You're in one of your moods, so it's no good trying to reason with you when you're like this. Still, the body slave idea has merit."

"Go ahead, make jokes. All I want is for us to be back in present day Greece, doing what we were trained to do. This is science fiction, and I want no part of it. I'm sorry to rain on your parade, but I'm having a hard time processing all of this."

I stood up and paced the length of our hut. "And what guarantee do we have that we can get back to where we belong? What if we're stuck here forever?"

She waited until my movement stopped, then she took me in her arms and rubbed my back, bringing me gently back to an even keel. "Easy does it, honey. Do you feel better now?"

I took a deep breath and resolved to change the subject to a more pleasurable topic. "I think so, for now anyway. Besides, we have to start thinking about this evening's shindig. I wonder who this important guest is and what makes her so special."

"See, you are better, and at least part of you is back to normal. You're curious, so don't go giving me this you'd-rather-be-elsewhere story."

"I guess stuff like this doesn't happen every day, and the experience will be something to tell the grandchildren about."

Kim's eyes widened. "What grandchildren?"

"Not mine, for sure. Pup's maybe."

"Don't depend on him," she said. "His gun doesn't have any ammunition."

Chapter 15

"I'm hungry," PJ said, as we walked to the clearing where the fires were already burning brightly.

Several warriors passed us as we made our way to the center of the activity. One of the women walked with a pronounced limp, but they were wearing masks, so it was hard to identify anyone. To my surprise, PJ turned around and spoke to the limping warrior.

"Reena? Is that you?"

The woman lifted her mask to reveal a couple of fresh cuts on her cheek and jaw.

"What happened?"

"Ask her," Reena said, nodding at me, before continuing her walk in the other direction.

PJ grabbed my tunic, halting my forward progress. "Let me guess. Sword-fighting."

"Yeah."

"And your sword was bigger... and badder."

"What can I say? I whupped her ass, but good. I'm sorry about the facial cuts, though. That was unintentional."

Shaking her head, she poked her index finger into my stomach and chest, emphasizing her words. "Dangerous, reckless disregard for human life."

"Ouch! Hey, it was a fair fight."

"I'm talking about consequences, tiger." She abandoned the pointy finger in favor of a hands-on-hips posture of disgust. "You could have been seriously hurt."

Aw. She was worried.

"Me? Not a chance."

"And you're so modest, too."

I put my arm around her waist and nuzzled her neck. "That's what you like about me."

"Correction. That's what I love about you. And to be perfectly honest, I hoped someone would give her an attitude adjustment."

"Then I'm happy to have helped." We took some more steps toward the gathering.

"But it doesn't change my opinion on your fighting."

I stopped walking. "PJ, you can't have it both ways. Sometimes fighting is necessary. Sometimes it's the only option."

"Let's discuss it later. Right now, I'm drooling too much."

* * *

Joints of pork and venison turned slowly on spits above the red coals, and mouth-watering scents rose from the cooking pots. Hand in hand, we strolled along the path that led to the tribal activity area. Drums beat quietly in the background, adding to the surreal effect of our situation.

"I wonder who this mysterious guest is going to be." PJ stopped in her tracks. "Are you sure that Leeja didn't say anything to you earlier today? You wouldn't be holding back on me, would you?" Her voice held an accusatory tone, which I chose to ignore.

"I told you. I asked her, but she wouldn't tell me for fear you'd coax it out of me. Those were her words."

PJ narrowed her eyes.

"Honestly, honey, I have no idea."

"Then I believe you."

"Thank goodness. I was afraid you were going to shove bamboo slivers under my nails."

She took my hand, and kissed each fingertip. "You know how I hate surprises. I'd like to know ahead of time, so I can prepare."

"Prepare for what?"

"I don't know. That's the problem."

"If I knew anything, believe me, I would tell you."

"I know you would."

"Good. So, let's drop it for now. We'll both find out soon enough."

We continued toward the festivities.

"It's just that—"

"PJ, please. I've about reached the limits of my patience with this subject."

She stopped and raised an index finger toward me, as if preparing to debate the issue further, but then she lowered her hand. "You're right, as usual. Let's just go and enjoy some of this fantastic-smelling food."

We were directed to the queen's large oval table. Its rough hewn surface was covered with a silk cloth of many colors. Goblets and tankards were placed at each setting, waiting to be filled with ale and wine. Our seats were located across from the three set aside for Queen Leeja, Marna, and the mystery guest. We waited to be seated until the Her Majesty arrived. Before we could speculate further on who would occupy the guest seat, Leeja appeared, attired in a flowing silken, two-piece outfit, the color of cranberries. Marna followed with a tall, olive-skinned beauty on her arm. The woman had almond-shaped eyes, full sensuous lips, and dark hair, braided with flowers. She wore a simple dress of pale green with a cape of the finest weave. Leeja motioned for her to stand on one side of her, Marna the other. All of us were served wine, but we waited to drink until Leeja gave the order.

A drum roll sounded, and Leeja raised her goblet. "Honored guests," she said, smiling directly at PJ before turning to her guest and raising her goblet. "I propose a toast to the greatest poet of all time. I give you the one and only... Sappho."

I heard PJ's breath catch and could only watch as she and the poet gazed at each other. "Her eyes... are amazing," PJ whispered after she recovered from her shock. "They're pools to the depth of her soul."

They stared at each other until I nudged PJ. "For goodness sake, say something. Acknowledge her."

PJ inclined her head. Sappho returned the gesture with a sweeping bow. I knew then that Sappho was the consultant Leeja had spoken about. She was the one who was going to help PJ with her writing. And who better to do the teaching than the greatest ever of lyric poets? I was happy for PJ. Writing would open new vistas for her, and it would make a difference in her life, despite her struggles with verse. If chronicling the Amazons' place in history was to be her mission, she could have no better teacher. I didn't know much about Sappho because little remained of her work, but I knew that she loved her students, possibly too much. I tried unsuccessfully to swallow the taste of jealousy I felt when I thought of the hours PJ and Sappho would spend together.

The feasting and dancing continued through the evening. PJ and I exchanged a few words with Sappho, and Leeja made arrangements for PJ's writing sessions with the poet. From the expression of panic that flashed across PJ's face, I anticipated little sleep for us once we returned to our hut. Fortunately I had a plan for making the most of those sleepless hours, providing of course, that PJ could get her mind off the beautiful poet.

* * *

"You don't have to do this, you know." Without Kim's presence for support, I was intimidated, but I managed to hold up my part of a quiet conversation with Sappho, while a young warrior-in-training assembled our writing tools and readied our work area. The space was at the edge of the meadow and within sight of the main camp. A detail of bodyguards was posted at a discreet distance, and the queen had ordered a picnic lunch, complete with wine and cider.

Sappho watched me with what appeared to be an amused expression, her eyes assessing every inch of my ridiculously skimpy attire. She leaned over and whispered, "It would seem that Leeja wishes this to happen, so who are we to stand in her way?"

"I guess we're both stuck."

"I intend to make the most of the situation," Sappho said.

I wondered why Queen Leeja had joined us. Perhaps she, too, thought that she might learn something from the poet. Or maybe, knowing Sappho's reputation for loving women, she had taken on the role of chaperone. The thought tickled me, and I couldn't wait to tell Kim.

Sappho arranged herself on pillows and poured wine for all of us. Leeja had taken a seat on a pile of furs just to the poet's right. I resigned myself to the arduous task ahead. Poetry had always been an anathema to me, like a magic trick of sorts that I didn't know how to perform and really didn't care to be enlightened about. But within the metered lines of poetry, history was to be found. On that point, I was clear.

It had therapeutic qualities, too. I had to believe that because Susanna had first suggested verse as therapy, and now Leeja wanted me to try it. A conspiracy was brewing. I picked up my goblet and drained the contents. Sappho and Leeja exchanged startled glances.

I deposited the empty goblet on the mat in front of me. "Let's get this over with, shall we?"

If Leeja was irritated, she didn't show it. "I have assembled scrolls, quills, ink, along with your own notebook and writing stick, PJ. Feel free to use the tools of your choice."

I grabbed my journal and pen, folded my legs under me and sank onto a pillow.

"Told you she was a feisty one," she said to Sappho, loud enough for me to hear, adding to my already considerable discomfort.

The poet unrolled a fresh scroll and dipped her quill into the ink well with a flourish. Positioned as she was, directly across from me, she commanded our maximum attention. Leeja sat quietly beside her, eating grapes and taking an occasional sip of her wine. The seemingly relaxed atmosphere was tempered by the sight of the warrior guards, close by, keeping their vigil.

How was I supposed to concentrate on what I was doing? My agitation grew with each grape that Leeja popped into her mouth. Why was I being humiliated this way? First I was forced to impersonate an Amazon with this micro-mini leather ensemble, putting my physical attributes on display whether I wanted them to be or not. While I may have been proud of my body, I certainly wasn't comparing myself to the likes of Leeja or Marna. Just because it was a way of life with these women, in this time, didn't mean I'd ever get used to it. And now Sappho watched me like she could see right through my meager attire.

Mornings in the village had been on the chilly side, too. The weather was not conducive to wearing so little. I wondered how some of the skimpily-dressed Amazons managed to keep warm. While Kim and I had our modern day khaki pants and shirts to help ward off the cold, how did these women keep from freezing their asses off? They had to be hot-blooded babes, every last one of them. Luckily for me, the sun was sharing its warmth, and I was able to keep my shivering to a minimum.

I opened my journal to the poem I had started. As the next phase of my total mortification, I was to complete it with the most famous lyric poet of all time assisting me.

"Now then, little one, show me what you've got," Sappho said, "poetically speaking that is." She continued to study me with a mischievous sparkle in her eyes until Leeja slapped her arm.

"Play nicely, Sappho. PJ is trying to write a love poem about Kim, her lover. She seeks literary assistance from you, and that is all."

The poet glanced downward. "Forgive me, Leeja, PJ. Really, I am a harmless woman." She turned toward me. "A flirtatious, sensual being, but no threat to you, I promise. When I see beauty around me, I react accordingly. It is my nature, and you are so beautiful. I cannot help but overreact. Forgive me, and please read what you have written so far."

With burning cheeks, I read the three or four lines I had written.

"'It's you I love.'" Sappho mused. "Yes, that has possibilities, but there must be more. Tell me more about your Kim. She is the woman who sat beside you at the feast?"

"Yes."

"She is a regal being, and I must believe, a passionate and protective woman."

"Absolutely."

"She fills your life… your very soul. You are both so close, so loving. Go with that, my dear."

I stared inward, summoning words and phrases, sifting them, rejecting them, until a few took shape. Sappho wrote silently while I struggled with the words. Leeja, with eyes closed, stretched out serenely on a pile of furs that had been carefully arranged on the grass.

After a while, we shared ideas. While I had been consumed with thoughts of Kim, Sappho and Leeja had recalled loving memories that had touched their hearts. I gladly took their suggestions and added my own. Marna, as Leeja's soul mate, was like her other half, a part of what made her whole. I could see and feel the power behind that image. Sappho's lovers, and from what little I had read, there had been many, tapped into her mind and body affecting her physically as well as spiritually. I could picture that, too.

We scribbled on, pausing only for occasional sips of wine or bites of cheese, grapes, and bread. At one point, when I was reaching for a fat juicy grape, I caught Sappho's eyes on me. She leaned over and whispered something to Leeja. They clasped hands and whispered like children sharing deep secrets.

"Okay, what is it?" I examined my outfit. "Did I pop out of this stupid harness again? You look like cats spitting canary feathers."

"What a colorful image. I must remember that," Sappho said. "It's just that for a few moments, you reminded me of a student I once taught at the House of Muses." She tapped her quill along one prominent cheekbone. "Ah, but that was long ago, in another time."

In another time.

Her words reminded me that I, too, was a visitor from another time, and what I knew of Sappho was from the historical perspective. I imagined she would be saddened that so little of her work had survived the ages. I had a sudden urge to hug her and tell her that despite the great loss to the academic world, the snippets that had survived served only to increase the modern scholar's curiosity about her life as a person and a poet.

I felt a shiver skip along my spine. Just when I was getting comfortable with these two, something had to come along to remind me of how weird this situation was.

Seeming to sense my discomfort, Leeja said, "You had better put the finishing touches on your work, PJ. Sappho has made a wonderful suggestion. We must return to the village and set it in motion. Marna and Kim are off someplace and must be recalled. Give Sappho your poem when you are finished. It will be read at the appropriate time and—"

"Wait, Leeja, just what have you two cooked up?"

"It's so obvious, given the great love you have for each other and your ties to the Amazons. What you have written is a poetic tribute. Sappho says she writes this kind of poem for a lot of young women. They're very popular."

"Popular? How?" Unsure of what Leeja and Sappho were planning, I started to squirm. "Besides, you haven't—"

"Let's see. We'll have a feast with roasted pigs and maybe a pheasant or two. For entertainment, the drummers will play. And dancing. We must have—"

"Please, Your Majesty, what are you talking about?"

"A joining ceremony, naturally, for you and Kim, in front of the entire village."

"And I will read your poem." Sappho beamed with satisfaction.

"Oh, my God!" My stomach contents threatened to revolt.

Oh, Kimmy, what have I gotten us into now?

*　*　*

"A what?"

"A joining ceremony." PJ's voice was a high-pitched squeak. "It wasn't my idea," she said, her eyes wide.

"Then whose dumb idea was it?"

"Leeja and Sappho cooked it up between them. I had nothing to do with it. It shocked the hell out of me, too."

"Great, what next?"

"See, they were helping me with my poem—Sappho was— when they came up with the idea."

"Why didn't you choke it off right then and there?"

"I couldn't. I guess I lost my nerve. I'm sorry, but you know how they are."

"Maybe it's not too late. Plans can be cancelled." I stalked from the hut, leaving PJ to stare after me. I thought she might follow, but she didn't. Although it was quiet in the clearing, I could hear talking and laughing coming from the stream where some were bathing.

"Who do they think they are?" I asked myself, as I marched toward the sound. I hoped that I could catch Sappho and Leeja there, so I could put an end to this nonsense before it went any further.

Sappho was in the midst of a group of chattering young women. She was basking in the glow of their attention. All of them were naked, frolicking in the stream. I stood on the bluff above them, wondering how best to broach, in a delicate manner, the subject of my annoyance.

As I watched, fascinated at the water lapping around their breasts, Sappho looked up and caught me admiring the beautiful bodies, and hers in particular. She seemed to enjoy my embarrassment. I remembered my irritation and my mission, but thanks to Marna I had learned to control myself. The momentary anger I had felt faded into the shadows. I saluted the poet, and then returned to make amends with my own true love.

I found PJ sitting cross-legged on our bed, writing in her journal. When I sat down beside her, she didn't move.

"I'm sorry about what I said. I know it wasn't your fault."

She put down her writing materials and turned to face me. "They're your people, Kim. I thought maybe you'd want to go along with it."

"They're your people, too."

"Maybe so. That's what they say, but I'm not sure I'm ready to believe them. And they were yours long before I ever knew about them."

"If it's any consolation to you, I don't really know them at all. I'm finding their ways so primitive at times, so geared to survival. And then, it's like they can see into the future, as if there are oracles among them. They seem to have feasts and parties for any reason, no matter how insignificant."

"It's pretty clear that you consider this joining ceremony insignificant." Her eyes were moist.

When I put my arm around her, she shrugged it away. "It's not that I don't want a ceremony, it's just that I was thinking of something else, more personal. A private ceremony for just the two of us."

She stared down at her journal, twisting the cap on her pen. "You've always been so romantic, so caught up in your relationship with the Amazons. The Marna and Leeja we found in the Superstitions were locked in an eternal embrace. That was a ceremony that committed them forever." She wiped her eyes and sniffed. "It's only a few words we're talking about. Would it really be so bad?"

"I'm sorry, PJ. It was just so unexpected."

"It was for me, too, but whatever Brigadoon-type scenario we're experiencing right now shouldn't affect our love for each other, except to strengthen it."

"I'll do it."

"I guess you're not that romantic after all."

"PJ, I'll do it."

"But, if that's your final—Huh?" She raised her head; her eyes lit up. "You will?"

"Yes, darling, I will." I took her into my arms. "After all, we might never again have the opportunity to have a queen and a great poet officiate for us."

PJ kissed me soundly. "I love you, Kimberly Blair."

"I love you, too."

"Hey," she said, nibbling on my lower lip. "We can still have our own private commitment later, somewhere else, can't we?"

"Absolutely."

* * *

After last minute fittings on my gown for the joining ceremony, I was escorted to the river for ritual meditation and cleansing procedures with the tribe's most ancient member. Doubling as the healer and shaman, she allegedly had the ear of the Goddess Artemis, and a vast knowledge of medicinal plants and herbs. I had not spoken with her since she tended our wounds after our losing encounter with the overzealous Amazon scouting party, but Leeja had wanted a meeting of this sort for several days.

Kim and I had been injured and disoriented that first day. The shaman had helped to heal us then, but had spoken only with Kim about the purpose for transporting us to the Amazon village. Now, during this bathing ritual, I hoped she might give me some details of my future duties.

The meditation would take place in a shallow inlet of the river where the water would be calm and relatively warm. However, I was not informed that the shaman and I would be naked during the procedure, though I shouldn't have been surprised. The Amazons liked to get naked for all sorts of reasons, important or otherwise.

Solemnly, our escorts undressed us and placed our clothing next to drying cloths on the riverbank. The women stood guard over us, while the shaman led me into the water.

When the level was just above my waist, we stopped and held hands, facing each other. I averted my eyes from the old woman's pendulous breasts and focused instead on her weathered face. Pale blue eyes peered at me with a spirit and intensity that belied her age, and when she spoke, her voice, though hushed, possessed a confidence backed by years of accumulated wisdom in her capacity as the Goddess's confidante.

She had me float on my back while she supported my body underwater, placing one hand at my neck and the other at my buttocks. At first it was disturbing to feel her hands touching me, but I was soon able to relax and forget about everything as her voice directed me further into a meditative state.

"Sink into the water," she said. "Allow it to surround you, hold you, and breathe with you."

With my eyes closed, I felt the water gently cushioning my body, taking away all the stress.

"You and your soul mate are the future of the Amazons. Together, you and she will form a circle of strength. Your union will combine the four elements of our world. You, child, are Water and Air. She is Fire and Earth."

I had never thought of Kim in that way before, but I realized that it could be true. As for me being water and air, I had no idea, but I liked the concept of my parts complementing and completing Kim's. It made us a team... a formidable team.

The shaman slid one hand out of the water to sprinkle a few drops on my forehead. "As you experience the water moving beneath and above your body, feel too, the pull of the forces governing the seas of the earth and the rhythmic cycles of the moon. Let your muscles, skin, and bones fall away. Drift along to a peaceful place. Become a drop of water on the surface of a deep, flowing river. You are light and fast. Nothing stands in your way. The sun shines down on you from above and warms you. It calls to you. You are one with the air and the water."

My muscles went slack and my mind grew tranquil. I was no longer aware of the weight or temperature of my body, only the soft voice of the wise woman hovering over me.

"Discover your power now, my child. The water below, and the air and sun above have entered your body and filled your spirit. You are no longer a drop of water, but a strong, yet sensitive force."

She put one hand on my chest. "Experience the purity of your beating heart. The Goddess has given you a gift that some may think a weakness. You see others' pain, and it makes you weep. But you are not weak. Your tears do not diminish you. They enhance your sensitivity."

I felt stinging at the back of my eyelids.

"You are of the water. Water is emotion and the key to cleansing and healing. Use the quiet times and the healing times to develop your writing skills, and your ability to sense what is in the hearts of others. This recognition is a necessity. The Goddess challenges you and your soul mate to seek out Amazons—those who are lost in your time—and help restore the great nation from which they are estranged. Your spirit guides will assist both of you in this quest. Your soul mate will use her talents to comb the earth for missing medallions so that you and she can match these relics with their recipients, ensuring the continuation of the Amazon nation into the future."

She slid her hand from my chest to my cheek, turning my head towards her. "Open your eyes, Amazon Hunter."

When I complied, she leaned in and kissed my forehead. "May the Goddess bless this body and the spirit dwelling within it. May this child overcome all obstacles and succeed in helping to restore the Amazon heritage for future generations."

I opened my mouth to respond, but a clap of thunder sounded in the otherwise cloudless sky. The noise startled both of us. My arms and legs floundered and my head sank under the water. I came up sputtering.

The shaman recovered quickly. "The Goddess has spoken. My work is finished." She embraced me, drawing me to her bosom. "And your work has just begun."

Lucky me.

I tried to respond with confidence. "Thank you, wise woman. You have placed a heavy responsibility on me and my soul mate. We have a lot to think about."

After a final hug, she pushed me toward the shore. "Go now. Dry yourself and dress for the ceremony. Join with your soul mate and share your love and your strength. Together, you will not fail."

Chapter 16

The drums rolled, calling PJ and me to our destiny in front of the tribe. As if specifically ordered, a gloriously full moon rose in the east, casting a pale, otherworldly light over our assembly area. Queen Leeja was dressed in the trappings of her royal station, accessorized by feathers and medallions of hammered bronze. She first appeared with her face hidden behind a delicately carved mask, but she removed it when she stopped directly in front of me. To her left, Sappho slipped gracefully into position, wearing a gown of the finest silk in a shimmering, misty green. Marna took her customary stance at the queen's right hand. Dressed in her warrior outfit with a sweeping cloak of gold draped from her left shoulder, she looked equally regal.

Impressed as I was with the trio's regalia, I had eyes for only one woman as we turned toward the sound of the single drumbeat. I watched PJ march with her escorts along the path to my side. Her blonde hair, highlighted with jewel dust, glowed in the moonlight and enhanced her natural beauty to the point of taking my breath away. I caught many of the young, unattached warriors eyeing her with desire.

Feeling like a full-blooded Amazon warrior, I stood proudly in my tunic of the softest leather with leggings to match, knowing I would soon be formally united with the most beautiful woman in the village.

The undertone of conversation stopped when Leeja stepped forward.

"Distinguished guest and Amazon sisters," she said in a voice that was clear, but gentle. "We are here today to honor Kim and PJ and the bond they share. Having them live with us for a time and seeing them together reinforces our belief that love is the strongest of all emotions, and that it will always be so. Though Kim and PJ come to us from another time, we have witnessed their connection and recognized its powers. We know that love like theirs wins battles and brings old enemies together in peace and friendship. It dispels the clouds of loneliness, offers companionship and care, and gives sympathy and comfort in times of pain. It also provides the gift of pleasure when two come together as one."

Leeja stepped back, motioning Sappho forward.

The poet took our hands and held them before focusing her gaze on me. "Kim," she said, "PJ wrote the poem you are about to hear. It's fitting that it be shared with you now and form the basis for your commitment."

PJ tried unsuccessfully to keep a blush from coloring her cheeks. Sappho addressed the rest of the tribe. "Please form a circle around us." We waited for everyone to find a space and become silent.

"We stand in a circle," Sappho continued, "celebrating the love that these two women have for each other. When I have recited the poem, all of you will bear witness to their eternal union. I will release them to each other, for then, their love can never escape. The poem is entitled 'Only You.'

> It's you I love
> with all my heart.
> When you are gone,
> I am lost—
> a rudderless raft
> upon a river flowing.
> When you are here
> beside me,
> I am whole,
> as together forever
> we are joined—
> two links in the chain of life
> that cannot be broken
> by sword or strife.
> It's you I love,
> and only you
> with all my heart."

It was Sappho speaking, but I was aware only of the words, PJ's words. They came directly from her heart. Tears stung my eyes as I realized just how much I meant to her and how much she meant to me. Unfortunately, I lacked the talent to describe my feelings in so poetic a manner. It was little wonder, I thought, that the Amazons chose her as their chronicler... their historian.

Sappho retreated a few steps, and Queen Leeja and her consort came forward. Leeja produced a band of the purest white cloth, and Marna held a tiny gold-handled dagger. The firelight reflected off its shiny blade, scattering light like miniature stars.

PJ and I looked at each other. I wondered if my eyes were glistening as much as hers were.

Two young masked warriors moved to flank us; each held one of our hands, my left and PJ's right, palms upward. I heard PJ take a deep breath and glimpsed a hint of fear in her eyes, before she steadied herself.

"This will sting a bit," Marna said, making a tiny cut on my wrist and then on PJ's. The warriors dabbed the blood until Leeja pressed our wrists together and bound them tightly with the white band. "Now, you are truly one," she intoned as a single drum beat filled the clearing. "Your blood flows together as two streams join to become a river. You will forever be together."

Other drummers picked up the beat as Marna presented us with the dagger. "Keep this," she said. "It is the instrument of your perfect union."

I accepted the dagger from Marna and handed it to PJ, who held it briefly before sliding it into the belt at my waist. We stood together quietly, not knowing what else to expect.

After glancing at Leeja, Marna whispered to me, "We're all waiting for you to kiss her."

With pink cheeks and glistening eyes, PJ tilted her head up so I could press my lips to hers. The assembled women roared their approval, so I took the opportunity to deepen and prolong the event. Whistles and cries of delight rewarded me.

"The ceremony is not yet complete," Marna said. She removed the large band that bound our wrists and replaced it with small individual bands.

We watched her sprinkle some secret ingredient on the blood-soaked cloth before ceremoniously dropping it into the main fire, creating a multitude of brilliant flames.

"You two have become one," Leeja said, hugging each one of us in turn. "You are of but one mind and one body through which flows the blood of both. In a little while, you will honor me by sitting at my side for the feast."

* * *

I looked over at Kim and took a deep breath. "We made it. We're officially hitched, Amazon style."

"Something else to tell the grandkids. Whoever they may belong to."

I was about to continue that line of conversation, but we were interrupted by what must have been another quaint tradition of this Amazon tribe. A few of the younger Amazons, their arms full of flowers, had joined our group. Queen Leeja now stood before us with two vivid specimens. As she gave me one, she bent her head and kissed me firmly on the mouth.

"Relax, PJ," she said, amused by my shock. "This is customary at a joining ceremony."

"In that case, could you do it again? I wasn't prepared the first time."

She moved on to treat Kim to the same honor.

I watched to make sure it did not last too long, but was distracted by another flower and another kiss, this time from Marna. Hers was brief but just as breathtaking.

A line formed, and one by one, the women presented us with a kiss and a flower, or a piece of tall grass. The girls who had delivered the flowers stood to one side and wove the floral gifts into wreaths for our heads.

The custom continued. Some of the kisses were chaste, some rather bold. Once or twice I heard Kim clear her throat when I was kissed a little too long or, in her estimation, a little too fervently. I was relieved when Reena's offering was quick and platonic. "Congratulations," she said. She moved on to Kim, where she extended her arm for a warrior handshake, and Kim returned the gesture—two warriors honoring each other's prowess.

The wreaths grew into colorful rings of fragrant blossoms. When the line ended, Leeja came forward and crowned both of us. "And now, you may kiss each other once again," she said, glowing with the pleasure of our joining.

Once again the tribe appreciated our lengthy display of affection. We had just broken apart when Sappho approached. Not being a member of the tribe, she had not participated in the kissing ceremony. To the delight of the crowd, however, she put a wild pink cyclamen into my hands. I only had time to take a breath before she placed her hands on either side of my head, kissed my eyelids, forehead, and nose, and launched an all-out assault on my lips, even opening her mouth at one point long enough to slip her tongue between my teeth. Jesus, Mary, and Joseph. I've just been French-kissed by the greatest love poet in the known world. My knees weakened and threatened to collapse.

Once I had been kissed to her satisfaction, she moved to Kim and repeated her ministrations, much to Kim's delight and my consternation.

When Sappho released my spouse, she had us join hands and placed both of hers on top. "May your union be joyous and long-lived," she said. "May no danger befall you that cannot be conquered, and may you always remember how happy you were at this moment."

"Thank you," Kim and I both said.

Because we'd been focused on Sappho's antics and our involvement with each other, we failed to notice that the joyous mood of the watching Amazons had shifted from passive to active. These women were ready to boogie, all night long if necessary.

*   *   *

Fires flared and sparks flew as new wood was added to the blaze. Dancers in artistically crafted masks leapt into the clearing. The evening festivities were underway. Kim and I wanted nothing more than to sneak off to our hut, but it was obvious that it would be several hours before we could escape unnoticed. We resigned ourselves to being guests of honor in a village full of lusty, half-naked, party-loving women.

"If you can't fight them, join them," Kim said.

I found a wineskin and squirted some of the contents into her mouth. She plucked a few juicy grapes from a platter and fed them to me without using her hands.

"Goodness, you're just full of talent," I told her, after swallowing the first, slightly bruised grape. "Mind if I try to master your technique."

Her throaty chuckle had my blood sizzling. "Be my guest."

The grapes we consumed far into the night contained no wrath, only the tangy sweet discovery and delight of true love.

The party wound down as the first few streaks of daylight appeared in the eastern sky. Kim and I stumbled toward our hut, anticipating a long, passion-filled melding of our slippery, sweat-soaked bodies and lustful, but kindred, spirits.

Before we left the festivities, Leeja had instructed us to dress in our modern day clothing when we awoke in the morning. We were to bring our packs with us and meet Marna and her at the center fire pit. We had no idea what to expect after that, but for now, we had other things on our minds.

Our wedding bed beckoned. Yawning, I prepared for a long, leisurely session of lovemaking with my heart's desire.

Kim groaned sleepily from her prone position on our bed. She watched me slip out of my shimmering gown. "Ooh," she said, discovering that my Amazon dressmakers had apparently skipped the lesson on underwear construction when they created my wedding ensemble. "Now that makes it easy, doesn't it?"

"Easy for what, my big, bad warrior?" I extinguished the torches and slid under our bed covers.

"Come closer and find out, gorgeous."

In the dark, I tugged at her tunic until her body was delectably naked. My hands roamed freely over her torso and buttocks. I felt the first few notes of a slow, sensual symphony course between us. After letting my fingers play solo across her receptive flesh, Kim started a musical interlude of her own.

I felt her soft, seductive mouth find the hollow of my neck. I remember her tongue tickling the spots above and below my medallion, and then trailing downward. Her hands cupped and caressed my breasts with gentle, but urgent strokes. I recall whispering naughty things in her ear, nipping at her neck, and splaying my fingertips across her firm abdomen. I even remember stretching out on top of Kim's long, smooth body and pressing my breasts contentedly against hers.

That's all I remembered, though.

When I next opened my eyes, morning sunlight filtered into the hut. Kim and I were still naked and wrapped in a familiar tangle of cushioning warmth, but I felt no tingling in my lower body, no residual glow of shared passion.

What happened? Correction. What didn't happen?

Kim stirred and opened her eyes.

"Hey, wife," I said. "Sleep well?"

"Like a vat of grape mash was gurgling around in my belly."

"Okay, beyond that. Do you feel anything different?"

"What should I feel? Making love with you shouldn't feel any different just because we went through that ceremony yesterday."

"True. But what if it didn't happen quite that way?"

She pushed fingers through her sleep-tousled hair. "What are you talking about?"

"I don't think we got around to doing the deed, so to speak."

"Of course we did. I was so horny that I couldn't keep my hands off of you. I distinctly remember kissing and fondling you until your moans threatened to alert the whole village."

"True. And I remember nibbling and teasing you until you drooled, but it was all just foreplay."

"Impossible. You mean, we never got around to—"

"Consummating the marriage? Nope. We must have been too exhausted after all the festivities."

"Damn. I guess the honeymoon's already over."

I cupped her chin in my hands and put my heart and soul into kissing her. "Take heart, wife. I still love you."

"Thank the Goddess." She returned my kiss with a spectacular one of her own. "Hey, we can start the honeymoon right now."

"You're a genius. I'm awfully glad I married you."

"Mmm." Her kisses had migrated to my neck, starting a familiar warm tingle in my lower abdomen. "I'm the one who's glad."

Unfortunately, Reena took that moment to interrupt with a request from Leeja to get our butts covered and report for the meeting. We hastily washed and dressed, as instructed, in our modern-day clothes.

Minutes later, we were standing inside Leeja's hut, hearing that the time had come to return to our regularly scheduled lives in our own century.

I was surprised at the sadness I felt about leaving. We had just picked up our day packs when we heard a whistling sound overhead, followed by a streak of flame that thudded into the ground outside the hut. Reflexively, we ducked before following Marna and Leeja outside. Their signal sent the women scurrying in all directions. Apparently, we were under attack. Shouts rang out, and Amazons rushed for their weapons as more flaming arrows landed nearby.

"Get back in the hut and stay down," Marna cried, snatching up more weapons from the back wall.

Kim pulled me down and covered my body with hers.

Leeja was torn between racing after Marna and staying to protect us. She left us in the hut and, armed with a short sword and crescent-shaped shield, she left to join the fight.

We could hear the sounds of battle. Metal against metal echoed around the compound. Every so often a cry or a gasp sounded as a sword struck flesh. I cringed at the thought of who might be injured, or worse, by this unseen and unexpected enemy. Male voices told us that the Amazons were up against an army of trained soldiers.

"I can't just hide in here while they're fighting all around us," Kim said. "You stay put. I'm going out there."

"Not without me, you're not."

"Okay, but you stick close to me, you hear?"

"Like glue, kiddo."

We peeked through the door of the hut to discover that the Amazons had rallied behind Marna with a strong counterattack. Several warriors had circled around Leeja and were returning fire with crossbows. They seemed quite willing to give their lives to protect their queen.

Smoke obscured the compound as the fire mortars slammed into the ground around us. One hit the hut we had just vacated, setting it on fire.

Once outside, Kim drew her sword, and I found a staff with a broken spear tip. We left our packs on the ground and joined the battle. We sensed that the Amazons were severely outnumbered, and sooner or later, we'd be staging a back-to-back last stand, waiting for the inevitable.

Our movements were tentative and uncoordinated at first, but Kim found her rhythm and used her sword skillfully to drive several men back and into the strongest of our warriors. I swung the staff at anyone who tried to get on Kim's unprotected side, sometimes tripping, sometimes slamming an arm or a leg enough to weaken an attacker until Kim or another Amazon could do more damage.

During a momentary lull, I glanced at my spouse. "If I don't get the chance to say this later, I love you, tiger."

She gave me a tired roar. "I love, you, too, short stuff."

Leeja and two formidable-looking warriors approached. Blood and sweat coated their bodies, evidence of earlier conflicts. "I'm sending you back to your world," Leeja said. "I intended to do it with more ceremony and happy tears, but it's too dangerous for you to remain here any longer."

I opened my mouth to respond, but she cut me off.

"Don't argue with me. It was time for you to go anyway. You both know what you have to do. Remember your promise. Fulfill your legacy."

"Where's Marna?" Kim asked, her eyes darting about the smoke-filled compound.

"She had to escort Sappho and her party away from this. They're safe now."

I breathed a sigh of relief. I'd come to love the poet despite the fact that she delighted in teasing me.

"What about you?" I asked, ducking a fireball that landed too close for comfort.

"I'll be fine. Don't you worry."

Before she could say anything more, a half dozen men in heavy armor stormed into our midst, swords drawn. I had no idea who these raiders were, but I knew they were bent on hurting my Amazon friends, and they had to be stopped. The dizzying heat of rage built up inside me. I was not a trained warrior, but these women had taught me something about defending myself. I didn't know if I could go on the offensive, though, or if I'd ever be able.

"Here comes round two." Leeja took a defensive stance, with Kim close behind her. I stayed in back of Kim, searching for a new weapon. The staff I was using had splintered over one soldier's particularly hard skull.

Flaming arrows continued to strike huts and brush, filling the air with fire and smoke. Individual battles raged and, for a time, we were separated from Leeja. Kim used her sword skills to protect both of us. I tried swinging one half of the broken staff, but it was of little use against armor. Fortunately, a reinforcement of women warriors came to our rescue.

The odds improved until one of the women fell with a sword wound to the chest. I tore a piece off my T-shirt and pressed it tightly against her injury, trying to staunch the heavy flow of blood. The healer was somewhere in the compound, but I had no idea if she would arrive in time, and I felt helpless as I searched through the curtain of smoke for a sign of her.

"Easy, take it easy," I said, when the wounded warrior tried to speak. It was Alaina, the Amazon who had given me such wonderful backrubs in the grotto. Tears spilled down my cheeks. "Hang on. You're going to be okay."

Another warrior raced by, but stopped when she saw us.

"Help me get her to the healer."

"There isn't time, PJ. You aren't safe here."

As if to prove her right, a man with a battle ax charged us. The Amazon used her sword to deflect most of the blow and then slashed his arm to the bone. He cried out and dropped his weapon, but reached for a dagger which he threw in my direction. I felt it slice across my upper arm, but managed to fall out of the way, while more warriors fired arrows into his chest from close range. He lay dead at my feet.

The contents of my stomach scorched and burned a path up the back of my throat. I picked up a piece of wood to act as a club and crawled back to Alaina. The front of her tunic had turned crimson, and she shivered with pain and shock. We shared a look and the realization that she would bleed out before any help would arrive.

"Water, please."

Her raspy plea forced me to move again. I found a skin with a few ounces left in it and dribbled some liquid between her cracked lips. She swallowed and made another effort to speak. "Go. Be safe."

"I'm not leaving you." I blinked back tears, picked up her sword, and stood over her body. My fingers sticky with Alaina's blood, I gripped the handle with both hands and swung it like a baseball bat, smacking attackers with the flat part of the blade. At the sound of running feet behind me, I turned, and Kim deflected the blade just as I was about to brain her.

"God, Kim, I'm sorry."

She reached for my shoulder. "You're hurt."

"Just a scratch." I noted a bloody, torn section of her pant leg.

"You've been injured, too." She waved me off and bent to examine Alaina.

"Kim, we have to get—"

"Honey, she's dead." Kim gently closed the warrior's eyes and stood.

I started to shake, and she pulled me close. "Come on. We have to get out of here."

"We can't leave them now. They need us." I couldn't believe what I was saying, and that these Amazon women were now so real to me.

We searched for Leeja at the last location we'd seen her, but the air was thick with smoke and fire. Cries of the wounded and dying filled our ears. The coppery smell of blood burned our nostrils. I remembered the saying about war being hell and thoroughly agreed.

Several more armor-clad raiders blocked our path. Kim still clutched her sword. Now it was stained crimson. Carrying Alaina's sword, I pressed my back against Kim's, and we engaged the enemy again. Blood and other body fluids splattered over us. Curses and cries assaulted our ears. Sweat streamed into our eyes, poured from our bodies, and made the swords slippery in our hands.

My upper body ached with the exertion of swinging and colliding with enemy body parts. It was terrifying, but in spite of the imminent danger, I was comforted by the warmth of Kim's back against mine. I knew beyond any doubt that she would kill or be killed to save me, and I would do no less for her. If we had to die here, I believed we would die together, and that reassured me.

Our technique lacked skill and finesse when we first had engaged the enemy, but practice improved our ability. Thanks to the Amazons' training, we too, had become warriors, in my case at least long enough to defend myself. The men attacked, delivered blows, and wounded us, but they didn't defeat us. They were battered, too. Unfortunately, they had superior numbers and continued to come at us. We knew it was just a matter of time, just minutes, if not seconds, before they would prevail. Just when we thought it was over, Marna and Leeja burst on the scene with several of their warriors.

A soldier picked that moment to thrust his sword at Kim, driving her to her knees. Before I could move, a young Amazon flew at him with her dagger poised. She sank it into his chest up to the hilt just as his sword slashed downward through her body. She and he collapsed on top of Kim.

While Marna and Leeja rebuffed the attack around us, Kim and I rolled the brave Amazon over and away from the dying raider. I spared him a brief glance, just long enough to see his eyes glaze and blood bubble from the corner of his mouth.

Kim's savior had been dealt a mortal blow. Kim cradled her in her arms during her last few breaths. I dropped to my knees beside them, and it took me a moment to recognize her.

"Oh, God... Sheena!" Tears flowed freely down Kim's cheeks. She held the young warrior-in-training who had been our guide during our first day with the Amazons. I put my arms around both of them.

"You truly are a Lion King," Kim said. We shivered and wept at the sheer senselessness of what we had experienced. With maddening speed, life had become death, and we couldn't do a damn thing about it.

We staggered to our feet, clutching each other. With a roar, another soldier raised his sword and rushed at us. Kim shoved me down and turned to meet the attack, barehanded. A blood-covered crossbow and several arrows lay on the ground near me. Remembering the day of the archery contest and the brief bit of instruction I got in using the weapon, I snatched it up, loaded an arrow, and fired point blank at Kim's attacker. Though I aimed at his torso, the arrow hit his sword arm, just above the elbow. He shrieked and his weapon clattered to the ground. Marna rushed over and finished him off with a wicked slash across his neck.

Leeja appeared at our side, breathing hard. "Go." She pointed to a hut that had not been burned. "You'll find your packs inside. Get them now. I must send you both back while there's still time."

"But what about Sheena and the rest of you?"

"I said now, Kim. There's nothing more you can do for us here."

We made our way as swiftly as possible through a path of fallen bodies. The air reeked of smoke and bloodshed. Once inside the hut, we settled our packs against our weary backs. Leeja told us to join hands. We gave each other the once-over by torchlight, and I was sure that all the horror of what I had witnessed was reflected in Kim's eyes. We had seen evil close-up, and we wanted no further part of it.

"I will touch your medallions now. Do not let go of each other." Considering the circumstances, Leeja's voice was remarkably steady.

In the few seconds remaining, I marveled at the amount of devastation and destruction that Leeja and Marna must have experienced during their lifetimes. Unfortunately, I knew what the future held, and the global outcome wasn't going to be much better. The weapons would be different, but the result would be more bloodshed, destruction, and waste. "What about you and Marna?"

"Pay attention, PJ," Leeja commanded. "Fill your lungs with air and try to remember the good times. Are you both ready?"

We nodded.

"Good." She took a deep breath. "Thank you for being with us, even though it was for a short while. The love you share was a joy to behold."

Kim and I glanced at each other before turning our attention to the Amazon queen. "We had the best of role models," Kim said, her voice cracking.

"We did. And we love you and Marna, and all your wonderful, courageous warriors."

"It's been our pleasure. Don't worry about us. After we relocate to the west or across the sea, we'll send spirit guides to help you with your mission. It will not fail."

Leeja kissed our cheeks and gave us hugs. "Now the time has come for you to go."

I opened my mouth, but her look silenced me.

"There's nothing more to be said."

She held my medallion in her left hand and Kim's in her right. I gripped Kim's hand tightly and closed my eyes against the sudden, rushing, whirling wind. It grew increasingly louder and more violent, until we were pulled apart, and the walls of the hut fell away.

The air darkened, filled with a choking dust, and flashed with bright, white lights. I was buffeted by falling stones and bits of wood that drove me to my knees. I couldn't tell where I was, or where Kim had gone. Then, mercifully, the terrible wind died, and all was quiet.

"Kim... Kim, where are you?"

Chapter 17

I tried to move, to feel for PJ, but I couldn't budge. When I called out, my mouth filled with choking dust. Where were we? What had happened?

I remembered the battle and how Leeja was trying to rush us back to the twenty-first century. In those last moments, everything had blurred with the noise of battle and the cries of the wounded. Worst of all was the agonizing silence of friends who had lost their lives defending their queen and us.

But where was I now? And where was PJ? Had we been caught in a time warp somewhere between then and the present day and been separated? Forever? Oh, my God, no. Not that. I tried again to move but couldn't. Was I—were we—trapped in the rubble of ages?

I could hear voices, distant, but voices nevertheless, and Pup's barks and howls. I would recognize him anywhere. Rocks and dirt moved; people were scratching and clawing through this barrier, furiously trying to free me.

"Hang on, we get you quick."

It was a man's voice with a heavy Greek accent. After what seemed like an hour, some of the debris above me was shoved to the side, leaving me coughing and spluttering in a shower of dust. I could see Sandy's face peering through the space, and then others. Pup poked his muzzle into a tiny opening and licked my face, but he was pulled back so the crew could move the rest of the rubble.

"What happened?" I asked Sandy, when we could hear each other.

"The roof caved in. You okay?"

"I think so. But, PJ... We got separated on our way back from... I don't know where she is."

"I'm over here." Two of the Greek laborers were carefully pulling her out of the rubble.

"Oh, thank God."

She and I were carried to the main passageway, where we sat side-by-side, waiting for the camp medical staff to examine us.

"You're a mess," I said, noting her dirty hair and face, and her torn, filthy clothing.

"You won't make the cover of *Vogue* any time soon, either, I hate to tell you."

When she reacted to my joke, her teeth shone like beacons. She had been smart enough to keep her mouth shut during our ordeal.

The expedition's medical team, which consisted of Dr. Allen Greenfield and his assistant, Beverly Kennedy, arrived and took over. Considering what had fallen on top of us, our injuries were relatively minor. My slashed leg and the wound on PJ's shoulder seemed to cause some curiosity, though, along with our blood-spattered clothing—spatters that appeared from their pattern to have come from a source other than our injuries. PJ had a bump on her head, and we both had plenty of bruises. The doctor insisted that we be immobilized and transported to the infirmary on stretchers. He wanted to take x-rays and perform a more complete examination on both of us. As we left the labyrinth, the Greek sunshine warmed us, and Frederick, Susanna, and the others greeted us with relieved cheers.

Our beds were in the same room, but a curtain was drawn between us. I could hear Beverly, the young, African-American Physician's Assistant, questioning PJ, as the doctor checked my heart and lungs. He was frowning.

"Is there a problem?" I asked.

"Not so much a problem as a mystery. Your injuries are not consistent with what you've experienced. Both you and Dr. Curtis have deep cuts that resemble stab wounds more than anything else. It's as if you two tangled with bayonets or long knives, not a roof collapse."

"Can't imagine why that is."

Beverly pulled back the curtain dividing our beds. It allowed me to see PJ. She had heard the doctor's comments, and we shared a questioning look.

"I'm afraid I don't remember much after cleaning that fresco," PJ said.

I decided to follow her lead, keeping my comments vague for the time being. "That's about when I lost touch with things, too. We went into the small chamber and saw that animal with the intriguing eyes."

"And I took out my soft-bristled brush to get a better view."

"Right. Then we heard a rumbling sound, and everything went black."

The doctor took the stethoscope from his neck and had me lean back against a couple of pillows. "I'll check the films again, but nothing seems to be broken." He turned his attention to PJ. "You have a slight concussion, but I want both of you to remain here overnight for observation. While your injuries are not life-threatening, they may cause you discomfort. We'll need to clean your wounds and suture your lacerations. I'll have to check your medical records to see if you need Tetanus shots."

PJ groaned. "I think I'm up to date on the shots, Dr. Greenfield."

"Let me consult your records to confirm that." He looked over at me. "Are you going to try to weasel out, too, Dr. Blair?"

"Come to think of it, I probably got one after the landslide in Arizona last fall."

"Landslides and roof collapses." Shaking his head, he flipped through the pages of our medical histories. "I didn't know archaeology could be such a dangerous occupation."

PJ and I shared another look. "You'd be surprised," I said, keeping my voice low.

Beverly, apparently catching my comment, asked, "Are you leaving something out of the story, Dr. Blair?"

"Nothing significant. Lately, it seems that we've needed nine lives to do our work, that's all."

"You've had your fair share of excitement, if this latest trauma is any indication. She turned her attention back to PJ. "Dr. Greenfield is right about those cuts, though. During my rotation in the ER at Mass General, I saw a lot of stabbings, and there's a resemblance. I can't figure out what sharp objects could have fallen on you and left such injuries. It doesn't make any sense."

PJ winced as Beverly peeled the remnants of her shirt away from her wound. "I guess it's like Murphy's Law. We seem to have a knack for being in the wrong place at the wrong time. If it's possible to get cuts like that from falling debris, then it'll happen to us."

"Sounds pretty difficult to me," the PA said, "but I'm not an archaeologist, and I didn't see into that room you explored. And the aftermath of the collapse won't tell me much." She examined PJ's shoulder and swabbed the wound with antiseptic.

"What if we told you that we had taken a short vacation to ancient Greece and sided with the Amazons in a battle?" PJ asked, innocently.

I choked on the sip of water I had just taken.

Beverly laughed. "It would explain the wounds, and it would make a great story. Remind me to buy the book, when it comes out."

Dr. Greenfield finished reading his charts and moved to the sink to scrub up. "Neither of you will need any shots. That's the good news."

"Great. What's the bad news?" PJ asked him, as he numbed the site of her cut and stitched her up.

"Beverly and I honed our suturing skills by stitching up domestic dispute victims and gang fight losers, but we're not plastic surgeons, so it's possible both of you will have some scarring. You may need further work done in the future."

"Don't worry about me," I said. "A few more scars won't bother me at all."

"And I've already got the scar from the bullet wound. If I need plastic surgery, I'll have both areas done at the same time." PJ sounded positively practical. "On the other hand, I think I'll keep the scars and be proud of them."

"That's right," Dr. Greenfield said. "I read about that in your files. Landslides, roof collapses, and flying bullets. I'm really glad I'm a physician and not an archaeologist. Way too lively for me."

"It does have its moments," I said.

He finished working on PJ and prepared to join Beverly in suturing my wound.

*　*　*

"You two know better than to enter a room not pre-checked for safety." Sandy sounded like a teacher scolding a couple of naughty children. "What were you thinking?" He had made certain we weren't seriously injured before he gave us the tongue-lashing.

"I know. We took unnecessary chances, and it won't happen again."

"It was my fault. I talked Kim into it."

"No, PJ, we were equally foolish."

"Yeah," Sandy said, pointing his finger at PJ, "but I'll bet my last dime that it was your idea."

She fiddled with her bandage, ignoring him.

"I'm going to let you guys rest awhile," he said, turning towards the open tent flap. "It's just a good thing we got to you soon enough."

"How soon?" I asked, knowing we had a lot of missing time to account for.

"It's hard to tell exactly. Several hours."

"What?" PJ's astonished expression probably mirrored my own.

"Yeah. Gregor was on his scooter, returning from town early when Pup met him on the road. The poor animal was covered with dirt, barking like crazy. Gregor figured something was up and called us on his cell phone. When he got back to camp, he alerted the others. There weren't many of the laborers around, since it was the weekend, but they started moving rock right away. We estimated it had been a couple of hours past the time of the cave-in when Gregor met up with Pup on the road. That's assuming Pup came out of there as soon as it happened."

"My God," PJ said.

Sandy didn't notice that her face had paled. "Lucky for us, there must have been some pockets of air under all that rubble, or you might've suffocated. You two must live right, you know that."

I was still absorbing the time difference. "That's all? A few hours… max?"

"Yeah, thanks to Gregor and your friend here." Sandy rubbed Pup's ears.

I looked at my four-legged pal whose life I had saved seven years ago. He had more than returned the favor. He trotted over to me and licked my face, then moved on to PJ, affording her the same treatment.

After Sandy left with Pup, PJ and I stared at each other for several seconds before speaking.

"Okay, if what Sandy said is true, then I had the strangest dream while I was under the rubble," she said.

"I did, too."

"About Marna and Leeja."

"Mine was also."

"I don't believe it. Now we're even dreaming alike." Her forehead crinkled.

"Better keep that ice pack on your head. You're losing it, sweetie. But it did seem so real."

"I know. It was like—"

"You two certainly can put the fear of God into people."
Frederick entered the tent with Susanna right behind him.

"Sorry about that." He and PJ hugged.

Susanna stood, hands in pockets, studying us. "Are you sure
you're both okay?" She took my wrist and checked my pulse to
satisfy herself.

"We're fine," PJ said. "We're banged up and sore, but other
than that there's no permanent damage."

"Mostly bruises," I added.

"We have some news for you, but we'll talk later." Frederick
brushed PJ's bangs off her forehead. "The doctor gave us
permission to peek in on you for only a minute, and then we must
let you rest."

"What news?"

"Later, princess. Later."

Susanna squeezed my hand. "What you both need now is
plenty of rest." She moved to PJ's bed, noted the icepack and peered
into her eyes.

"It's only a slight concussion, honest," PJ told her.

"Mmm. I see that." Susanna scanned the rest of her body. "Any
pain?"

"Just a bit sore and stiff."

"You were very lucky." She glanced at me. "You both were."

When they had left, we speculated briefly about their news
before dropping off to sleep, though, for me it was hardly restful. So
much had happened, but we'd only been away a few hours. How
could that be? It made no sense at all. My brain couldn't resolve the
contradiction in time.

I checked on PJ who appeared to be sleeping peacefully. What
a dream! I recalled some of the visions I had experienced while I
was searching for the Lost Tribe of Amazons in the Superstition
Mountains of Arizona. That seemed so long ago now, but at the
time, it was as if I had been there with those women and part of
what was happening to them. This was the same kind of reality. I
remembered the battle and was suddenly filled with concern for
Marna and Leeja and for the many friends I had made in that dream
world.

* * *

Two days after our rescue, we were back in our own tent and
healing nicely. Dr. Greenfield didn't want us to return to work yet,

for fear of breaking open our wounds. Frederick and Susanna had gone to Athens for a few days during our convalescence, so we had not been able to get together with them.

PJ spent some of the downtime writing in her journal and organizing her reports. When all of that was up-to-date, she sat cross-legged on the floor, cleaning out her very grubby daypack, while I worked on the computer.

"Oh, my God." The color drained from her face.

"What is it? What's the matter?"

"This." She held up the tiny gold-handled dagger. "It was at the bottom of my pack."

I heard buzzing in my ears and was forced to swallow before I could speak. Scenes from our joining ceremony replayed in my mind, and when I peered at my left wrist, I could see a tiny, well-healed scar. As if tuning into my wavelength, PJ raised her right wrist, revealing a matching scar.

We couldn't speak for several more seconds.

PJ eventually found her voice. "It really happened. But Sandy said we were missing for only a few hours. This is a case for the Sci-Fi channel."

"I'm concerned about them."

"Who? Marna and Leeja?"

"Yes. And the other women. Their warriors."

"I'm concerned about our sanity." PJ looked at me as if begging for an explanation. "If it really happened, then Sheena gave her life for us."

"And Alaina, too."

PJ pressed a trembling hand to her lips. Her eyes glistened with tears. I took her in my arms, stroking her hair, kissing her temple. "Easy. I can't begin to explain what happened to us, but I know we have some very good friends in Ancient Greece."

"Nobody will believe this. We can't share our story with anyone, not even Susanna."

"Maybe you could relate it as a dream."

"I don't know. I guess so." PJ stretched out on our bedroll, and I joined her. We lay there with only our thoughts and each other for company, but that was enough for now. We were together, and together we'd go with the flow of our lives. We were a team, forever and always.

* * *

When Dad and Susanna returned from their trip, they invited us to dine with them, away from camp, in Eresos. We assembled around a large table on one of the raised platforms at Bennett's, a restaurant owned by an English couple, Max and Jackie Bennett. In addition to Greek cuisine, Bennett's offered English and Italian entrées. Kim, Susanna, and I ordered vegetarian lasagna, while Dad tried the prime rib.

Conversation focused on routine matters during the main course. We had just requested dessert when the waiter brought a large bottle of chilled champagne to our table and set about filling our glasses. Kim and I eyed each other, anticipating the big news. We had been speculating for the past few days, and the only logical explanation was that Dad had proposed to Susanna. With this announcement in mind, we got haircuts, pressed our best khakis, slipped blazers over sleeveless tops, and even dabbed some makeup on our sun-baked faces. For a couple of dirt-diggers, we cleaned up pretty well.

Susanna looked fantastic in a long printed skirt, silk blouse, and a loose, open-weave vest. Gold earrings and a matching necklace were the perfect enhancements to the honey blonde of her hair. Just a light bit of gray streaked the strands framing her face. She kept her eyes on my father for most of the meal. He was quite dapper in a British-made sport coat that I recognized as an old favorite. His wavy silver hair, suntanned skin, and clear blue-green eyes belied his sixty-six years. Though he had gained a little weight, I had to admit he seemed happier and more energized than he'd been in years. Together, he and Susanna were a handsome couple. I resolved to accept their news with as much delight as possible, though a few nagging worries plagued me. It wasn't that I thought she was after his money. She was wealthy in her own right. I just needed some more time to get used to the idea that Dad could be sharing his love and attention with someone besides me.

"Priscilla, Kim, we have some exiting news to share with you." Dad allowed his comment a moment to sink in before continuing. "How should I phrase this? You are both invited to a... I guess you'd call it a recitation of wedding vows."

"A what?" I asked, puzzled.

"At the camp, in a few weeks."

I was still confused. Apparently, from her expression, so was Kim. "Do you mean a wedding, Frederick?"

"It's a bit more complicated than that." Susanna turned to Dad. "Should I explain further, Freddie?"

Kim and I looked at each other. Freddie?

"Go ahead, Susie." Dad raised her hand and kissed it.

It was then that I noticed a band of gold with a glint of diamonds on the ring finger of her left hand, but I was still processing the Freddie and Susie part. Who were these people?

"A few weeks before we came to Greece to visit you both and see Sandy's project, your father proposed to me."

"Ah." I said, sensing what was coming.

"I accepted," Susanna said, "and we decided to plan a wedding for next year in Boston. We planned to tell you when the time seemed right."

Dad took up the story. "Once we had a look around, we fell in love with the Greek islands and decided to get married right here, but we ran into so much red tape. We knew you two were busy helping Sandy, but we figured we'd do it later when your work was finished. Then, you were almost crushed when the ceiling collapsed, and you needed time to recover. We decided that life was just too short to risk waiting until next year. Instead of flying to Athens like we told you, we went back to Boston and were married by my old friend, Judge Evans. We hoped you'd forgive us. You do, don't you?"

Kim broke the silence that followed. She held her glass high. "So, you're married. Congratulations."

I was speechless.

"Yes, we're married," Frederick said, "but we don't want to exclude you. We'd like to have a small ceremony for family and friends here on Lesvos. Afterwards, we'll have a party with music and dancing and food catered by Demitri and his son." He looked at me, waiting for some kind of response. "Is that okay?"

"Okay? It's wonderful. It's just that you caught me off guard." After much hugging and kissing, we raised our glasses in a toast to the newlyweds. "Geia sas! Best wishes!"

We sipped our champagne and dug into the apple crumble with thick cream, chattering about shopping for outfits for the ceremony, and planning what the couple would do in the future.

"This is the perfect time to tell them about your other news," Susanna said, putting down her napkin. "I'll just go to the powder room and give you time to talk privately."

"No need for you to leave."

"Ah, but I need to repair my makeup. In case you hadn't noticed, I got kind of teary with all that hugging and kissing."

When she rose from her chair, Dad got up, too, giving her a peck on the cheek before she left.

"Dad, what gives?"

"Wait," Kim said. "I'm not sure I can take another surprise tonight."

"Just one more thing. It's something I've been pondering for a while now, ever since Susie and I started seriously planning for a future together. And now, with us getting married, it seems just the right time to do it."

"Good grief, Dad, what is it?"

"We want to travel a bit, so I want to take more time off. I'm easing way back on my workload at Curtis Enterprises."

"Oh."

"And I plan to step down as head of the Foundation."

I gasped and Kim gripped my hand. "I don't believe this, Dad. You've always been a workaholic. Is there some medical reason that you're not telling us about?"

"No. I'm fine. My blood pressure is up slightly, but I'm taking care of that. And I suppose I could stand to lose a few pounds. Other than that, I'm in fine fettle. I'm better than I have been in years."

"Who will be taking over the Foundation for you?" Kim asked.

"Malcolm Goodrich. He's been there the longest, and he's a good friend and colleague."

I knew Goodrich and heartily approved his choice.

"What I would really like, though," Dad continued, "is for you both to accept appointments to sit on the board and to represent the Curtis family."

"What?" I was stunned.

"My God!" Kim seemed equally surprised.

"You don't have to decide anything tonight, but I would like you to let me know soon. That way, I can set things in motion."

Susanna returned to a very quiet table. "Judging from the silence and shocked expressions, I presume you've asked them."

"They're going to think it over, and I want them to do just that." He took her hand and held it. "Since they're still in shock, maybe this is a good time to leave them with the bill for this dinner." He and Susanna seemed amused by his joke, but Kim and I were still blown away, and must have looked like deer caught in some car's headlights.

* * *

I went to Dad's on-site office tent the next morning with a couple of concerns about the board appointments.

To avoid any possibility of catching Susanna and him on the daybed again, I coughed loudly before entering.

"Don't worry, Priscilla. The coast is clear." Dad wasn't very successful at keeping a straight face.

"Very funny. I guess I'm never going to live that down."

"Not for a while, yet. I'm having too much fun teasing you." He pushed his chair away from the table that doubled as a desk and stretched out his legs. "Have you two made a decision?"

I stood facing him across the table. "Almost. There are a couple of issues that worry us, though."

"Let's hear them."

"Can you guarantee that the members of the board will accept us if our lifestyle becomes common knowledge?"

He stood, circled the table, and wrapped his arms around me. "You mean, will they understand if they find out that you two are a couple?"

"That's exactly what I mean. You and Susanna have been wonderful, but somehow I don't see all of them being quite as tolerant. I'm used to controversy, but Kim shuns the limelight. She keeps her personal life private, and I don't want her hurt."

He tilted my head up so we could see into each other's eyes. "Princess, I wish I could prevent any possible trouble you both may encounter, but you know as well as I do that I can't promise anything. Right now, those who know us or suspect that you two are together have been fine about it."

"Yes, but right now we're in the background. We're just working archaeologists. Coming into the boardroom, well, that's a different matter."

"True." His hands came around my shoulders. "Our position in the community affords you some insulation."

"If you're saying that our wealth can force even the most intolerant of them to keep quiet, I'm not sure we can be comfortable with that."

"Why don't you try it and see how things work out? You can always resign later, if you feel it's necessary. You and Kim are respected professionals who live quietly. You don't call attention to yourselves, except when kidnappers attack you, photographers get in your way, or walls cave in."

"Or we're attacked by marauding raiders."

"What?"

"Nothing. Just joking. But you did forget to mention earthquakes and rattlesnakes."

"Those, too."

"Okay, I guess we can work around that problem, if and when it occurs. But there is one other issue."

Dad steered us back around the table and sat down, pulling me onto his lap.

"Hey, I haven't done this since I was a child. I'm way too big now." I tried to get up, but he had me in a tight grip.

"Nonsense. You're still my princess."

"I'm your thirty-six-year-old daughter who messed up half her life and almost destroyed you in the process, before finding love and making amends."

"We all make mistakes, and that wasn't entirely your fault, you know." He tucked my head under his chin and held me close. I felt his jaw working, and I blinked back tears. His arms were strong and comforting. "I'm so damn sorry, honey."

"I know. I'm sorry, too."

"We were so happy when your mother was alive. We were the perfect family. Then, when she died, I couldn't stand it. You resembled her so much. Same hair and eyes. It hurt to look at you. I threw myself into work because it was the only way I could get through the day." He sniffed, released me, and wiped his eyes.

"I needed you, too, so badly, but you hardly ever came home from work. I thought you didn't love me any more." Tears slid down my cheeks. "All that acting up was to make you notice me."

"I know. I was a lousy father."

"Your heart was broken, just like mine. We couldn't help each other because we were too badly hurt ourselves. It wasn't anybody's fault. I know that now."

When I got up, Dad shifted to a more comfortable position. "I'm sorry anyway," he said. "If I could do it over again, I'd make things right. We lost so much time."

"But now you have a new life. You have Susanna, and that means you've found love again."

"She can never take your mother's place. You know that, don't you? But she loves us both very much."

"She's a wonderful woman, and I know I will come to love her." I fished a tissue from my pocket.

I blew my nose before kissing him on the cheek. "And I love you very much, too."

"I've always loved you, princess, even though I didn't always show it. Susanna wanted us to have this talk. She felt it was way overdue, and I agreed with her."

"Me, too. And now I'd better get back to Kim. She'll be wondering where I am."

"You said you had another issue to discuss."

I tapped my forehead. "Right. If we accept the board positions, will it restrict us from taking part in any further expeditions? Are there any rules or conflicts of interest about that?"

His easy laughter warmed my heart. "There aren't, but even if there were, you'd find a way to break them. Wild horses couldn't prevent you two from following your dreams."

"Hey, what can I say? I'm your daughter, and I can be as stubborn as you are. Some of that attitude must have rubbed off on Kim, too."

I could still hear him laughing as I exited the tent.

Chapter 18

PJ and I eased back into our routine in the labyrinth. I was relieved that Sandy and the rest of the team had decided to leave the caved-in room undisturbed for the time being. I thought that was just as well, for PJ's sake and my own. Keeping safe was the crew's main reason, but neither PJ nor I were ready for a return to the land of the Amazons. We had left them in such a precarious state that we feared a return would mean finding most of them dead.

Our explorations continued along the main passage, but progress was slowed by the keen sense of danger that lurked so far into the tunnels. Safety was our top priority. "We don't want anyone else getting hurt," Sandy told us on our first day back to work. He focused on PJ.

"Don't look at me," she said, holding her hands up in surrender. "I'm not taking any more chances."

"Where have I heard that before?" I whispered in her ear.

"Hey, I'm ready to stay in the present for a while. The good old days weren't always that good."

A short side passage ended at a wall constructed of huge blocks. How the builders of that wall ever got the blocks into the passage and lifted them into position was a mystery to all of us.

Sandy consulted with Frederick, who suggested the use of a small, specially designed forklift to disassemble the wall. Sandy was not in favor, however, and after some discussion, they decided to hire expert stonemasons and more laborers to help the rest of us in cutting away individual blocks, without disturbing the integrity of the labyrinth walls. Using manpower and hand tools also prevented excessive dust and engine fumes from entering and accumulating in the work area.

Slowly and painstakingly, the men chiseled the first block out from the upper corner of the left side and deposited it on the ground. After the second block was extracted in the same fashion, Sandy switched on his powerful flashlight, climbed up on the stack, and peered into the opening. We heard his sharp intake of breath. "Kim, PJ, you've got to see this."

I joined him at the opening and felt the same exhilaration that had gripped me when we first viewed the interior of that cave in the Superstitions. My gasp echoed off the walls. "That's amazing."

"What's in there? Come on, Kim, let me see." I jumped down to allow PJ access. Since she was shorter, I bent down and gave her butt a boost upward. "Watch it," she said. "No fair pinching."

PJ took a quick peek and called down to Sandy. "Congratulations, buddy, you've hit the jackpot."

He struggled to keep his voice calm. "It's a little soon for that. We need to know more about what we're looking at here."

One by one, the team took turns at the opening.

After the initial exclamations of awe at finding a massive golden door behind the wall of blocks, an uneasy silence fell over the group. We settled into a routine of removing, photographing, and numbering all the stones so that they could be replaced later, but nobody speculated openly about the significance of a door in that location and what it might be guarding. In private, however, if the crew members were anything like PJ and me, imaginations ran rampant, conjuring up all sorts of precious finds behind that mysterious barrier.

Sandy had the electricians run bright lights into the area so the team could work in shifts around the clock. After all the blocks had been removed, the sheer majesty of the golden door was revealed. Its face was a series of squares, each containing designs of carved figures. When light played across the squares, the figures appeared to move.

A few more days passed while Sandy and Frederick conferred with experts and government officials. The rest of us spent our time measuring, taking pictures, making sketches, and researching the carvings on the door. When all the careful preparation was finished, Sandy decided it could be opened, but that feat proved more difficult than we imagined. The structure had no obvious lock or latch, and more experts were called in. They huddled with the team's engineers, seeking a way to gain entry without damaging the door itself. Almost anti-climactically, Alexander tripped a tiny panel deep within the design, and the massive barrier swung freely on its hinges. The huge door operated so smoothly, it was as if it had only recently been closed.

Sandy, Alexander, PJ, and I donned shoe covers, dust masks, and gloves before entering the room in single file. A sense of quiet reverence kept our bubbling excitement in check.

The room, some three meters by five, was crammed with an astonishing assortment of artifacts and treasure, most from ancient Greece, but others, we determined as we explored, from other parts of the Mediterranean.

"My God," Sandy said, "where do you suppose all this stuff came from?"

It was as if this valuable cache had been gathered from somewhere else, the mainland perhaps, and stored there, for safekeeping.

PJ stooped to examine two effigies of the Goddess in one corner. "These are similar to, but smaller than the one found on Knossos."

Sandy and Alexander peered closely at two frescoes on opposite walls where images of dancers seemed to leap outwards in a three-dimensional effect. Tablets covered with ancient script were piled in a corner as if hurriedly dropped in place. Beautiful pottery, most of it intact, lined one of the walls. Kraters, amphorae, bowls, vases, and cups were piled haphazardly in the middle of the floor. A small gold chest contained piles of ancient Greek coins; another was filled with jewelry fit for royalty.

I looked at Sandy. "Congratulations, Dr. Arnold, you've stumbled on a treasure trove."

PJ slipped her gloved hands into the chest and let a fistful of coins cascade through her fingers. "It's like pirate's hidden loot, just waiting for the thieves to return."

"Something like that. There's stuff here from around the ancient known world." I fingered a cartouche. "For example, this is Egyptian."

"It's going to take ages to go through all this stuff." PJ looked around in wonderment.

"Just the recording, photographing, and dating will take months," Sandy said, "maybe years."

"Definitely years." I was on my knees studying the tablets. "We'll have to get experts in to decipher all this script."

Sandy appeared to be in daze. It was as if he couldn't comprehend the enormity of his discovery. He was a kid discovering a furry caterpillar for the first time. Looking over at me, he said, "Guess I'm going to be around here for a long time."

"Very convenient," PJ quipped, "with Irini being here and all."

The visible parts of Sandy's face reddened above his dust mask. "I guess it will work out okay at that."

Alexander laughed. "I'm sure you'll manage, boss."

"One thing I'd better manage right away," Sandy said, his forehead wrinkling, "is talking to Frederick about tightening security around here."

"Good idea," PJ said.

"Yes." He rubbed his wispy mustache. "We've had a lot of people in here lately, and while we've checked them out, the sight of all that wealth is quite a temptation."

"Talk to Frederick," I said. "He'll get right on it." If anybody knew about security, Frederick Curtis did.

Within an hour of Sandy's meeting with Frederick, Greek armed guards appeared at the labyrinth entrance. Within twenty-four hours, an American security detail joined them, and a day after that, workers began installing a chain link fence, with surveillance cameras and sensing monitors around the site's perimeter. If word leaked out about the value of the find and all the gold, we could be targeted by all sorts of less than honest citizens.

"I don't like living and working in an armed camp," PJ told me, when we retired to our tent the evening after the compound had been fenced in.

"I don't either, but considering what we have here, it's a necessary evil."

Despite my having other things in mind, we were both so weary that we were asleep in minutes.

*   *   *

Our work had taken on a new sense of urgency. Kim and I spent all of our free time conducting research to help Sandy identify the contents of the treasure room. One evening, just before bedtime, I stood in our tent, zipped my sweatshirt jacket, and grabbed a paper from our make-shift desk. "I'll be right back. I downloaded that list of experts in Linear B writing. I know Sandy hasn't had the opportunity to contact anybody, and I'm sure he'll want to get right on it."

"Okay." Kim, absorbed in what she was reading, didn't even look up. She answered so automatically that I wasn't even sure she had heard me. It had been like this for both of us since our discovery, and I was feeling a bit ignored. I guess I was neglecting her just as much, but it didn't make me feel any better.

When I started out, Pup raised his head, stood up and wagged his tail. "Later, buddy, okay? We'll take a walk when I get back, I promise." He sank down onto his bed with what sounded like an exasperated huff, sounding just like Kim when she was put out about something. That made them two of a kind, but what a lovable pair they were.

A large quadrant of moon gave me plenty of light, but I stuck my flashlight into my pocket anyway.

Sandy's tent was illuminated from within by a soft, yellow glow, and I heard music playing at a low volume.

"Sandy. You around?"

"Yes." Sandy's reply was muffled, and I heard a feminine voice say something.

Uh-oh. I must be interrupting something. "Sandy, it's PJ. If it's not a good time, I can come back later."

"No problem, PJ. Come on in."

"Okay, if you're sure." I pulled aside the door flap and walked into the tent. "Hey, you two. Are you sure this is no bother? It can wait."

I was glad to see that they were both dressed. Stumbling in on my father and Susanna that time had made me gun-shy about visiting couples in their private sanctuaries. Sandy didn't look upset. He was sitting with Irini on their bedroll, holding her hand, and gazing dreamily into her eyes.

"I... uh... have a list of experts on ancient tablet interpretation. If you want, I can contact any of them for you." I waved the paper at Sandy. He was still lost in the depths of Irini's eyes. "Earth to Sandy. Come in, please."

"Sorry." He dropped her hand just long enough to reach for the list. "Thanks, it will save me a lot of time." Their hands clasped again, and I became invisible.

Okay, I'm obviously in the way.

"That'll be all, then." I turned to leave the tent. "Carry on... uh... I mean have a good night."

Sandy cleared his throat. "Wait, PJ. You can tell Kim, but nobody else, okay?"

"Tell her what?"

"Not even our folks know yet."

"Ookay."

"I just proposed to Irini." He looked like he'd just won the Lotto.

"And I accepted. We're going to be married." Irini's eyes gleamed with joyful anticipation.

Boy, was my timing in need of adjustment, or what?

"Fantastic news. No wonder you both seem so goofy." I rushed over to hug them and give Sandy a big kiss. "Cowboy, we thought you'd take forever to catch a clue. Way to go."

"Well…" He blushed.

"He caught on real fast," Irini said, giving her new fiancé a possessive hug.

"This is so great. Let me get out of here and tell Kim." I hugged each of them again.

As I rushed across the compound, I couldn't stop a goofy grin from plastering itself on my own face. And when I told Kim, she would have the look, too. Love was in the air, or maybe it was in the water.

* * *

"What?" PJ's question was sharp.

We'd discussed the news about Sandy and Irini, expressing our delight in their happiness and good fortune. Then she'd gone silent, her expression reflective. I couldn't help watching her, waiting for a return of her extroverted self. "Was I staring? I'm sorry."

"No need to apologize, Kim. Just tell me what's on your mind."

"I was about to ask you what was on yours."

PJ's expression lightened. She smiled. "How about we take turns with the questions? I'll ask, you answer. Then you ask, and I'll answer."

"Okay." I took her hands in mine. "I love you."

"And I love you, too. But why were you staring?"

"You've been quiet, inward, if you like. Is something the matter?"

She blew out a breath, and her gaze drifted off to one side. "Nothing's the matter, really. It's just that when I think about Frederick and Susanna, and Sandy and Irini, I can't help asking myself if our love is any less than theirs."

"Of course not." I led her to our bed and pulled her down beside me. "And don't you mean Freddie and Susie?"

"I know." PJ momentarily forgot her seriousness. "Can you believe it? They're acting like a couple of teenagers. It's as if they've gone through a metamorphosis."

"I think it's great."

"I do, too. Dad happy again is something I never thought I'd live to see. Susanna is good for him, even though I admit I had some pangs of jealousy at first. I know it was childish to feel that way, but I've been the only woman in his life for some time, despite our having been at odds with each other."

"Your feelings are perfectly understandable." I took PJ's face in my hands, gently caressing it as I looked deeply into her eyes. "But, to answer your question, our love is no less than theirs. If anything, it's greater. It has to be, in order to flourish among people who consider it the very essence of evil."

"That's the whole thing. No matter how strong our love is, its value is less in the eyes of society. It's something to be pushed into a closet like a broken tennis racket and kept there, out of the sight."

"As far as I'm concerned, society can go to hell. It's no one's business whom we love or what goes on in the privacy of our bedrooms. We can't change what or who we are. We're consenting adults, and our love is just as precious as anyone else's."

"I know, but I want to be able to shout it from the mountaintops and let everyone know how much I love you."

Seeing tears in PJ's eyes, I softened my tone. "The important thing is that we do love, because without love, hearts shrivel, and souls surrender all hope." I watched two tears trail down her cheeks. "You do still want to be with me, don't you?"

She nestled her head under my chin, sniffling. "I love you, and I want us to be together forever."

"That goes for me, too." I rubbed my cheek against her head, breathing in the sweet fragrance of her hair.

PJ broke away from our embrace long enough to pull a tissue from her pocket and dab her eyes. "It's just not fair."

"What can I do to make you feel better?"

She snuggled back against my chest, wrapping both arms around my waist. "I'll be okay. It's just that Dad and Susanna will be having their ceremony, and Sandy and Irini will have theirs. But for us, it's not allowed."

"Have you forgotten that we are joined in the eyes of the Amazon Nation, and our blood flows in each other's veins?"

"I haven't forgotten. It's just that it happened in another world, another time. It would be nice to declare our love here and now, in our time."

"Yes, it would." I kissed her temple and a tiny seed of an idea took root in my mind.

"Thank you for understanding." PJ turned her head so she could kiss my cheek. "That Amazon ceremony was like a dream, and I'm not sure to this day that it wasn't just that."

"What about the dagger you found in your pack?"

"I can't explain that," she said.

"Neither can I, but I'm sure that someday, we'll know the truth."

PJ appeared to feel better after we had talked about it. She pulled me to her again and kissed me slowly and lovingly, taking great pleasure in the act. "We don't need words, do we, for our love to thrive? It'll do so because of the strong bond between us. And while we've had some rough spots here and there, and probably will again, it's strong enough to weather all storms. You're my soul mate, and that's all that matters."

I held her close to me, rocking us both for several minutes. Neither one of us spoke. Just feeling her warm breath tickling my neck and the steady beating of her heart against my chest was enough.

Chapter 19

I stood just behind Kim at the base of a small hill overlooking our camp. Above us, on the top of the hill, a white trellis of red roses formed an arbor where Dad and Susanna planned to recite their wedding vows. Below the arbor, in a naturally curved earthen amphitheater, a small orchestra played for guests seated on wooden benches. Just behind us, a tent had been erected to provide privacy for the bride before her grand entrance.

Kim tugged at her outfit for the fifth or sixth time in the last minute. I didn't know if it was the fact that she was wearing unfamiliar clothing or the solemnity of the occasion, but something had her twitching. It was the first time I had ever seen Kim in a skirt, and the sight of the colorful fabric accentuating her slim waist and firm butt flooded me with all sorts of inappropriate thoughts.

"Some latecomers," she said, bringing my thoughts back to what was happening. She put her hand behind her back, and I gave her palm a tickle, before squeezing her fingers.

"Irini's family," I said. "They had food to drop off." I watched as they greeted friends and relatives before locating places to sit.

"Wow! There's a bunch of them."

"Uh-huh. Sandy's going to have in-laws crawling out of the woodwork."

"I hope they appreciate him."

I was touched by the note of concern in her voice. Even though he was now a grown man and in charge of his own destiny, she still worried about him.

"They seem nice. The ones I've met anyway."

We watched the family shuffle back and forth, trying to find enough empty seats in one area.

"How are you holding up, PJ?"

"I'll be fine, thanks to our discussion last night."

She shifted again. "All part of the service."

"I wish you'd calm down, though. You look sensational, by the way."

"What, the skirt? And the flowers? I feel like Zorba the Greek meets the hippie generation."

"Do I have to throw you down on the ground and ravish you to prove how sexy you are?"

"Ha! Now that would excite the crowd."

"Dad would have an attack for sure, and it would embarrass Susanna on her big day, so I'll try to restrain myself."

"Good thinking."

"Just remember the thought's there in the back of my mind."

"What a mind you've got," Kim said.

"You know what we talked about last night. All that and more is floating around in my head right now. The biggest thought, though, is how much I love you and how thankful I am that we found each other."

Kim turned completely around and smiled down at me, eyes glistening. "Right back at you, kiddo."

The orchestra started the last of its introductory music. When it finished this piece, we'd begin the processional. I tried to focus on the event about to take place, but my thoughts flittered in all directions. Cupid had definitely visited my world recently and wreaked havoc on it. His amorous arrows had pierced the hearts of several targets close to me. As a result, Dad and Susanna had married, Sandy had proposed to Irini, and Kim and I had been joined in a mythical village's equivalent of a wedding.

I thought about how I'd be forced to share the love Dad and I had just reclaimed, and I realized that I wasn't the love of Sandy's life any more. Last night it all came to a head, and I needed Kim's help to soothe my raw emotions. She helped me admit that a tinge of jealousy was behind my emotional upheaval, and that Cupid's arrows had first made loving pincushions of both of us.

I'd be forever grateful for that. Kim was my rock. She was fair-minded, tender, thoughtful, brave, sexy, smart, and clearly the best lover I'd ever had. Shit. I was back to thinking lecherous thoughts again, but I guess that was better than allowing jealousy to consume me.

* * *

The first few notes of Pachelbel's Canon in D major sounded. Kim's skirt swayed gently as she started up the slope to where my father and Sandy stood waiting. Shake your booty, tiger. I took a deep breath and pushed my thoughts in another direction, remembering all the work we'd accomplished in such a short time to bring this ceremony together.

During the past week we'd shifted into high gear, setting up the site, ordering flowers, arranging for food and musicians, shopping for clothing, and decorating the dining hall tent. Susanna's vision for the event was to mix the best of Greek Island foods, clothing, and dance, with traditional American favorites. So far, it had all come together beautifully.

Even though it was November, the weather had also cooperated. Not only had the rains held off, but the sun still held some warmth as it shone through thin, white clouds against a blue-gray sky. The temperature was a comfortable sixty-two.

Salt-laden sea breezes rustled my long, flowing skirt. As bridesmaids, Kim and I were dressed in matching gold skirts with Greek motifs in green along the hemline and dark green bolero jackets over long-sleeved white silk blouses.

Susanna's outfit reversed the colors of our skirts to give her gold trim on a green background. She also wore a long tunic top that was ivory with gold brocade at the edges, over a gold blouse.

Debate over head coverings raged for several days. Irini inadvertently solved the problem when she presented Susanna with a book of Sappho's poetry. While my stepmother was thumbing through it, she found a fragment of verse that resolved the controversy perfectly.

"'She who wears flowers, attracts the happy Graces: They turn back from a bare head.' There you have it, ladies," Susanna said. "Right from the poet herself. Number nineteen from the Mary Barnard translation."

Kim and I were startled when we heard those words. It was as if Sappho had spoken to us, adding her own unique touch to the ceremony. We were only too happy to comply with Susanna's request that we wear flowers in our hair, and wished that we could share with her what we knew about the historical poet. In private, we wondered about our Amazon joining ceremony and the custom of weaving wreaths for our heads. Had it really been an Amazon tradition, or had it been Sappho's idea? And what about all that kissing? We decided that Sappho could easily have suggested that quaint idea, too.

However, now wasn't the time to get sidetracked. Susanna beckoned me from the staging tent, and I ducked inside to help her button one of the cuffs of her blouse. Together, we watched Kim give Dad a kiss on the cheek and hand him the slender white candle she carried. I had one also, and would give it to Susanna once we all assembled under the rose trellis.

"Almost time," I said. "Last chance to back out."

She put her hand on my arm. "Not on your life. I'm crazy about your father... and his lovely daughter."

"I'm happy, too, that you've become a member of our family. I can't think of anyone I'd rather have for a stepmother. Should I call you Mom, or Susanna, or what?"

"Why don't we stick with Susanna, or even Sue. Either is familiar and works well for me."

"Works for me, too, Susanna."

She gave me a peck on the cheek, and a light scent of Chanel mingled with the fragrance of the roses.

My cue came. After making sure my ringlet of baby's breath and red rosebuds was secure on my head, I started up the slope toward Kim. She was gazing my way with such a tender look on her face, my heart turned cartwheels in my chest.

All of the assembled students, friends, relatives, and laborers turned their attention to me as I made my way slowly up the slope to the arbor. Glancing sideways at them, I could see they were dressed in their finery and made a colorful addition to the landscape. I heard whispers and an undercurrent of anticipation as they looked beyond me to catch the first glimpse of the bride.

When I reached the arbor and stood in front of Dad, he leaned forward to let me kiss his cheek. "Relax," I whispered, "she didn't chicken out." He kissed my forehead and pretended to be relieved. I stepped back to stand in front of Kim, feeling the warmth of her hand on my back. Along with everyone else, we turned our heads toward the staging tent, waiting for Susanna to appear.

The music paused and started again, repeating the hauntingly beautiful notes. Susanna stepped out, carrying a bouquet of baby's breath and roses, wearing a ringlet of matching rosebuds in her hair.

Appreciative murmurs greeted my beautiful stepmother as she walked toward her waiting groom. When she reached us, Susanna exchanged her bouquet for the candle I carried.

Sporting a brand-new navy-blue suit and tie, Sandy stepped forward to address the guests. I felt a little bit of a tug on my heartstrings, remembering how I had been tempted to have a fling with this handsome guy. That was when I first joined Kim's excavation in Arizona's Superstition Mountains, and I was still in my love 'em and leave 'em days. Fortunately, his maturity kept me from acting on a misguided attraction, and we formed a lasting friendship instead. I couldn't speak for Sandy, but I'd come to love and cherish that bond between us. He was the brother I never had, and a genuinely good guy.

"Welcome all of you, to this joyous occasion." Sandy's voice was clear and deep. "We're gathered here today to join with Frederick and Susanna as they stand before us to exchange expressions of their love. After the ceremony, you're all invited to a celebration in their honor. There'll be food, music, and dancing, combining the best of Greek and American traditions. And now, let's begin."

He lit both of their candles, and then stepped to one side. Dad and Susanna faced each other, holding lighted candles, gripping each other's free hand. The breeze dropped, allowing the flames to flicker brightly.

My Dad looked so handsome in a black business suit, pearl-grey shirt, and white striped cravat. A bright red rosebud was pinned to his lapel. I noticed that his candle shook as he spoke, but otherwise he looked calm and collected.

"Susanna," he said, seeming to caress her name with the tone of his voice. "At a time in my life when I thought I'd never again feel love, you appeared. We began as friends who shared common interests, and I thought that was enough. Then, before I knew it, I was finding any excuse to talk to you, just to be with you.

"Thank you for your friendship, your strength, your kindness, and your love. You have saved me from a lonely old age. I pledge to you, in front of our family and friends, my friendship, my protection, my devotion, and my love, now and as long as I live."

Susanna blinked back tears. I saw her squeeze Dad's hand. "Frederick, I've admired you and your family for many years. You were a handsome, dynamic presence at all the otherwise boring social functions that I was required to attend." Several of the guests chuckled.

"As our friendship deepened, I tried to deny my feelings for you. I thought I had no need for marriage. I had my work for comfort in my old age. How wrong I was. Your thoughtful attention and romantic gestures broke down all my defenses. With quiet tenderness, you captured my heart." Her voice broke and she paused to take a deep breath. Dad rubbed the back of her hand with his thumb.

"I pledge to you my love, and I promise to cherish you for all the days of my life."

A few sniffling sounds drifted upward from the guests and murmured words of approval. My eyes filled, and Kim shoved a tissue into my hand at just the right moment.

Dad and Susanna, using their separate tapirs, lit a single tall candle that sat on a glass-topped table behind them in the arbor. Once the single flame was burning brightly, they extinguished their individual ones, symbolically proclaiming that from this day onward, the two were one and would move forward as a single entity.

They melted into each others embrace and kissed. Cheers erupted from below, briefly drowning out the orchestra's soft music. Two people—two hearts and minds—had come together in the arbor to stand under an arch of sweet smelling roses. They'd arrived as two people, but left as a couple to be showered with rose petals as they looked confidently to their future together.

I saw a vision hovering in the sky, and I blinked, thinking it was a weird cloud formation, but it took the shape of a woman's face. Blonde hair, green eyes, and a tender expression I hadn't seen since I was fourteen. I must have swayed, because Kim's hand clamped on my elbow, supporting me.

"Don't panic," she said. "I see her, too."

Tears dribbled down my cheeks. "It's my mother. I feel her warmth, her love. She's giving her approval to Dad and Susanna." I turned to Kim. "But if you see her, too, then maybe she's blessing us, as well."

"I think so." Kim used her thumb to blot my tears. "Please don't cry. I don't have any more tissues. And you can't use your shirt sleeve, it's silk."

The thought of her making a perceptive fashion statement had me giggling. "Now, I've heard everything. This has truly been an amazing day."

"Hey, the fun's just beginning."

* * *

The Greek musicians rose and began a lively tune. We fell into step behind the newlyweds to walk to the reception. Our utilitarian food tent had been transformed into a banquet hall with a buffet area of extravagant proportions. Demitri and Pietro had outdone themselves. I swear I heard the tables creaking under the weight of it all.

Appetizers, or mezedes, were offered of taramosalata, which was Greek style caviar, tsatziki, cucumber dip that goes with everything, and tyropita, cheese filled pastries.

The entrées consisted of: hoirino me selino, which I discovered was lemon pork with celery, moussaka, an eggplant casserole, spetsiota, a Greek style fish dish, and exohiko, a delicious roast lamb with herbs.

Representing the American cuisine, I saw fried chicken, a huge steamship round of beef, mashed potatoes, and gravy. Assorted Greek and American vegetable dishes accompanied the entrées.

An array of desserts awaited us on a side table. A huge wedding cake that Irini's family bakery had created for the occasion was in the center. It featured red rosebuds with olive leaves and was decorated with the sentiment, "Happy New Life, Frederick and Susanna."

"Kali oreksi! Bon appétit!" Demitri shouted, as the bride and groom reached the far end of the room and approached their places at the head table.

* * *

In a quiet moment during our meal, I slipped an envelope into Dad's hand. He looked surprised.

"Go ahead and open it."

Dad tore open the envelope before handing it to Susanna to examine the contents.

"Oh, PJ, Kim. What a wonderful gift." Tears filled her eyes and threatened to spill over.

My dad was uncharacteristically speechless.

"Kim and I did some phoning and faxing. We knew you wanted to travel and haven't had time to plan a honeymoon, so we thought this would be a good place to start your new lives together." They both covered their mouths as I spoke, seeming happy, but quite surprised and astonished by the extent of our plans. "For the next three nights, you're booked into a villa at the Paradise Hotel and resort at Gavatha. Sauna, heated pool, spas, room service... all the amenities. Oh, and I put the directions, phone numbers, everything you need, in the envelope."

"Thank you both so much," Dad said, after finding his voice. He pulled us into bear hugs. "I've not one, but two daughters, and I love them both."

"But wait, there's more," Kim added, sounding like a late night TV infomercial. "Contact Joanna at the number on the sheet, and when you're ready to go, she'll fix you up with an all-expenses-paid week's tour of the islands in the Northern Aegean. Your headquarters will be on board a private, fully-rigged sailing ship."

Dad was so excited, I was afraid he'd hyperventilate. He grabbed Susanna and hugged her fiercely. Then he turned and hugged each of us again.

Any further conversation was drowned out by the Greek orchestra, consisting of clarinets, violins, lute, lyre, santouri, the two-headed Greek drum—the daouli, and tambourines. They played a variety of traditional dances.

We drafted Demitri and Pietro to give lessons and organize the guests into groups. The men performed a lively dance while in a big half circle, with arms across their shoulders. Alexander explained that the dance was called Geranos, or the dance of the labyrinth. According to legend, Theseus, after killing the Minotaur at Knosses, stopped at Delos and offered a sacrifice to the gods for sparing his life. Afterward, he performed this dance of serpentine movement. Dances of this type were often performed by grooms at weddings to illustrate the difficulty of getting out of the labyrinth of life.

The women danced in a half circle of their own. Irini helped us learn some of the shuffling steps and turns to a series of slow dances called Surtoi. We practiced these with plenty of stumbling missteps and laughter.

The men were supposed to do their dancing with leaps and fast footwork, while the women remained graceful and slow in their movement. After a while, and with a few Greek beverages under our belts, we joined both half circles and tried a blend of lively and slow steps.

Consuming too much alcohol was a concern for me ever since my fiasco in Arizona. The night I went out partying with the boys and Sandy had to drop me off at Kim's place was still vivid in my memory. I, in my inebriated state, managed to make a pass at him, insult Kim who was my boss at the time, and vomit all over the solitary cactus that grew on the RV lot she rented in Apache Junction. Sandy had brought me there, to Kim's motor home, to sober up because he didn't know what else to do with me. What an embarrassing time it was for all of us. If someone had told me then that Kim and I would become a loving couple and that today I'd be on a Greek island, celebrating my father's wedding, I would've thought they were crazy.

The orchestra switched gears and played a variety of American dance tunes. And when I heard the familiar strains of the Anne Murray favorite, "Could I Have This Dance", I grabbed Kim.

"It's our turn."

Her eyes widened. "Whatever you say."

The lights were dim. We found a quiet spot in the shadows where we could indulge ourselves with a slow, romantic dance together as an Amazon-style, married couple. I stole a few sweet kisses and leaned my head against Kim's chest while wishing that the dance would never end.

She hummed along with the music.

"Are you happy?" I asked her.

Her lips pressed against my temple. "I'm blissfully happy."

"Me too. I only wish…"

"What?"

"I only wish that it would stay like this forever, but I know it can't."

* * *

After Dad and Susanna left on the first leg of their honeymoon trip and the festivities wound down, Kim and I retired to our tent. I put away my wedding finery and slipped into a shirt and sweat pants. Kim, who had already changed into her old scrubs that doubled for sleepwear, wanted to enter some data into her laptop. I took out my journal and I wrote a few paragraphs about the day's events and then sat back, contemplating.

Thoughts I'd kept bottled up for most of the day surfaced. I was happy for Dad. He'd found someone to love again, and Susanna would be a true friend and advisor to all of us as we settled into our lives as a family unit. I rejoiced at Sandy and Irini's double blessing—his great archaeological discovery and their future marriage.

So much love was in the air, so many public demonstrations of that love. I thought of the love that centered me and the joy I felt when Kim and I had pledged ourselves to each other in the Amazon village with Leeja and Marna and Sappho. But that wasn't real life. A wedding in real life would never happen for us.

Don't dwell on that, I thought. It's been a terrific day; don't ruin it now.

"Fifty thousand drachmas for your thoughts." Kim had left the computer and was kneeling in front of me on the bedroll. Her brow wrinkled.

"That'd be a whole lot more than they're worth right now."

"Oh, but there's inflation, you know. It's probably just a buck ninety-nine in U.S. funds. Come on, PJ, what's wrong?"

"Nothing really. The champagne has my mind wandering all over the place tonight. I was careful, but I probably drank too much."

She leaned forward to kiss my forehead and nuzzle my neck, drawing me close. "Do you feel sick?"

"No. Nothing like that. I'm fine." I stood up. "I'll take Pup for his final evening walk and get some fresh air. You don't have to wait up for us."

Pup gave his own impression of a Geranos when he saw me grab the leash.

"PJ."

I turned at the tent opening to look back at her.

"Don't shut me out, okay? I love you."

Tears burned my eyelids. I didn't want her to worry unnecessarily, but I also didn't want to explain my feelings right now. She couldn't do anything. This was the way life was going to be for us. I knew it going into the relationship, and I had no regrets. I just didn't think it would hurt so much.

"I know, and I love you, too. It's just that I need some alone time."

"I understand."

Chapter 20

"Kim, this isn't necessary."

"I disagree."

"But you know how I hate surprises. Besides, I'm over my mood. Please don't think you have to make me feel better."

"I want to do this, sweetheart. It'll be for both of us, believe me."

We were in our tent, stuffing last minute items into our travel bags. PJ was right. She'd talked to me about her insecurities and jealousies and was in a much better frame of mind, but nothing was going to change my plans. Sandy had agreed to take care of Pup for us while we were gone, so there was no reason we couldn't slip away for a few days.

"Are you ready?" I asked her, a touch of impatience creeping into my voice.

"I guess so." Her forehead creased. "It would have been easier to pack, if I'd known where we were going and what we'd be doing there."

"Did you pack the blouse and skirt I asked you to?"

PJ zipped her bag, and saluted. "As ordered."

"And that new shawl your Dad brought from Athens for you? We've been so busy you haven't had a chance to wear it."

"Yes, I have it."

"Good." Evenings would be chilly. I'd already packed my red Andean wool poncho. It was one I had acquired years ago while searching for Amazons in South America.

"So, either we're going to a colder climate, or we plan to be out late at night." She folded her arms and waited, hoping, I guess, that I'd divulge more information. When I didn't, she stuck her tongue out at me. "Crap. You aren't going to tell me anything more, are you?"

"Nope. You'll know everything soon enough."

She shrugged. "Then I guess I'm ready, boss."

Outside, Sandy's pickup awaited us. He would use Irini's Fiat for the couple of days we would be gone. While the truck—a ten year old, faded red Toyota—wasn't exactly a status symbol, it provided us with basic, dependable transportation. Its bed, covered with a camper shell, was crammed with tools, maps, and other paraphernalia. We tossed our bags on top of everything else in the back and climbed inside the cab.

"Wait."

"What?" I withdrew the key from the ignition.

"You're not taking me on some sort of time-travel trip, are you? Like back to Amazon Land?"

"No, dear, not yet."

"Oh good." She blew out a breath, then grabbed my wrist. "What do you mean not yet?"

"Why don't you just relax, and try to enjoy the scenery."

"Are you certain that Pup will be okay with Sandy?"

"He'll be just fine." .

"Oh, God." PJ leaned back, pinching the bridge of her nose. "I think I feel a headache coming on."

* * *

I pulled into the entrance of a large seaside estate, the walls of which were so white, they were nearly blinding in the bright sunshine. Multi-colored flowers and olive and pistachio trees formed a well-landscaped border for the narrow road that led to several adjacent white-walled cottages. Each cottage overlooked the brilliant blue water and had its own pristine beach front. PJ waited in the truck while I checked us in. The doorman frowned at me, casting a scornful glance in the direction of Sandy's vehicle, apparently fearing its shabby presence would infect all the other vehicles parked near it in the lot. Like a lonely little onion in a petunia patch, the truck was easy to spot, positioned fourth in line after the Jaguar, Mercedes, and Lexus.

"It's a loaner," I told the doorman. "The Rolls is in the shop."

Once the reservation was confirmed and I had the cottage keys in hand, I drove to the far end of the beach where our secluded, two-story vacation retreat awaited.

PJ was still confused. "Are you going to tell me what's going on? What we're doing here?"

"A little R and R, my dear." I gave her what I thought was a rather saucy look. "Don't you think we deserve it?"

"Sure." Her eyes were shining. "But this place is so ritzy. And our own private cottage." She bounced on the seat. "Why didn't you tell me? Here I am arriving in jeans, plain old jeans."

"Jeans are acceptable everywhere."

"Not this pair, they're so worn. Cripes, they're not even designer."

I gasped. "Horrors. How will you ever live it down?"

She found my attempt at humor only mildly amusing. "Hey, it's a reflection on you if I'm not properly attired."

"Believe me, proper attire for you is going to be a lot less than jeans, if I have anything to say about it."

Our bungalow was not large, but it had sleek Danish-modern furniture and the solid wood floors gleamed with fresh polish. The downstairs consisted of a compact kitchen with its own eating alcove, a small living room, and a bathroom. A curved wooden staircase led upstairs to a small bedroom containing a twin bed and futon couch, and a large master bedroom that featured a canopied double bed with filmy white curtains that, once pulled into place, would close us off from any worldly distractions. French doors opened onto a balcony with a swinging love seat that overlooked the water. From somewhere close by, the sounds of a bouzouki could be heard. The online site for this vacation spot had advertised a popular band with these three and four-stringed instruments that sounded like lutes. PJ and I had enjoyed hearing them earlier at an outdoor cinema. Perhaps we'd catch the dinner show, if we decided to eat at the estate's four-star restaurant.

After we'd disposed of our luggage, PJ locked me in a fierce embrace. "What am I going to do with you? You're always surprising me, and you know I don't like surprises."

"You don't?"

"Surprises like this I could get used to, but it must have cost a fortune."

I kissed her gently. "You don't think you're worth a little extra effort?"

Her happy expression held the promise of a wonderful couple of days. "Right now, I'm thanking my lucky stars that I fell in love with someone so understanding and generous."

I kissed her again, longer and with more intensity. "Want to take off those tacky non-designer jeans and try the bed?"

"Can't wait."

We disrobed quickly, leaving articles of clothing scattered about the bedroom. By unspoken agreement, the curtains remained open so the sea breezes coming through the open French doors could caress our heated skin as we explored each other, our fingers tracing backs, breasts, and thighs. Our kisses were urgent, our tongues hungry for the taste of each other. Throughout the afternoon, we made love and dozed, a cycle that left us utterly spent and lying in a tangle of arms and legs, enveloping ourselves in tender and loving dreams.

Late in the afternoon, I awoke before PJ, lifted myself onto my elbow, and stared in wonder at her naked body. It was a work of art, consisting of inviting curves that led to a hard, flat belly. I wanted to make love to her again, to tease her breasts with my tongue, and immerse myself in the exotic fragrance of her heated passion, but I didn't have the strength.

I wondered what I'd done to deserve such a remarkable woman.

Giving in to my desire, I moistened my lips and pressed my mouth to her right breast. She stirred, and I felt her fingers move through my hair.

"Come here, you." Her voice was husky.

Somehow, I knew I would find the strength.

* * *

When I next awakened, PJ was on top of me, her breath warm against my neck and her fingers curled around my breast. What bliss. The only problem was that I was starving, and I still had plans for us. I gently lifted my arm to check my watch. Her warm body shifted and stretched.

Her fingers uncurled and a palm now caressed my breast.

"Mmm. I may never leave this bed. Everything I need is right here." Still struggling against sleep, her words were slow and sexy.

I blew out a contented breath. "Not that I'm complaining, but what about food? We've slept the afternoon away. Aren't you getting hungry?"

PJ's stomach rumbled. "Did that answer your question?"

"Then let's decide where we want to eat dinner."

She rolled off my body and pulled the sheet up as far as our hips. The breeze coming into our room had grown cooler without the sun to warm it.

"Dinner? Oh, I don't care, Kimmy. You decide." She tickled my ear with her tongue.

"We have a few choices. There's a restaurant in the main house of the estate, or if you feel like walking along the beach a bit further, there are several small restaurants right along the water's edge."

"Let's walk along the beach and take our chances with one of the smaller restaurants, but not the tavernas or coffee houses. They'll be too noisy, and the ouzo will be flowing like water. I don't want to be with a crowd anyway, just you."

I turned my head and kissed her, touching her cheek with my fingertips. "Sounds good to me. But you must wear the outfit for me tonight. Okay?"

"Okay."

"Great. Let's grab a shower and get dressed."

"Whoa. What's your hurry? Have you got a hot date later on?"

"I sure do." Playing along, I checked my watch again. "And we're running behind schedule."

She threw back the covers and hopped out of bed. "Okay, I'm up. I suppose, to save time, we'll be forced to share a shower."

I slipped on my robe and picked up some of our discarded clothing. "Good thinking. That'll also conserve water."

A knock sounded on the cottage door.

"Who could that be?"

PJ snickered. "Maybe your hot date got tired of waiting." Still naked, she spread her arms wide. "Shall I go and let her in?"

I tossed a robe in her direction. "Put that on. I'll check the door."

By the time I reached the entrance, there was no one around, but a long, white box—similar to a florist's delivery carton—was on the top step. I picked it up, finding it much too heavy for flowers.

PJ had come downstairs to satisfy her curiosity. "Aww. Your date had to cancel, so she sent some long-stemmed roses as a consolation. Guess you're stuck with me all evening."

I handed her the box.

"Wow," she said, shifting to balance its weight. "Much too heavy for roses, even long-stemmed ones. Must be a whole bush, or even a small fruit tree."

"Okay, enough joking. I really have no idea what it could be, or who sent it."

PJ eased the box onto the glass-topped coffee table. "One way to find out."

"Do you want to look? There doesn't seem to be any name or address on the box, so I don't know if it's meant for you or me."

"You're the one with the hot date and all the surprises. You open it."

I lifted the lid and pulled away the inner cloth wrapping to reveal a shiny, familiar, ornately carved sword.

PJ peered into the box and looked at me. "Kinky. Your hot date must be with Queen Boudica."

"I wish it were, because the real explanation is way more complicated."

We shared a look.

"Amazons," she said. "It's always about Amazons."

"Uh-huh."

She folded her arms across her chest. "Which one this time? A spirit guide?"

"Marna. She had this sword made especially for me and told me that when we returned to our world she'd find a way to get it to me. She said I might need it."

PJ sank onto the sofa and held her head. "I guess I should be thankful it isn't an assault rifle. Maybe there'll be a crossbow under my pillow in the morning."

I rewrapped the sword and left the box on the table, sensing the evening and my romantic plans had suffered a serious blow. PJ denounced weaponry of all kinds, and she wasn't really sure if our mission to help the Amazon Nation was a noble cause or a waste of time. I had to admit that I wasn't certain what the future would hold on that score, either. However, my main concern was PJ and what I wanted to happen this evening. I sat down and put my arms around her.

"Forget this for now, okay? Let's shower and dress for a nice dinner. I think I can hear some calamari calling your name right now."

"At this point, I'd settle for some gyros, or souvlaki, or whatever they're called."

"No. We're going to forget about the Amazons, take a nice hot shower together, dress up, and stroll along the beach until we smell some great grilled meat or fish cooking and stop for a quiet meal."

She took my hand and led the way to our shower. "Okay, but I'm not eating squid, and you can't make me."

* * *

"Do you think it was as beautiful in Sappho's time as it is now?"

"I suspect it was even more so," I said, my eyes feasting on PJ who looked deliciously lovely in a low cut silk blouse of the softest pink and a black, mid-calf length skirt. Her outfit was accentuated with a silver-buckled, brocaded belt.

Our beach stroll had landed us on the terrace of the estate's main house. The aroma of grilled meat and fish lured us from the moment we stepped outside the cottage. We were sitting across from each other at a small round table, enjoying a glass of local muscat, snacking on fruit and cheese, waiting for our entrées of grilled shrimp, balsamic rice, and sautéed vegetables.

"Let's take a walk along the beach after we eat," I suggested, sipping my second glass of wine.

PJ's eyes widened. "Dressed up like this? I couldn't have made it here if they hadn't built that stone walkway."

"We can take off our shoes and hike our skirts up a bit." I, too, was dressed up in a long-sleeved white blouse and a navy-blue, knee-length, tailored skirt. "I feel like doing something off-the-wall."

"I think you've had a wee too much nectar of the grape." PJ said. "By the way, what on earth are you carrying in that sling bag that you're guarding so carefully?"

"All in good time, my darling. All in good time."

"Come on."

"Okay, if you must know. I have my poncho in it, as well as some snacks in case we get hungry on the walk."

"Hungry!" She rolled her eyes. "We've been sitting here, stuffing our faces with fruit and cheese while anticipating a platter of shrimp. What makes you think we'll be hungry after that?"

"You never know, do you?"

"Sometimes I wonder about you," PJ said, grabbing my arm. "Okay, if we can still move when we finish our meal, we'll take this dressed-up walk on the beach with our supply of snacks and our cover-ups. There's nothing wrong with either one of us that a little insanity wouldn't cure."

"I knew you'd come around to my way of thinking."

* * *

I was pleased to see the beach was quite deserted, probably because it was cooler, though not uncomfortably so. PJ drew her new Greek shawl around her shoulders, and I took out my poncho and pulled it over my head. Hand-in-hand, we strolled along the fine-grained, sandy beach, enjoying the feel of it beneath our bare feet.

"What are you thinking so hard about?"

"Something Sappho wrote," PJ said. "Let me see if I can remember it." She scrunched up her face for a second or two. "'If you come, I shall put out new pillows for you to rest on.'"

"Sappho really impressed you, didn't she?"

"She was the goddess of lyric poetry, and having the opportunity to work with her was an honor I don't feel I deserve. I'm still not sure it really happened, but I'd like to believe it did."

"Then it did. But what was she saying to you in the poem?"

"She was just reading her own work, showing me, as a teacher to student."

I chuckled. "Sometimes, PJ, you can be so naïve."

"Me, naïve? That's a good one."

"I think Sappho, in her own subtle way, was propositioning you."

"Come off it."

"No, really. Read into her words. She was a mistress of flirtation, and I know for a fact that she was quite taken with you."

"Holy shit!"

We'd almost reached the headland where we'd need to turn around and return to the cottage. I kept glancing to the east, hoping my timing was right. It was, because just as we reached the point, I saw the glow that heralded the rise of the full moon. To our right, the crystal clear blue water gradually changed to reflect the ivory colored path of its ascending light.

"Hungry?" I asked, digging into the bag.

"You've got to be kidding." She stopped when she saw that I hadn't pulled out any food. "Ooh, for me?"

"Yes, for you." I opened the small white box and pinned the corsage of miniature red roses to her shawl, and although my hand was shaking, I managed to do it without pricking her with the pin. Then I dug into the bag again and pulled out a small bottle of champagne and two plastic goblets.

"What's the occasion? It's not like an anniversary or anything, is it?" The shine in PJ's eyes mirrored the rising moon.

"The occasion, sweetheart, is our commitment to each other. I know it hurts you that we can't be joined together like any two people in love."

I poured us each a glass and we linked arms to drink a silent toast. PJ got a case of the giggles.

"I can't wait to see what else you've got hidden in that bag."

I put it down on the sand and took her hand as I stood up. "Nothing more in there. Just gifts from my heart."

We looked at each other for a few seconds. PJ inhaled and, sensing the mood had turned serious, she went still.

I turned her hand over and kissed her palm. "I pledge to you now, on this perfectly lovely night on Sappho's island, in the presence of this full moon and Sappho's ghost, that I'll care for you always. I'll protect you and die for you if I have to because I love you so very much." I reached into my pocket for the tiny, velvet covered ring box. Inside was a set of matching bands inscribed with our names looped together.

"With this ring comes my heart." I slid one of the bands on PJ's finger. "For without you, my heart will certainly shrivel and die."

"Oh, Kimmy." Her eyes filled to overflowing.

I kissed her, tasting the sweetness of her lips and the salty flavor of her tears. "Will you be mine forever?"

The moon was riding higher in the sky, spreading its light along the beach and over the headland. In the not too far distance, the lights of Eresos twinkled like candles in the night.

PJ had been unnaturally quiet, but she took the other ring and reached for my hand. "I'll be proud to take you forever as my own. I shall love you with all my heart for as long as I live on this earth and forever afterwards. Recent experience has shown us that we can be together throughout eternity, and that we'll follow the path that's already laid out for us. Ours is a never ending journey."

I knew she was referring to our destiny as Leeja and Marna had explained it. Although in her more down-to-earth moments, she still insisted it was a dream, she was coming to accept that not all things could be so easily explained.

We held each other in the moonlight. PJ stood with her back to the cliff. I leaned in to her and my lips sought hers. Without hesitancy, she responded, the tip of her tongue teasing mine and warming me to the core.

"Time to go back to the cottage," I whispered hoarsely.

"I thought you had a hot date for later on."

"I do." I found the soft spot under her throat and kissed her there. "With you."

"Then we'd better go, before I take you here and now in the moonlight."

"And allow the waters of the Aegean to wash over us, bathing us in our moment of passion."

"You can be so romantic at times."

"Only at times?"

PJ put her arms around my neck and gazed into my eyes. "How can I ever thank you for this evening, for marrying me in the here and now? And thank you, too, for all the other evenings and days that have made my life so complete."

"Having you share my life is all the thanks I'll ever need or want." I kissed her, gently at first, then passionately.

"Whoa there, tiger. Let's get back to the cottage where there's some privacy."

We started back, two dressed up women strolling arm in arm along the beach in one of the most romantic places on earth, carrying our shoes and the bag with the now empty corsage box and the remains of our commitment celebration.

"It's so beautiful," PJ said, stopping and gazing out to sea. She took my hand and touched it to her lips, then stood quietly at my side.

"What is it?" I asked, seeing her eyes misting in the moonlight. "What are you thinking about?"

"I'm thinking that it would've been nice if Leeja and Marna had been here tonight to share all this."

"What makes you think they weren't?"

"We didn't see them."

"No, but they seem to know all that goes on with us."

"Spooky, isn't it? I wonder if Sappho sees all, too."

"Hmm. I think I'm a little jealous of Sappho."

PJ's arm came around my waist. "You don't need to be."

We kissed there, in the moonlight, our bare feet cooling in the moist sand. Gentle waves broke against the shore, splashing our ankles with foamy surf. Lost in our warm embrace, we forgot about everything but each other and the bond of love that held us together.

Laughter sounded from a great distance and a sudden clap of thunder startled us.

"What the hell was that?" I asked looking skyward. Two figures emerged along the moon's reflected pathway to the horizon. They sat astride horses who tossed their heads until their long and beautiful manes became one with the surf and spray.

"Whoa."

"What? Is something the matter?" PJ turned and looked in the same direction, but the image had faded. In its place, a pair of sea birds soared low over the waters.

"Nothing's the matter. Everything's fine." I rubbed my eyes and peered into the spray-laden air. As soon as PJ turned away, the image changed again, and was that of a pair of dolphins leaping gracefully into the air, guided by two masked riders, their swords held high, glinting in the moon beam's path.

What the hell was going on? Was it the shape-changing shaman, paying us a visit? Or had I sipped too much champagne?

I became aware that PJ was asking a question. She had not, it seemed, seen what I had seen. "But how can there be thunder when there isn't a cloud in sight?"

Before I could respond, the sand shifted beneath our feet, and a strong tug threw us off balance.

"Kim, the waves are breaking higher now. We'd better—"

"Yeow!"

A wall of cold seawater doused us and dumped us on the beach.

Laughing, sputtering, and soaked to the skin, we helped each other up and stumbled toward the cottage.

"Still think that Marna and Leeja didn't drop in and visit us back there?" I asked PJ, when we reached our sanctuary.

She shivered. When she spoke, her teeth chattered. "Of all the d-dirty, low-down, des-despicable, pranks. Yeah, it had to be them. And Sappho probably p-put them up to it."

"Oh, I know she did. That blouse of yours is transparent when it's wet."

PJ gasped and shook her fist at the sky. "Pervert!"

I held her tightly. "Come on, let's go inside and get out of these wet things. We can dry off in front of a roaring fire. You can doubt them or accept them, but one thing is certain. The Amazons have made our lives interesting."

"Definitely. And we can be sure that wherever our future takes us, our lives will never be dull."

I wiped wet bangs from her forehead. "I knew my life would never be dull the moment I first met you."

"You rocked my world, too, Kim, though I had no idea what I was in for when I fell in love with you."

I opened the door and we stepped inside, quickly peeling off our clothing, trying not to drip too much on the polished floors.

PJ hung our soggy garments in the bathroom, allowing them to dry over the tub. She grabbed a couple of large, fluffy towels to wrap around our bodies and hair. I lit the logs in the fireplace, and we stretched out on the sofa under a thick quilt.

"Ah, this is perfect," I said, sliding my hand inside the flap of PJ's towel, tickling her belly.

She launched a retaliatory strike on my ribcage, and before we knew it, the towels were gone and some serious lip-locking ensued.

"If we're heading where I think we're heading," PJ said, as my hands cupped her breasts, "I'd just like to say that I loved the ceremony you planned, and the corsage, and the ring, and the vows we said. Most of all, I loved that you understood that I needed something to make our love valid."

"You're welcome."

She shifted her body so that her head was tucked under my chin and her cheek pressed against my breast. "I can't say positively that ancient warrior women came out of the shadows, took us back to their world, and made us a part of their legacy. It's still possible that when we were caught in the cave-in, and in an unconscious state, we somehow dreamed the event."

"But how could we both have had the same dream?"

"I haven't figured that part out yet. Maybe, just maybe, we were caught up in some sort of time warp and—"

"Your doubts are my hopes."

"One thing you should never doubt, Kim. I love you, and I'll follow you anywhere our life together takes us."

"How about we take up where we left off this afternoon? We're already naked and warm."

"Mmm. And this time, our tummies are full."

I slid my fingers down her smooth, firm torso. "We should be good until morning, then, Mrs. Blair."

Her head lifted. Desire shone in her eyes. "Let the loving begin, Mrs. Curtis."

K.C. West

Victoria Welsh

About the Authors

K.C. West and **Victoria Welsh** met online several years ago. Despite living practically on opposite coasts of the United States, they found plenty of common ground in their interest in writing. K.C. lives in the east with her husband and two daughters. Victoria, a poet and writer, resides with her life partner in the southwestern United States.

The authors are hard at work on the next book in the *Shadow* series, but they'd love to hear from you.

Kcwest2004@hotmail.com
vctrwelsh@gmail.com

Coming Soon from Blue Feather Books

From Hell to Breakfast, by Joan Opyr

Wilhelmina "Bil" Hardy is at loose ends—and in the small college-town of Cowslip, Idaho, that's a mighty short length of rope.

After a long struggle with non-Hodgkin's lymphoma, and an even longer struggle with the law, Bil's brother Sam has died. Bil is devastated, but she has no time grieve. Her sisters, Sarah and Naomi, seem to be dating the same cowboy, but neither knows they're sharing. Her girlfriend Sylvie is having mother troubles. Her role model, lesbian separatist and commune-builder Captain Schwartz, is having ex-husband troubles. And, worst of all, Bil's parents have sold the family home and bought 200 acres on a remote hillside from a notoriously crooked businessman. Bil's mother, Emma, is looking forward to evicting local drug dealer and Sam's erstwhile pot supplier, Jake the Snake, from a run-down shack on the hillside, but someone beats her to it—with a shotgun.

Who killed Jake? What's the unwelcome news from Captain Schwartz's ex-husband? Who is pushy preacher George Knox and what does he want? And, most puzzling of all, what do Bil's sisters see in bow-legged two-timer Buck DeWitt? Bil must answer all of these questions and more while trying to keep her relationship with Sylvie from going AWOL. Holy Cowslip! It's business as unusual for Bil and her crazy Idaho cadre.

Accidental Rebels, by Kelly Sinclair

It's the summer of 1989, and in the small Texas town of Tantona, to be openly gay is to be notorious. But three closeted women are about to shake things up.

Mandy, a young reporter, is hung up on God and women. Librarian Tina is eager to ditch old personal dramas, and rocker Cat is struggling to get her band off the ground.

Unanticipated connections bring the women together... and then there's Sherron, a reckless blonde who becomes the talk of the town.

When secrets come doused in Texas barbecue sauce, all the ingredients are present for a surprising and spicy mix.

Check out these other exciting titles from Blue Feather Books:

Tempus Fugit	Mavis Applewater	978-0-9794120-0-4
Whispering Pines	Mavis Applewater	978-0-9794120-6-6
Yesterday Once More	Karen Badger	978-0-9794120-3-5
Addison Black and the Eye of Bastet	M.J. Walker	978-0-9794120-2-8
The Thirty-Ninth Victim	Arleen Williams	978-0-9794120-4-2
Merker's Outpost	I. Christie	978-0-9794120-1-1
The Fifth Stage	Margaret Helms	0-9770318-7-X
Celtic Shadows	K.C. West and Vi Welsh	0-97703186-1

www.bluefeatherbooks.com

Printed in the United States
132638LV00003B/132/P